GASPAR BROWN

ADVENTURE 5

MORE GASPAR BROWN ADVENTURES

by

HUTTON WILKINSON

*Gaspar Brown and the Mystery of
the Gasparilla Succession*
ADVENTURE 1

*Gaspar Brown and the Mystery of
the Seminole Spring*
ADVENTURE 2

*Gaspar Brown and the Mystery of
the Necronomicon*
ADVENTURE 3

Gaspar Brown and the House of Mystery
ADVENTURE 4

Gaspar Brown and the Mystery of the Yucatán Legacy
ADVENTURE 5

*Gaspar Brown and the Mystery of
the Ashkenazi Acquisition*
ADVENTURE 6 (COMING SOON)

*Gaspar Brown and the Mystery of
Uncle Ting's Garden*
ADVENTURE 7 (COMING SOON)

GASPAR BROWN

AND

THE MYSTERY OF

THE YUCATAN LEGACY

ADVENTURE 5

HUTTON WILKINSON

Book design by Sue Campbell Book Design

ISBN 13: 978-1-7325653-4-0 (print)

Contents

PROLOGUE:

GASPAR BROWN, THE BOY BILLIONAIRE, AND HIS BUDDY, ALEX MENDOZA, COULDN'T WAIT FOR SCHOOL TO end and summer vacation to begin. Both boys were students at Andrew Jackson Junior High in the town of Calaluna, Perdido Isle, Florida. They'd met last year when Gaspar and his mother Elvira moved from California to Florida to accept an inheritance from their cousin, Eugenia Floride Mendoza Munoz-Flores y Gaspar. Eugenia Floride's adopted father, Charles Munoz-Flores y Gaspar, the mysterious millionaire had amassed a secret fortune in pirate treasure and that treasure was young Gaspar's best kept secret. Uncle Charlie was Gaspar's mom's great-uncle, whose jovial ghost still haunted *La Rinconada*, the seaside villa on the Gulf of Mexico which the old boy had built in the roaring twenties. Uncle Charlie only made his presence felt to those he loved … and the old ghost considered Gaspar his best friend and was always around to guide and mentor the inquisitive and acquisitive teenager.

From the moment Gaspar and his mom took up residence on the island, their life had changed into one of adventure, discovery and no end of complications. Upon receiving his initial inheritance, Gaspar had taken steps to restore Uncle Charlie's extraordinary estate, as well as to raise his great-uncle's sunken yacht *Argente*. Young Gaspar's most audacious plan to date was to restore the magnificent ship to its original Edwardian splendor. Now with summer vacation quickly approaching, he was making plans for the yacht's maiden voyage, which was to take place following the marriage of his mom, Elvira Brown to family friend and attorney, Peter Cawthorne. The wedding was scheduled to take place on June fifthteeth at St. Anna's Catholic Church, a structure built on La Rinconada property several hundred years ago by Spanish explorers.

Since school started nine months ago life had been full of study and play for Gaspar and Alex, and plenty of work for Alex's parents, Felix and Angela, who were the official caretakers of La Rinconada. It was they who kept the whole place running like clockwork. Peter Cawthorne had also had his hands full working with Gaspar's accountants trying to figure out how best to avoid the enormous inheritance taxes still looming over the estate.

Gaspar ruled the roost at La Rinconada and was nothing if not practical. Not yet old enough to drive, he hired Lamar Washington, from the Grand Hotel Floride to chauffeur him and Alex and their buddies in the old Ford Woody Gaspar had found rotting in the stables on his first day on the property. The old station wagon had subsequently been restored with Lamar and Alex's help. Besides being a great driver, Lamar was also an expert mechanic. It had only taken the clever man less than a month before he had the cool old car ready to roll. The restored Woody was what Gaspar and Alex rode to school in each morning and tooled around the island in each afternoon and on the weekends.

The boys' school was particularly great because the playground extended right out onto the beach without walls or fences, leaving the kids free to play on the sand and even in the water during recess. Gaspar and Alex were the kingpins of a group of boys whom they'd organized into a water polo team that practiced every day after school in La Rinconada's almost Olympic-sized swimming pool. Some upper classmen had organized a rival team in hopes of thumping the younger kids. So far Gaspar's *Jackson Sharks* had won the day every time the two teams competed. News of the Sharks superiority had traveled fast, and it wasn't too long before the Jackson Sharks were being invited to compete against teams as far west as Pensacola as well as in Tampa, Miami, and Naples.

Besides their interest in water polo, Gaspar and Alex took tennis lessons from their pal Brewster Wharton's brother Scott and sailing lessons from their pal Craig Cadawalader. When they weren't messing around after school, the two friends always studied together up in Gaspar's office, which he'd transformed from the former blue bedroom in the old house. This was their headquarters, complete with dual computers and all the equipment they needed to do their homework. More often than not, they also used the computers to figure out how best to accomplish some of Gaspar's more creative schemes. Between the two of them, Gaspar was by far the more inventive, and Alex had the practical sense of how to really get things done. Gaspar dreamed of a career in business, while Alex dreamed of being an architect. Gaspar admired his friend's desire to build edifices that would last. Gaspar's father had been an architect, and until his premature death Gaspar had spent most of his spare time in his father's offices. The draftsmen there had called him *The Little Architect*, which he never thought he was. Gaspar hadn't told Alex yet but when the time was right, he had big plans for his pal's career.

Alex lived with his parents, Felix and Angela, in a charming apartment over the stables at La Rinconada. More and more, he was hanging out with Gaspar in the big house, and that was exactly the way Gaspar liked it. They were like brothers, and from the moment of their first meeting only twelve months before, they had been inseparable.

It was only last January that Gaspar's mom, Elvira had decided to move out of La Rinconada in favor of a smaller house they owned in the nearby town of Calaluna.

She preferred the smaller house and because she was soon to marry Peter Cawthorne, Gaspar figured she wanted a more manageable place that they could call their own. Gaspar on the other hand had no intention of ever leaving La Rinconada. For the past few months, he'd been living on his own, bachelor style, doing as he pleased along with the newest member of his family, his faithful standard poodle, Mr. Peugeot. Being his own boss was nothing new … Gaspar rarely asked for parental approval anyway. With his mother's wedding coming up, Gaspar had his hands full with all of the special arrangements he was planning to surprise the bride and groom with on their big day. He'd not only made special plans for the wedding itself, but also for the reception afterwards and the honeymoon, too.

F. Cath.

CHAPTER 1

SCHOOLDAYS

GASPAR SAT AT HIS SCHOOL DESK FULL OF ANTICIPA-TION, WAITING FOR HIS TEACHER, MRS. LAKER, TO finish her English lesson so that he and Alex could head home. Today was the day that his fully restored yacht, *Argente*, now re-registered under its original name, *Floridablanca*, would sail into the canal at La Rinconada, completely refurbished down to its new decor by The Tony Duquette Studios of Beverly Hills. Gaspar had chosen these designers because they'd been his father's favorites, although his dad never had the opportunity of working with them. Gaspar hired them as a nod to his father's exceptional style and taste and couldn't wait to see the finished product.

Craig Cadawalader, Gaspar's sailing instructor whom he'd hired to captain *Floridablanca*, had promised to bring the ship in at four o'clock this afternoon, on the button. Gaspar looked forward to standing on the terrace of La Rinconada with his mother and his entire extended family to watch the magnificent ship, originally built in Liverpool for his great-uncle Charlie in 1918, as she sailed up to her dock. The school bell didn't ring a minute too soon and as if shot from a canon, Gaspar and Alex grabbed their backpacks and ran for the street where his driver Lamar Washington and Gaspar's handsome French poodle, Mr. Peugeot were waiting patiently for them in the Woody.

When the boys and Peugeot arrived back home to La Rinconada, they found many of the invited guests already assembled. Waiting for them were Elvira and Peter, Brewster Wharton and his brother Scott, Al's parents, Felix and Angela and even Bishop du Bon Secours, who was on hand to bless the restored yacht the minute she docked. Drinks and finger sandwiches had been placed on a buffet set up between the swimming pool and the balustrade, which separated the beach along the Gulf of Mexico from the garden. A four-piece combo from *The Grand Hotel Floride* in Llojeta played Cole Porter tunes lending a celebratory atmosphere to the occasion. As the group of friends mingled and laughed, a cry rose up, first from Gaspar and then from Alex and one by one from the others while Mr. Peugeot barked enthusiastically.

"Here she comes," passed back and forth between the enthusiastic guests and the prancing pup.

The beautiful, sleek, one-hundred and fifty-foot yacht sailed quickly past the spit of land separating the Rinconada Cove from the Smuggler's Cove, to the east. Smuggler's Cove had been the scene of the big drug bust which took place at the end of last summer. That was when Gaspar and his buddies had been instrumental in alerting the authorities to the illicit running of drugs across the Rinconada property. The boys' quick actions caused the hated drug smuggler, Unzega to be scared off. Although the authorities believed that the evil man had escaped scott free, Gaspar knew otherwise, having solved *The Mystery of the Gasparilla Succession*, almost singlehandedly. In any event, Unzega's gang of conniving goons had been arrested, and the drug lords big black yacht *Revenge*, impounded by the Coast Guard.

Floridablanca dazzled white against the turquoise waters of the Gulf of Mexico. Her new crisp white canvas billowed in the balmy tropical breeze, and her polished brasses glinted in the Florida sunlight.

"What a beauty she is," bragged Gaspar to everyone's delight.

"You certainly had vision, son," his mother congratulated him. "Only you could figure out how to raise her from her watery grave and bring her back to life. She's so beautiful, Gasp. Thank you for fixing her up for us." She thanked her son before kissing him sweetly on the cheek.

"Bravo, Gaspar," Peter Cawthorne enthused, clapping his teenaged client and soon to be stepson on the shoulder. "What a beautiful sight, to see her back at sea again. I remember sailing on her with my father and your cousin Eugenia Floride when I was your age. This is such a thrill. I know your great-uncle Charles and Cousin Eugenia would be proud of you if they could only be here.

Gaspar looked around and instantly saw Uncle Charlie, or at least his ghost, standing on the widow's walk of the Tombs, the octagon-shaped structure that sat at the end of the yacht canal. Most people thought that structure was a boat house, but only Gaspar knew that it marked the spot where the pirate Jose Gaspar, better known as Gasparilla, had hidden his legendary treasure way back in the eighteenth century. Below the tombs lay the secret tunnel Uncle Charlie had used to transfer the treasure to the new vault he had built specifically for the purpose of keeping his extraordinary treasure safe. Standing on top of the roof terrace of the octagonal boat house called The Tombs, Uncle Charlie's ghost, who was invisible to all but Gaspar, was as usual wearing the most outlandish Admiral Nelson-like uniform with gold epaulets, lots of gold braid and a huge multi-plumed tricorn hat. From the widows' walk, Charlie waved wildly at Gaspar, but Gaspar only smiled and nodded discreetly, not wanting to give the old ghost away. Gaspar planned to seek Uncle Charlie out later and couldn't wait to discuss the excitement of the ship's homecoming with him privately.

Craig Cadawalader ordered his handpicked crew to

furl the sails, as he slowly brought the great yacht to its dock. Two sailors in white uniforms standing on the sea wall caught the lines that their colleagues threw over to them from the deck of the still-moving ship. Immediately the sailors worked the lines to double her up to the huge bronze cleats attached to the coral stone dock of La Rinconada's Grand Canal. Spontaneous applause broke out from the assembled onlookers, which included the household help and the gardeners. When the yacht was tied-off, the crew lowered her brow or staircase so that everyone could scramble aboard and look around. Captain Craig Cadawalader strode forward and greeted Elvira and Gaspar, who were the first onboard with Peugeot hard on their heels. When Gaspar stepped on deck, he offered Craig his hand in congratulations.

"How'd she handle, Captain?" Gaspar inquired.

"She's a honey, sir," Cadawalader replied formally to his young master.

The captain had earlier informed Gaspar that whenever he was aboard *Floridablanca* as her captain, he insisted that they enforce formal Navy protocol and that all manner of proper address would be strictly adhered to. Gaspar thought this was a reasonable request and looked forward to playing Fletcher Christian to Craig's Captain Bly. "Captain, please escort Mrs. Brown and her friends around, and point out all the improvements we've made to *Floridablanca*," Gaspar insisted.

"Aye, aye, sir," was Cadawalader's immediate response.

"Please, Mrs. Brown," he said offering Elvira his arm. "It will be my pleasure."

With Elvira in tow, Captain Craig Cadawalader led the entire assembly around the deck. He pointed out the tubs of flowering white chrysanthemums, which the decorators had insisted upon. Also of note was the black and white striped canvas awning extending over the poop deck which shaded several groupings of large-scaled natural colored wicker furniture, including sofas, chairs and tables, upholstered in a printed linen in a pattern of coral branches, seashells and ocean waves. There was also a long teak dining table with twelve chairs arranged around it. The decorators had placed shiny brass Moroccan lanterns everywhere, as well as arrangements of seashells, and dozens of throw pillows in shades of blue, coral and yellow. Under all of this comfortable furniture, jute area rugs with navy, black and white bindings designated the different areas.

The tour proceeded around the deck and up the stairs to the bridge which was all shiny bright with mahogany details and polished brass fittings. Off the bridge was a dormitory for four crew, a tidy head and a closet to hold uniforms.

Continuing down the other side of the bridge, the visitors proceeded to the ship's bow to see how *ship-shape* Captain Cadawalader had made that area. Here the decorators had placed four chaise lounges for sunbathing, with blue and white Chinese porcelain garden seats between them to hold drinks.

Inside the main cabin, guests visited the newly redecorated saloon and its adjoining dining saloon. Both of these areas had been furnished with long, low banquettes and deep comfortable club chairs upholstered in bright printed linens. Kilim carpets covered the polished mahogany floors and lamps made of antique Chinese porcelains topped by shades made of raw linen sat here and there on tabletops. Besides the banquettes in the dining saloon, there was also a large oval table surrounded by twelve antique carved teak planter's chairs from Thailand.

Moving below to the staterooms, the procession of guests oohed and aahed as each cabin was revealed. There were seven double cabins in all, six of which were decorated in nautical variations of blue and white, coral and white, black and white, white on white, and beige and white. The cabin which the decorators had been told *not to hold back on,* was the owner's stateroom, the one which Gaspar had reserved for his mother. This magnificent room, besides being decorated in shades of ivory, rose and pale aquamarine, had its own wood burning fireplace sporting the original Louis XV antique marble fireplace selected by Uncle Charlie when he'd had the yacht commissioned over a hundred years ago.

THE SHAKEDOWN CRUISE

Having inspected the magnificent yacht from stem to stern with Mr. Peugeot at his side, Gaspar was itching to get the show on the road. "Come on, mom," he beckoned. "I want you to christen the ship. Remember this isn't Cousin Eugenia's *Argente* anymore. I want you to christen her *Floridablanca*," he insisted leading his mother back towards the ship's brow, which they climbed back down following Peugeot who led them onto the dock.

A vintage bottle of Dom Perignon champagne had been hung by the crew from a long grosgrain ribbon near the ship's prow. Bishop du Bon Secours stood by, and when the guests had assembled at the rail overhead, he spoke an invocation asking God to protect the ship and all those who sailed on her. After the bishop splashed holy water on her prow and gunnels, Gaspar reached out and pulled the bottle of champagne forward, handing it to his mother.

"I christen you *Floridablanca*," Elvira Brown invoked, allowing the dark green bottle to shatter against the ship's prow, splashing its vintage nectar over the glistening white hull. The festive occasion was chronicled by three photographers, two from the local newspapers and one that Gaspar had hired from Naples, to make a record of the happy event. The photographers had been Uncle Charlie's idea. The old ghost had insisted that Gaspar start his own series of albums chronicling his time at La Rinconada, just like Uncle Charlie had done, starting as far back as 1918.

Gaspar and his friends applauded loudly, and a cheer rose up, led by Gaspar's best friend, Alex.

"Hip, hip, hooray! Hip, hip, hooray! Hip, hip, hooray!" the assembly shouted in unison taking up Alex's *cri de coeur* as Peugeot joined them, barking in unison to the happy cries.

Captain Craig Cadawaladar blew the ship's horn and started the mighty engines, as the jazz combo on the poop deck struck up a lively medley from Cole Porter's "Anything Goes". With Cole Porter playing in the background, Gaspar and Elvira danced up the stairs and back onto the deck with Peugeot bringing up the rear. The bishop and his two attendant altar boys picked up the hems of their cassocks and sprinted for the stairs, before the crew hauled them up.

"Take her out, Captain Cadawalader," Gaspar called up to his skipper up on the bridge.

"Aye, aye, Sir," Captain Cadawalader replied before calling, "Shove off men."

With that the *Floridablanca* began to float slowly down La Rinconada's Grand Canal and out into the Gulf of Mexico. The sailors quickly responded to their captain's commands and before long *Floridablanca* was under full sail, heading for a tour of Perdido Isle's coastline along the Gulf of Mexico between the towns of Calaluna and Llojeta, which formed the east and west boundaries of the privately owned island.

"Let's take her once around the block, captain," Gaspar suggested, knowing that his former sailing instructor would understand that he wanted to sail her once around the entire island.

Being on board the magnificently restored yacht and sailing around Perdido Isle was Gaspar's dream come true. Being surrounded by all the new friends he'd made in the short first year that he and his mother had moved to west Florida, was evidence that they had arrived exactly where they were supposed to be despite many fears, trials and tribulations. Even Al's father Felix, who was deathly afraid of drowning, seemed relaxed and happy to be part of this celebratory cruise. Al's mother, Angela, kept herself busy making sure that the provisions, which Gaspar had ordered were being served in the dining saloon. The many adult guests milling around the buffet included Gaspar's antiquarian, Jason Steinmeyer and his librarian, Margaret Stewart who were soon joined by Gaspar's school chums Pat, Sancho, Mark and Kevin, along with Kevin's sister, June. Gaspar was close to these four chums who'd helped him thwart the evil Unzega back at Smugglers Cove, and June, who'd been so instrumental in helping him not only with *The Mystery of The Seminole Spring* but also at *The House of Mystery* along with Jason and Margaret too.

The tour around the island took just four hours. As they passed the marinas of Calaluna and Llojeta it seemed as if anyone on the island with a boat or with access to a boat, had come out with blow horns and bells including the Coast Guard who were equipped with fire hoses spouting fountains of water to welcome the sparklingly restored white and gold yacht. By the time they finally sailed back, between the two huge carved alabaster lanterns which marked the entrance to La Rinconada's Grand Canal, the sun had completely set, and a Saracen moon surrounded by diamond-like stars filled the sky. Tied up once again at her dock, the festive party taking place on board continued far into the night.

It wasn't until midnight that the last guest left La Rinconada, and Gaspar and Mr. Peugeot finally got to bed. Because *Floridablanca* was his new toy, Gaspar decided to spend the night onboard and made himself and Peugeot at home in the big stateroom with the marble fireplace. When they walked into the room, the first thing they saw was Uncle Charlie sitting in the big club chair by the fireplace, waiting for them. Mr. Peugeot who didn't like spirits greeted Uncle Charlie's presence with a loud barrage of his angriest barks which Gaspar and Charlie both knew were more bluster than bite!

"Congratulations, Gaspar." Uncle Charlie greeted his nephew, while ignoring the pup. "It's great to see my pride and joy looking like new again. I have to compliment you on the decorations, they're simply marvelous," the old boy expressed his pleasure.

"Thank you, Uncle Charlie. I'm glad you're as pleased as I am. I couldn't be happier with the christening of the ship and the entire celebration." Gaspar enthused.

"Are you bunking in here tonight?" Charlie asked.

"Yes, I am," Gaspar said throwing himself down on the bed next to where Peugeot had already claimed his personal space.

"I don't blame you, boy." Uncle Charlie exclaimed looking askance at the sprawling poodle dog. It's exactly what I did right in this very room the first time I saw her finished and at dock in Liverpool." Uncle Charlie reminisced. "I wish you'd been with me on that maiden voyage across the Atlantic." Uncle Charlie waxed sentimental. "Have a good night's sleep, Gasp and we'll catch up tomorrow." Uncle Charlie promised, but Gaspar never heard him … he was out like a light, fully dressed on top of the covers with Peugeot snoring beside him.

CHAPTER 3

THE WEDDING

GASPAR HAD WITNESSED THE GROWING LOVE BETWEEN HIS MOTHER AND PETER CAWTHORNE, THEIR FRIEND and family attorney. He was happy for his parent, who he understood needed the love and security of a good man. Having had daily contact with Peter for the past year, Gaspar couldn't think of anyone better suited to the task. Peter was an extremely competent attorney, businessman and mentor to Gaspar, and Gaspar considered Peter to be one of his most loyal friends. Gaspar couldn't have been more pleased with the love affair, engagement and looming wedding and did everything in his power over the past few months to give the lovebirds room and not get in their way.

Their wedding was scheduled for Saturday, June fifthteenth and it would take place at the Catholic

15

church on La Rinconada's property. The church was a huge Hispano Moresque pile of architecture whose interior Gaspar could only describe as a "Storm-At-Sea" motif. What had been an abandoned church was getting near completion under the capable hands of Gaspar's Beverly Hills decorators. For the time being Bishop du Bon Secours was in charge of all things spiritual at La Rinconada until a suitable priest could be found to take up residency in the old rectory. It was the bishop who would preside at Elvira and Peter's wedding. Gaspar had plans for making his mother's wedding into a major event. He had told Elvira to find a dress that she wanted and that he would take care of all the rest of the arrangements including the honeymoon which would be an extended trip on *Floridablanca* to a secret destination which he and Alex intended to go on with them. Gaspar was happy that his suggestion, as always, had suited his mother just fine.

The afternoon of the wedding had arrived. Lamar Washington was waiting in La Rinconada's motor court with his shiny old silver Cadillac limousine to drive Gaspar and Elvira to the church. Gaspar waited for his mother at the bottom of La Rinconada's double coral-stone staircase. When Elvira appeared on the landing, a vision in white lace beaded with pearls, wearing a wreath of pearls and diamonds in her hair which held in place her gossamer veil of the finest white tulle, she looked to Gaspar, just like an angel. Angela, Alex's mother, stood behind her beaming. As matron of honor, Angela had helped Elvira dress. Slowly the two beautiful young women descended the staircase one in front of the other.

Mr. Peugeot heralded the ladies' descent to the entrance hall by barking loudly, wagging his tail.

"Mom, you look gorgeous," Gaspar expounded enthusiastically. "Here are your flowers," he said, gallantly handing her the bouquet of white orchids, gardenias and lilies of the valley which had been tied with a wide, double-faced, ivory-colored, silk-satin ribbon, exactly as the teenager had instructed the florist to arrange them.

"Thank you, Gaspar," Elvira breathed. "You'll always be my cavalier."

"I have something special for you, mom ... a present." he said picking up a leather case off the table near to where the flowers had been. Opening the box to show her what was inside, Gaspar heard both his mother and Angela gasp.

"They're rubies, mom," he said, "or almost rubies. They were Cousin Eugenia's. I'm not sure if they're real or not, but it doesn't matter. I read someplace that if you have to sniff it, taste it or touch it to find out if it's real, then it doesn't matter if they are or if they're not, because even if they're fake they're just as beautiful as the real thing," he informed the ladies wisely knowing full well that the jewels were indeed the real McCoy.

"Oh, Gaspar," Elvira cried. "Put them on me, honey!" she said crouching down in front of her four-foot eleven-inch-tall son, while stroking the base of her neck with her fluttering hands.

"Remember, ma, that day in the kitchen when I told you I'd cover you in rubies? Well here they are." Gaspar stood up behind her on tiptoes and clasped the precious necklace around his mother's throat. "Let's get going, mom," he urged her. "Peter's not the type of guy who likes to be kept waiting."

Since early morning, an army of florists had been filling the house with garlands of *stephanotis* and *rubrum* lilies under Gaspar's previous instructions. Months ago, he had asked Mr. Wilson, the manager at the Grand Hotel Floride in Llojeta, to supervise his catering staff and to "pull out all the stops" for this special occasion. Gaspar had told the seasoned hotelier that he wanted the buffets to look like the ones in the 1961 MGM film *Pocketful of Miracles*, where Bette Davis plays Apple Annie pretending to be Mrs. J. Worthington Manville, and gives a major party for Count Romero of Madrid.

"I want everything you can think of on those buffets," Gaspar told the astonished old innkeeper at their initial meeting. "Lobster, roast beef, chicken, crab, oysters, shrimp, squid, octopus, turkey, a suckling pig with an apple in its mouth, pheasants stuffed with apricots displayed with full plumage, sand dabs, mussels, clams, scallops, quail, salmon, even peacock, complete with feathers ... if you think anyone will eat it," Gaspar finished up. "And Mr. Wilson, throw in some potatoes, all kinds of potatoes, boiled, steamed, fried, hash browns, scalloped … whatever and rice, lots of rice in all different colors."

"How about vegetables, sir?" Wilson asked dubiously.

"Vegetables!" Gaspar shrieked, "You've gotta be kidding!" It was only Wilson's sad look that convinced the teenager that he'd have to relent. "Okay, Mr. Wilson, vegetables," he said resignedly. "But not too many, and no Brussels sprouts or cauliflower. Serve a lot of raw vegetables and salads, bring a lot of salad. Use your own discretion." Gaspar knew when to give in where adults were concerned. "Just remember, I'm an anti-vegetarian," he confessed to the bemused man, "Meat and potatoes are my thing."

"We'll bring a full bar, plenty of champagne, fruit punch and soft drinks for the young folk and people who don't drink, lots of ice and plenty of silver trays and crystal glasses," the thoughtful man enthused.

"Great," Gaspar was really getting into it. "How about some ice sculptures in the shapes of pirate ships, sea monsters, giant seashells, mermaids and tritons too."

"If you like, sir, but we'll need to keep them in the shade," Wilson warned.

"Maybe we need a tent, that's it, an air-conditioned tent. Call my pal Dave from Lagomar Party Rentals. He's the guy we always use for these kinds of things." Gaspar hoped that he sounded like a professional party giver, never having planned anything more extravagant in his young life than cake and ice cream before.

"Very well, sir, and the tablecloths, centerpieces and flowers?" he asked solicitously.

"All taken care of. I've got our decorators from Beverly Hills on board. The same ones who did the yacht. Not to worry, they're always throwing big parties for their best clients!"

"And the music," asked Mr. Wilson. "Will you have dancing?"

"Like crazy!" came Gaspar's response. "My mom and I love to dance. Get us your best dance orchestra, at least ten pieces, and find me a Hawaiian who'll sing loves songs on a ukulele from an outrigger in the swimming pool. And hey, Mr. Wilson, how 'bout some synchronized swimmers in the pool too, you know, like they have in the old Esther Williams movies." Now he was really on a roll. "And Mr. Wilson, hire a combo too. I don't want any lull in the music when the big orchestra goes on a break. Also, I've been reading about this guy, Johnny Holiday, on the internet. He lives in Hollywood. I've seen him perform on YouTube. He's really great. Could you call him for me and fly him and his show out here for this? I think it would be great to have a floor show and a real vintage forties kind of experience for our guests."

Wilson looked over served, as he frantically scribbled all of this down in his leather notebook. "How about dessert, sir?" he asked exhausted.

"Just wedding cake," was Gaspar's simple answer, "and ice cream, coffee, liqueurs, chocolate caramels. I don't want to overdo it," he said facetiously, hoping to get a reaction from the weary man.

Now the afternoon of the big day had finally arrived. Earlier this morning Gaspar and Peugeot had surveyed the tent and approved of the amazing decorations which the designers had transported from Los Angeles. To his joy, the interior of the tent had been lined with a specially printed fabric in a giant pattern taken from several antique maps of the world in a brilliant ivory, blue and yellow coloration. The tables had been covered in pink cloths with gauze overlays in soft jeweled tones of amethyst, citrine, aquamarine and peridot. In the middle of each table a small island of sand had been constructed, out of which sprang coral branches in blues, purples and pinks, sea urchins, and anemones, seashells and other formations normally found underwater, rather than on top of a dining table. Centered amidst this mass of colored sea life had been placed the most beautiful models of pirate ships made of wood, but painted to look like ivory, as if they'd been made in the eighteenth century by prisoners of war. Each of these fantastic crafts were individual. The designers had furled the sails so that one could look between the masts and rigging at the guests across the table. Each ship had its name on a stiffened banner undulating on the sand between the sea shells so that the guests would know which table they were assigned to, whether it be the *Floridablanca*, *Fortune's Galley*,

Bachelor's Delight, Fancy, Whydah, Gift, or *Golden Hind.*

Each table, and there were twenty-four of them, had its own ship with its own name attached. Gaspar couldn't have asked for more, having told the decorators exactly what he wanted and they having made his wish their command. To top off all of this festive beauty they'd installed tall étagères holding giant clamshells all around the perimeter of the space and had these filled with cascading white *phalaenopsis* orchids. Gaspar had forbidden Elvira or Peter to look inside the tent while the decorations were being prepared. In fact, he hadn't told them anything about any of his extravagantly creative plans. The entire wedding was his present to his mother and his new stepfather, and he couldn't wait for them to unwrap it.

When the tall clock in the hall struck four o'clock, Gaspar told Angela that she better, "*hightail it to the church with Felix and Alex.*" He and Elvira would follow in the limo. Peter had better be there waiting with his best man and new law partner, Brewster Wharton. Gaspar fretted needlessly, knowing full well Peter would never let them down. "Come on Peugeot, get up front with Lamar," Gaspar instructed the canine ring bearer.

For today's occasion Gaspar wore white flannel pants, a blue striped shirt with white collar and cuffs, a pair of Uncle Charlie's gold and lapis lazuli cufflinks resembling Spanish galleons, a blue and white polka-dotted silk tie, (also from Uncle Charlie's closet) and a swell pair of new

Gucci loafers in coral colored suede. He topped all of this off with a new double-breasted blue blazer to which he had the tailor in Llojeta add Uncle Charlie's solid gold buttons emblazoned with ship's anchors entwining the letter "F" which was the official crest for *Floridablanca*. As the official ring bearer, Peugeot had been outfitted with a special vest with the wedding rings attached with satin ribbons.

With Peugeot safely in the car, Gaspar offered his mother his arm and together they sailed forth from La Rinconada and into the back of Lamar's waiting limo.

"This sho-is-a happy day," Lamar proclaimed, as he closed the door behind them.

The drive to the church was indeed a happy one with mother and son sitting close to each other, reminiscing while Peugeot rode shotgun, keeping a sharp lookout out the side window for squirrels.

"Your father would be so proud of you today," Elvira told Gaspar.

"He's also proud of you, mom. He'd want you to be happy, and he would have liked Peter a lot if he'd ever met him." Gaspar assured her.

"Your father was a very special person, Gaspar," Elvira told him. "He loved us, more than anything. If he could have seen this coming," she said, motioning out the car window at their new domain of Perdido Isle, "he would have been so happy and would have relished bringing this place back to its original glory, just like you're bringing it back to the way it was, and to someday developing these five-hundred-thousand acres into something beautiful for the future."

"That's going to be our job, mom. You and me … and Peugeot's … just wait and see." He assured her light-heartedly. "I won't let you and dad down, or even Uncle Charlie … or Peugeot for that matter. And I know Peter will help me anyway he can, too. He already told me so."

"Peter's your ally and a really good friend," Elvira assured him. "He won't let anything happen to you, or to me, or Perdido Isle or La Rinconada for that matter. I know we can put all our trust in him. I think you know that too."

"I do, mom. The three of us and Peugeot, of course, will be a real family. I know it," Gaspar beamed.

As the car pulled into the churchyard, the crunching of broken seashells could be heard coming from under its tires. Angela was waiting by the church's open door. Felix and Alex were already inside, in their roles as ushers. As they walked closer to the church, Gaspar and Elvira could hear the organ playing inside. Gaspar checked his watch, or Uncle Charlie's watch as he liked to think of it … 4:30 on the dot. Uncle Charlie had taught him that *punctuality is the courtesy of kings*. They were right on time, as usual. A trumpet sounded from inside the church and the organ started up again with the wedding march from Mendelssohn's *Midsummer Night's Dream*. Angela kissed

Elvira on the cheek and walked towards the big double doors that led into the church. The two ushers, Alex and Felix, one on each side, nodded to Gaspar and he nodded back. They threw the doors open in unison and Angela stepped forward carrying a mother of pearl-encased prayer book that Gaspar had found in Uncle Charlie's library. After five beats Gaspar, with Peugeot on a leash, and Elvira on his arm followed Angela ... very slowly. The assembled guests rose and turned towards the simple procession. First, Gaspar saw smiles, then he heard gasps. He happily escorted his mother towards an incredibly happy Peter Cawthorne, who stood beaming next to his best man, Brewster Wharton, who bent down to retrieve the rings from Peugeot's vest. Gaspar handed his mother into Peter's care and stepped back, Mr. Peugeot in hand.

"Who gives this lady to be wed?" Bishop du Bon Secours asked loudly.

"I do," Gaspar answered solemnly. "Her son, Gaspar Brown," he ad-libbed to his mother's delight, who looked back and blew him a kiss as Peugeot let out a loving bark.

Having read his lines, Gaspar stepped to the side and led Peugeot to their seats next to Alex and Felix, in the very first pew. Surveying the altar, as if for the first time, he saw that Elvira and Peter were now front and center, and that Brewster and Angela were on each side of them.

The rest of the ceremony was a blur. Before he could start daydreaming, as was his wont, Gaspar found himself and Peugeot following the bride and groom, matron of honor and best man down the aisle, followed by what he thought must be the entire population of Calaluna and Llojeta, combined. A happy throng of strangers were massed outside the church, throwing handfuls of rice and confetti at the newlyweds who fled for the safety of Lamar's waiting limo. They were no sooner inside the old Cadillac than Lamar sped off for La Rinconada and the reception that awaited them there. Brewster and his girlfriend Colleen offered Gaspar a ride, while Felix, Angela and Alex also sped as fast as they could back to the house.

Gaspar had the presence of mind to ask Captain Morgan of the Calaluna Police Department to send over eight detectives in plainclothes to guard the main gate, the back gate into the stables, and the entrance from the street which led to the tombs and yacht basin. Captain Morgan had also placed one of his men at the front door and two at the base of each staircase, as well as a man in the drawing room, library and of course dining room where all the presents were on display.

Lieutenant Carl Anderson had also stationed the Coast Guard cutter *Orion* offshore as a precaution, less enthusiastic boaters try and crash the party from the gulf.

When Gaspar and Peugeot got to the house, they found Elvira and Peter in each other's arms waiting to greet their guests.

"We haven't peeked at the tent yet, Gaspar," Elvira assured him. "We're waiting for you to show us."

"Okay, let's line up here just to get started and then we can move outside after most of the people have arrived," Gaspar suggested. "Brewster and Colleen can be our first guinea pigs," he giggled.

It wasn't too many minutes later that Felix and Angela arrived, kissed the bride and shook hands with the groom and Gaspar, with a pat on the head for Peugeot, before joining Brewster and Colleen outside to make sure everything was in order for the party. Alex was the next to arrive and got a lot of compliments from the assembled Brown - Cawthorne family and a little bit of teasing about his dapper new blue suit. Alex and Gaspar had gone shopping together, getting all their *yachting duds* together for the big trip they would soon be taking on *Floridablanca*.

"I never thought I'd see the day," Gaspar chuckled, shaking his head at his duded-up pal.

"Yeah, you should talk," Alex teased. "Wait till you wear that houndstooth plaid suit you insisted on buying the other day. Then we'll see who gets the last laugh."

A river of well-wishers flooded the entrance hall, spilled down the steps into the drawing room and poured from room to room oohing and aahing at all the paintings, antiques and special decorations which made up La Rinconada. For many, this would be their first, and possibly their last visit to the historic house, which only a year ago had sat vacant and neglected, in want of an heir. Now with Gaspar in residence, the house and garden had blossomed into a real family home, cozy and warm despite its very grand proportions.

When the time was right, Gaspar and Peugeot escorted the newlyweds into the party tent. Standing in the curtained opening he watched his mother's and stepfather's faces as they took in the scene.

"I've never seen anything like it in my life," Elvira blurted out in happy disbelief.

"Amazing," was the only word Peter could utter. Then, "where did you find this incredible collection of pirate ships?" he asked Gaspar.

"You can thank the decorators for those," Gaspar confessed. "They did it all. I just gave them the idea."

"They're all made of ivory," Elvira admired the collection of model ships spread about the tent, a different one on each table,

"Yeah!" Gaspar lied, not wanting to burst her bubble and tell her that they were just painted to look like ivory … an idea he gave the decorators in hopes that the ships would look like they'd been made by long-gone prisoners of war.

"Extraordinary," was the most used word being whispered around the tent.

The reception was swinging. Peugeot was let loose to make the rounds, romp on the beach and beg treats from the guests. Gaspar and his pals hung out at the *Floridablanca* table and stuffed themselves from the plentiful buffet. They watched, laughed, and listened as Johnny Holiday did his *schtick* from the stage to the accompaniment of Dean Mora's ten-piece orchestra. Then to his friends' surprise, Gaspar got up and asked his mother to dance. He loved to dance, and so did she. They had a rip-roaring time out on the black and white checkered dance floor. Other couples stopped, just to watch mother and son tripping the light fantastic. When he got back to the table, Gaspar told Alex that it was his duty to not only dance with the bride, but also with his own mother, Angela as well. He also told Kevin, Sancho and Pat the exact same thing. It's your duty as guests to dance with the ladies, *all of them*. Alex and the rest of the gang were terrified at the thought, which pleased Gaspar to no end. He now watched and laughed as they obeyed him, and for the first time he realized the power of entertaining. Thinking their duties done, the boys all slunk back to their *stag* table, but Gaspar wasn't going to let them off the hook that easily.

"Okay, guys, big deal. You danced with the bride and you danced with your own mothers, now it's time to dance with some chicks our own age. Get up, follow me. We've just started," he told them in no uncertain terms.

And so, they danced and danced, and ate cake, and joked around until it was almost ten o'clock at night. That's when Gaspar gave the signal to start the fireworks, which he had placed on a barge anchored about four-hundred feet offshore. There, the famous Cicogna family of pyrotechnicians, who he'd flown in from Italy, presented their display of *faux de artifice*, as a special surprise for the bride and groom and of course for his guests' pleasure. With an enormous *boom*, which sent revelers running out of the tent to see what the commotion was, the sky ignited into a rainbow of colored streamers, exploding stars and giant chrysanthemums. To Gaspar's delight the Cicogna launched missiles that skipped along the Gulf of Mexico in front of them exploding in beauty with each skip across the water. Everyone lined the balustrade looking out to sea to enjoy the spectacle, while waiters passed trays of champagne, coffee, and liqueurs. Forty-five minutes later, when the fireworks ended, another fanfare announced the synchronized swimmers in the pool. Gaspar was pretty sure that nobody from Perdido Isle had ever seen anything as glorious as this party, not since Gatsby, or MGM, or Uncle Charlie's day, that's for sure!

The party surged on and the orchestra continued playing, while Elvira, Peter, Gaspar, Peugeot and Alex climbed aboard *Floridablanca* where Captain Craig Cadawalader and his crew stood at attention to welcome them. With a massive toot of the yacht's horn, all of the guests came running to the seawall, and the ship departed for the honeymoon cruise. The passengers' luggage had been on board for days, and all of their provisions too. Guests watched and waved handkerchiefs and threw paper streamers, which waiters with baskets passed around, as the beautiful ship slipped down the grand canal, prow first. Gaspar appreciated that Captain Craig Cadawalader had earlier docked her, prow forward in order to make an elegant getaway that evening. As *Floridablanca*, pennants waving in the tropical breeze, passed in front of the house, with cheering guests lined up along the balustrade of the terrace, the Coast Guard cruiser *Orion* gave the newlyweds a twenty-one-gun salute. It was a thunderous send-off that nobody present that night, especially Gaspar and his parents would ever forget.

CHAPTER 4

THE YUCATÁN

GASPAR HADN'T TOLD ANYONE EXCEPT FOR HIS CAPTAIN WHERE THEY WERE GOING. HE'D TOLD Peter, Elvira and Alex to pack for the tropics and to bring things suitable for a glamorous yachting trip, but that was all.

"Where are we headed, Gaspar?" Peter finally asked as they all stood near the rail, looking back at the party lights growing smaller and smaller in the distance.

"We're going to my place in the Yucatán," Gaspar disclosed his plan with just a bit of reluctance.

"Your place in the Yucatán?" Elvira parroted her son.

"Yeah, you guys haven't forgotten about the old house on the beach that belonged to Uncle Charlie's friend and protector Dr. Mendoza y Mendoza, have you?" Gaspar asked, feigning disbelief.

33

"Of course not," answered Peter. "But Gaspar, nobody has ever been there, not after 1975 at least," Peter reminded him.

"If we get there and don't like it," Gaspar assured them, "we can just stay on the yacht, or go on down to Punta del Este. I hear that's a nice place to visit this time of year."

"Sounds like fun, Gasp," Alex piped up. "I've always wanted to see the land of my ancestors and who knows, maybe I have a rich Uncle Charlie down there too."

"I hope you're not disappointed with my choice. I thought it would be fun … and romantic," Gaspar explained. "If you'd rather go to Paris or something, I'll just tell Craig to head east. No problem. I do have Angela and Felix meeting us down there. They leave tomorrow by jet for Mérida. I would have brought them with us, but you know how scared Felix is of drowning. Anyway, they'll get there long before we will, and get the lay of the land and see what the house looks like and everything." Gaspar was starting to second guess the soundness of his decision for this trip.

"Gosh, if I'd known, I would have telegraphed the caretakers and told them to expect us," Peter threw in, wearing his business hat.

"It's okay, Peter. I asked Brewster to do that for us. I didn't want to spoil the surprise. It's all set. Brewster says the caretaker, Juano and his wife Carmen can't wait to meet us, and they said that the house is all ship-shape and ready for our arrival. Like I said, if we don't like it, we don't have to stay, but there's all kinds of neat stuff to see in the Yucatán." He told them with as much enthusiasm as he could muster. "I've put lots of books on the subject in each of our state rooms so if you're interested … you have plenty of homework, if you want to do it."

"Gaspar, you always think of everything," Elvira complimented her son. "This is going to be the best trip we've had since our road trip last summer, when we drove out here from California to see Perdido Isle for the first time. Thank you, darling, for taking such good care of us. And thank you, for that beautiful reception too. I've never been to anything like it, and I've certainly never heard of anything like it or seen anything like it, not even on TCM. Gaspar, you never cease to amaze me. Kiss me goodnight. Mama's going to turn in." Elvira proclaimed, hoping she'd allied her son's fears of defeat.

"Goodnight, mom," Gaspar kissed her goodnight.

"Goodnight, dad," Gaspar gave Peter a big abrazo.

"Goodnight, Mr. and Mrs. Cawthorne, Alex smiled at the newlyweds. "See you in the morning."

"Goodnight, boys," the newlyweds called in unison as they headed to their cabin below deck.

Gaspar and Alex and Peugeot stayed up, walking back out onto the poopdeck. It was a balmy night, and the stars spangled against the black velvet sky. "This is the life," Gaspar took a deep breath hoping to chase all negative thoughts from his mind as he, sprawled with

Peugeot on the built-in sofa at the fantail.

"You said it, brother," Alex agreed. "Thanks, Gasp … for choosing the Yucatán for *Floridablanca*'s maiden voyage, and thanks for taking me along for the ride. I'm the luckiest guy in the world." Alex hoped his words would cheer his pal up.

"Don't give it another thought, Al. I wouldn't have done it without you. Just wait till we get there. We'll get a car and go to all the ruins, and eat lunch on the beach, and parasail and jet-ski, and explore ancient Mayan sites and visit all the museums and the churches, and we'll meet interesting people … I can't wait!" Gaspar finished breathlessly. "You'll see, it's gonna be a great trip." He was still trying to convince himself, as Peugeot cuddled closer, sensing his master's disheartened mood.

"It was a great party, Gasp," Alex complimented his host. "I've never danced with my mother before. Heck, I've practically never danced with a girl before except for the big dance you gave at the clubhouse. You're always opening my eyes, man."

"Yeah, well besides my mother and your mother, who'd you like dancing with best?" Gaspar wondered. Rehashing the party had an effect on him and he started to feel a little more like his old self.

"June, of course … stupid," was Alex's reply.

"Yeah, well she barely comes up to your belly button, you *spongy, reeling ripe snot locker*." Gaspar couldn't believe that Alex actually thought June could be at all interested in him or vice-a-versa.

"You gotta admit, June definitely has the moves," Alex defended his position. "And she's certainly never gonna fall for *a spleeny, rough-hewn, pigeon-egg* like you, you *rump-fed, sheep-biting puttock.*" Alex chuckled through the insults he hurled at his best friend.

"She's too good for you … you stupid idiot. I hope you're not falling for her. June would never put up with a *clown-dressed, potato-faced phylloxera*, and that's what you are." Gaspar Haddocked.

"Falling for her. I'm not falling for her. What would I want to hang out with girls for anyway, *You ruttish, pox-marked, hairy cucumber?*" Alex retreated.

"That's good, cause *I like her a lot*, and I think *she likes me a lot too*. So, stay away from her, you *tottering, shard-borne, mumble-news*," Gaspar romanced.

"*By my beard, get out of here, you two-timing, rotten, toad-spotted banana-seller.* June … Ha … She doesn't even know you exist, *You wayward son of a skain's mate.* That lovely lassie wouldn't give you the time of day." Alex stared his friend down.

"*Dart not scornful glances from those eyes, Al.* June wouldn't be so crass as to swear by *a false deity*, such as yourself *Alejandro*," Gaspar called his friend by his Spanish name which he knew Al hated.

"Oh, yeah, well you obviously didn't see me dancing with her tonight or you would have noticed that *June* was all over *me* on the dance floor, you *beslubbering, beef-witted, barnacle*." Alex exaggerated as best he could.

"Oh, yeah, you *bitter blockhead*. Well you've never been diving with her either like I have, you *artless, base-court apple-john*. When I was diving with her the other day, I pretended to get a cramp and June dragged me through the water and up onto the sand and kneaded my leg. Basically, I was manhandled by that beautiful *feline filly*," Gaspar bragged.

"You *faithless filthy bandit*. Now you've gone too far. Besides, you're such a liar. Come on, you *pig-headed goat*, let's hit the sack. It's been a big day and listening to your love life is not how I want to end it," Alex scolded Gaspar while heading inside.

Peugeot had watched and listened to this exchange between friends, turning his head back and forth, confusion in his bright black eyes. When his pals finished their argument and started for bed, he jumped up and joined them. Walking shoulder to shoulder towards their respective cabins, the two boys with Peugeot trotting behind them continued to Captain Haddock their way down the companionway, tossing even more ridiculous insults at each other all the way to their staterooms.

CHAPTER 5

SAILING, SAILING, OVER THE BOUNDING MAINE

THE TRIP FROM PERDIDO ISLE, FLORIDA, TO MÉRIDA, YUCATÁN TOOK FOUR DAYS UNDER FULL SAIL. CRAIG charted a direct route, assisted by cooperative breezes and favorable gulf streams. The family's days were filled with reading, eating, sleeping, sunning, playing cards and checkers, as well as chess, shuffleboard, and many formidable games of Monopoly. Gaspar also had a comprehensive collection of old MGM films brought on board, which they projected onto a big screen. Life on *Floridablanca* was nothing if not stress-free. Craig had hired a chef named Murray, who turned out phenomenal meals for the family and crew. At Gaspar's invitation, Craig joined them for all meals and in turn, Craig regaled the family with tales of the sea, which had been passed down to him from his family of trophy-winning yachts-men. One of the best stories he told was how back in 1914 his great-grandfather had taken a party of friends to the Crimea on his yacht and how while there, they were trapped in the Black Sea when America joined the allies in World War I. Craig said that his great-grandfather asked the Americans on board if they wanted to spend the war in the Crimea or make a run for it. They all agreed to make a run for it and assembled all the weapons on board that they could muster. The yacht, with its motley crew of grand dames, debutantes, dilettantes and yachtsmen, ran a German blockade and got out through the Mediterranean. The tale was a tall one, but it kept the captive listeners on the edge of their seats throughout the telling. The days whizzed by and before they knew it, *land ho* was heard shouted by one of the sailors up on the bridge. Gaspar, his parents and Alex ran to the rail to see Yucatán looming in the distance. It had been a quick and very pleasant trip, but now that they'd made landfall, Gaspar had a sudden sense of foreboding.

So, this was the famous bay that supposedly was the site of the impact of the meteorite that killed the dinosaurs, Gaspar thought ominously. *But what does that have to do with this trip?* Shaking off his feelings of trepidation, he put his arm around Alex's shoulder and mumbled, "Now we're really gonna have some fun, Al."

CHAPTER 6

CELESTÚN, YUCATÁN

WHILE PLANNING THE RESTORATION OF *FLORIDABLANCA*, GASPAR MADE SURE THAT CRAIG HAD A RELIABLE GPS system installed and that he'd brought very accurate maps on board too. Before raising anchor after the wedding on Perdido Isle, Brewster had informed Craig exactly where The Doctor's House was located, and how best to find it. Sailing to the southwest of Mérida, they continued along the coast towards the town of Celestún. Reaching the coordinates 20°51.5'N 90°24'W / 20.8583°N 90.400°W / 20.8583; -90.400., they soon came to a clearing in the tropical fringe of jungle which framed the small village of 6,000 souls. This was their destination.

Celestún was the name of the village, and Huayrocondo was the ancient name of the hacienda that

Gaspar had inherited from Uncle Charlie along with Perdido Isle and La Rinconada. The Doctor's House was the name used by the family and Uncle Charlie when referring to this particular property. From where Gaspar watched from *Floridablanca*'s railing, The Doctor's House, stood out as one of the larger structures along the expansive stretch of beach.

As the travelers made their preparations for going ashore, Captain Cadawalader anchored *Floridablanca* about three hundred yards out in the bay. From the deck they could see that a formidable crowd of onlookers had come down to the beach to see the beautiful Edwardian yacht bobbing at anchor. Gaspar wondered if there might be some old people in the town who actually remembered the yacht coming to port years ago. *Floridablanca*'s new motorized tender took Craig and his four passengers ashore where they were met by the harbor master of Celestún. Felix and Angela were standing with the official who was wearing an old threadbare, sweat-stained uniform, but who looked the part with his long sideburns and mustachioed upper lip.

"Welcome to Celestún, Señors y Señora," the harbor master greeted them cordially. "It is good to at last meet the new owners of Huayrocondo y La Casa del Doctore. The hacienda has been vacant for many, many years, and we feared that the family might never return again."

"Is it an important house?" Elvira asked, confused.

"Si, si, Señora," the official replied. "When he lived

here, Doctor Mendoza y Mendoza was the most important man in the village. He owned not only the house, but the biggest hacienda in the area. The hacienda land is situated around the Pico de Huayrocondo," he told them, proudly pointing towards the towering peak off in the distance. "The entire hacienda was a land grant from the King of Spain to an ancestor of the doctor's, El Capitan Ignacio de Mendoza y Mendoza. He was not only a conquistador but also the perpetual governor of Yucatán. The royal land grant was said to be so vast that no white man has to this day ever crossed it from one end to the other." He told them with astonishment and raised eyebrows. "Your land is bordered by two rivers which run on each side of the Pico de Huayrocondo, but some say that the hacienda actually has no boundaries, and that it extends all the way to Chichén Itzá or maybe even as far as the Pacific Ocean," he told them breathlessly. Today is a great day for our town, Celestún … now that Los Patrones, the family of the doctor, have returned to claim their patrimony," the man explained, bowing low. "Come, captain," he insisted guiding Craig Cadawalader by the elbow. "You will need to fill out some papers in my office. Buenos tardes, Señores," he said bowing again to Elvira, Peter, Gaspar, and Alex. "Your friends, Angela and Felix, will take you to your house."

After happy hellos with Angela and Felix and without any further ado, the travelers followed Alex's parents to The Doctor's House. There they met Huayrocondo's caretakers, Juano and Carmen Mendoza, who Felix and Angela introduced to Alex as his cousins. What the actual relationship of these people were to Alex was anyone's guess? For now, cousins were cousins and the Mendozas, all of them, were very happy to be together again on the Gulf coast of Yucatán.

The house was a big, low-slung, Spanish Colonial hacienda with thick adobe walls, deep overhanging porches and a sweeping red-tiled roof that had been patched so many times that the red clay tiles were now stacked five and eight high in some places. While being shown around their new *beach house*, as Gaspar dubbed it, they discovered five patios, twenty bedrooms, a double sala, a massive dining room, a completely antique, falling-down kitchen, hardly any bathrooms that worked and a stable yard attached complete with twenty empty stables full of filth.

Going back into the house after their hasty tour, they looked the place over one more time, albeit a little less politely.

"Gaspar, this is your house," his mother chided him. "You should be ashamed to bring us here with the place in this condition," she chuckled.

"Now, mom, you've seen worse," Gaspar joked. "But this definitely is a room in which a great deal of expense has been spared." He paraphrased his favorite mystery author Dashiell Hammett. "Of course, with a coat of fresh paint, some throw pillows and a few bouquets of fresh flowers, you'd be surprised how cozy we could make this." He chuckled, recalling Marty Feldman's hysterical line from *Young Frankenstein*.

"Your optimism is unbounded … it's what I've always liked about you, Gasp," Peter cut in.

"Okay, folks. Let's get real." Gaspar rallied his troops. "All we need are two bedrooms and two bathrooms. Angela and Felix have already settled in and they aren't unhappy …. Are you?" He asked his caretakers hopefully.

"We're very cozy, and we've fixed up two bedrooms and two bathrooms for you as well. We'll show you," Angela announced with a smile.

"There, you see, problem solved," Gaspar quipped. "Now this living room may be a little dusty, but it has charm. All of this old stuff is amazing … seventeenth-century Spanish Colonial, authentic. Let's look at it again, tomorrow, in the daylight and reappraise the situation" he told them, moving into the next room. "This dining room is dreamy. The table could use a good scrubbing and the chairs might need a cushion or two, but just pretend you're living in the seventeenth century. Believe me, this is so much better than anything any of the Spanish conquistadors had back in those days. If you really hate it here, we can all go back on board *Floridablanca* or, if you prefer, we can go inland to a hotel. I promise not to make you stay here if you hate it." Gaspar felt his grand plans had only slightly deflated.

Angela showed them to the bedrooms, which she

and Carmen had cleaned up for them. The honeymoon suite was beyond description with its sagging bed, broken-down old furniture and windows covered with faded sun-bleached curtains. Gaspar and Alex would gladly share a room but theirs was no better. One look at the amazingly barbaric bathroom with its cracked and stained toilet sent the two boys into gales of howling laughter.

"A thousand million-the dead of winter-storms!" Gaspar Captain Haddocked, while Alex fell down on the floor, laughing uncontrollably.

"Angela, are you and Felix really happy here or would you like to come on board the yacht with us or take a hotel room in town?" Gaspar asked her solicitously.

"We like it here, Gaspar. We are actually very happy staying with our cousins, meeting members of our family. We don't want to stay anywhere else," Angela insisted, nodding in the affirmative to her husband.

"Okay," Gaspar countered to the others. "I've got a plan. We'll go back to the yacht and spend the night. Tomorrow we'll make an excursion into town to have a look around. In the meantime, I have a surprise for us, which I'll tell you about at dinner."

Back on board the yacht, Gaspar went into conference with Craig. Together they got on the phone to California and spoke with a travel agent who was still at work, (California time being two hours earlier than Yucatán,) and formed a plan of action. Shortly after they hung up, an email came through which Craig printed out. By the time dinner was served, Gaspar was ready to spring his big news.

"Okay, boys and girls, here's the deal," Gaspar enthused. "I've contacted a travel agent who has laid out a brilliant itinerary for us. Tomorrow morning, we will be picked up in town by an SUV with an English-speaking driver, who is also a guide. He will take us to all the most amazing Mayan sites and places of historic importance or cultural interest in the Yucatán including Chichén Itzá, Uxmal, and Tulúm. When we get to Tulúm, Craig will have *Floridablanca* waiting for us. In the meantime, we'll be spending our nights in deluxe rooms at the most interesting places along the way. Then when we are completely happy with our little Yucatán adventure, we'll get back on *Floridablanca* and come back here, and take another look around."

"Oh, Gaspar. Leave it to you to save the day," Elvira smiled at Peter, then gave her son a big kiss on the cheek. "The itinerary sounds fantastic, and you know I've been doing my homework, too. I hope we'll get a chance to see Dzibilchaltún, Ek Balam and Valladolid too."

"And I definitely want to climb up inside the pyramid of El Castillo, and see the *Jade Jaguar*," Peter added, happy to be on board with Gaspar's new plan.

"And when we get to Tulúm, Craig, I thought you might like to take me diving at the Dos Ojos Cenote," Gaspar hoped. "Maybe Alex would like to go with us, as long as Felix and Angela don't find out," he winked at all assembled.

"*Code of silence, code of silence,*" Alex shouted, knowing his father would never approve of his going underwater. "I'd love to go diving with you guys."

"And, Gasp, don't forget you and I are going to the Isla de Mujeres. Remember, you promised," Alex whined.

"Al, you're always so horny. There are no women on the Isla de Mujeres. Didn't you read the guidebook? Peter, you gotta have a talk with Felix about this. I can't be Al's best friend and his father figure, too," Gaspar complained.

"I don't know why not," Peter said. "That's the way I feel about you, *best friend and father, too.*"

Gaspar just smiled. "You read my mind, Peter."

"It takes one to know one!" Peter shot back.

What Gaspar hadn't told his fellow travelers was that he'd called his decorators in Beverly Hills and told them to get on the next plane to Mérida, Yucatán. He told them that The Doctor's House needed a complete facelift without removing any of the charm, and that they needed to haul in the best decorator in Mérida to help them do the dirty work. He told them that they had only two weeks to make it happen.

"Just do the obvious stuff first, the stuff you see, on the surface. And get the existing bathrooms to work, and somehow make every bedroom have its own bathroom. The house needs an entirely new kitchen. New beds, new curtains, new upholstery. But don't throw out any of the antiques, just polish them up. I know you guys like a challenge, especially when the budget is unlimited," he joked. "Text me every day with updated reports. I want this to be our little secret. Your contacts will be Felix and Angela. You met them at La Rinconada. They'll be the only ones from our immediate group who will be in on this, along with my attorney Brewster Wharton, back at Perdido Isle. He'll provide the dough, just like last time! While you're at it, find a landscape gardener who can quickly spruce up the grounds. Nothing extravagant, just make it beautiful as if it's always been like that, you know, wild, and tropical like an MGM film ... *my* look." With that, Gaspar turned off the phone before going into dinner.

CHAPTER 7

FOUR INTREPID EXPLORERS

THE NEXT MORNING, AFTER A HEARTY BREAKFAST ON DECK, GASPAR, ALEX AND THE HONEYMOONERS WENT ashore in the bright morning sunlight. Gaspar had instructed his traveling companions to bring everything ashore that they would need for a two-week trip across the Yucatan peninsula to Tulúm, where he'd instructed Craig to have *Floridablanca* waiting for them. Before they piled into the waiting SUV, Gaspar asked them to take one last look around The Doctor's House to see if it looked as bad in the morning light as it had the previous afternoon. After they had a second look around, Gaspar could see by their combined reactions that as far as they were concerned the situation at Hacienda Huayrocondo was hopeless. As the others piled into the waiting car, Gaspar took Angela and Felix aside and informed them

51

that the decorators were on their way, and that it was to be their little secret. If they needed him, all they had to do was call or text his cell phone.

With a happy farewell, the travelers gladly left the ramshackle Doctor's House in the dust and headed for the Yucatán jungle.

Their driver, Roberto Ortiz, a young man who knew the country well, asked them if they had any special requests. Gaspar suggested heading first to Mérida so that they could see what the largest city in Yucatán looked like. Roberto informed them that Mérida had once been one of the richest cities in the world and that it was a town of mansions, cathedrals, and magnificent public buildings. He promised them that they would be in the city in about an hour and forty-five minutes.

The ride to Mérida passed smoothly along a well paved highway. Arriving at their destination, they drove through one of the ancient gates of the former walled city, marveling at the abundance of Spanish Colonial, seventeenth-, eighteenth-, and nineteenth-century architecture. Roberto proved to be a superlative guide, driving them to the historic center of town and escorting them around the various sites. In just a short time they visited the Palacio de Gobierno, The Catedral de San Ildefonso, which was the first cathedral built in the continental Americas way back in 1598. They next drove to the Barrio de Santa Lucia to see the chapel which the Spanish had built in 1575 before Roberto suggested they stop for lunch. They had been so engrossed in the magnificence of the old town and its charming barrios or neighborhoods that they hadn't realized it was well past one in the afternoon.

Roberto took them to what he assured them was the *best restaurant in town* and when they got there, the Casa de Piedra at Hacienda Xcanatun did not disappoint. Located in the Casa de Maquinas of the renovated old hacienda, they dined surrounded by old machinery in an amazingly decorated high-ceilinged room. The various dishes which Roberto had suggested they order were exotic and yet familiar to them, as many were reminiscent of the exceptional Yucateca cuisine Angela cooked for them back at La Rinconada.

After lunch, they took a leisurely stroll around the old hacienda. All the time Gaspar was pointing out how similar the layout was to The Doctor's House, and the potential of putting *that* house back in order, just like this one had been restored. Having fully explored the Hacienda Xcanatun they got back in the car to continue their sightseeing.

Besides Mérida's bustling shopping streets, elegant parks, towering municipal buildings, arches, fountains, and mansions galore, the city was filled with religious sites of importance, all of which Roberto insisted they see. When Roberto mentioned wanting to show them even more, everyone revolted and begged him to save something of interest for another day.

"Let's find a hotel," Gaspar suggested diplomatically. "Roberto, we need a tea party, and a *siesta*. I, for one am exhausted."

"You have reservations at The Hacienda Misne, Roberto announced with a big smile. It is a Yucatán hacienda from the nineteenth century. The hotel has a beautifully restored principal house surrounded by lush tropical gardens behind old walls. It is just four miles from here, near the highway to Cancun. I think you will like it, señor."

Gaspar looked back at his parents from his seat next to Roberto and smiled.

"Gaspar, you're amazing. How'd you get this trip arranged so perfectly?" Elvira asked.

"Don't speak too soon, ma. It's only our first day of touring. Let's wait and see what Roberto has wrought," Gaspar urged.

"Señor Gaspar, if there is anything you don't like or something you want to do, I am here to serve you, *para server te*," Roberto insisted.

"Don't fret, Roberto," Gaspar assured him. "So far so good. We trust you implicitly and defer to you on all things Yucateca.

Two very pleasant days later, after a thorough visit of Mérida and having enjoyed all of the first- class amenities of the Hacienda Misne, they decided to move back in time and explore some of the nearby Mayan ruins.

Their first stop after leaving Mérida was the Mayan

archaeological site of Dzibilchaltún. Roberto tried to teach them to pronounce its name properly. "Ts'íibil Cháaltun," he kept mouthing, but none of his passengers could quite copy his Mayan inflections. Finally giving up, he told them that the ancient builders of Dzibilchaltún chose the site of the city so as to be as close as possible to the coastal salt-producing region, while still being located on a reasonably fertile and habitable terrain."

Although Dzibilchaltún was only a ten mile drive, it took the travelers thirty minutes to get there from Mérida. The minute the car stopped, Gaspar, Peugeot and Alex bounded out and started heading for the biggest structure they could see.

"Have fun, guys," Elvira called after them.

"We'll stick with Roberto and learn what all of this is about", Peter added.

Together the newlyweds laughed out loud at the boys' enthusiasm for exploration.

While his parents watched and discussed with Roberto the logical way to visit the famous archaeological site, Gaspar with Alex and Peugeot beside him, disappeared in the direction of the temple they'd seen peeking over the top of the trees. When they reached their goal, they learned from reading the placard placed there that they were at the Temple of the Seven Dolls. The placard also stated that the structure was so named because of seven small effigies found under the ruins of a later pyramid when the temple was discovered by archaeologists in the 1950s.

"Gosh, Al," Gaspar wondered. "that means that underneath all of this there's a whole other temple. Let's figure out how you get into that one?"

"There's probably an entrance from up there," Alex said, pointing up to the pavilion perched on top of the pyramid. "I bet there's a trap door and a secret staircase leading down inside … from up there."

"Okay, let's go see," Gaspar shouted as he scrambled up the stairs on all fours, followed by Peugeot who climbed the first steps with trepidation before getting the knack of the steep climb up. The boys were as amazed as Peugeot at how really steep the pyramid was. Reaching the top, they couldn't believe that the descent appeared to be practically straight down.

"That's not gonna be much fun to climb down, Peugeot," Gaspar chuckled to his pooch.

Having reached the pinnacle of the pyramid, Gaspar and Alex searched and searched for the secret entrance that might possibly lead down into the other pyramid, while Peugeot sniffed around, but their collective efforts were to no avail. Turning their attention to the more obvious, they took in the view. From where they stood, they could look out in all directions over the jungle. They could see the tops of other temples protruding above the lush vegetation and they could also see the sun, glistening on the sea, twenty-two kilometers away. Up on top of the world, the boys realized that they were practically the only visitors to the sacred site. Below them, Peter and Elvira were walking slowly with Roberto, who was gesticulating enthusiastically, this way and that, telling them about the Maya and the archaeology all around them.

"Come on, Al. Let's go back down and explore some of the other structures," Gaspar suggested.

Very slowly, the two boys eased themselves down the steps which they'd climbed up on all fours … but now, going down they lowered themselves, step by step, bump, bump, bump … on their butts. Gaspar held a grateful Peugeot in his lap for the descent, Gaspar laughing and Peugeot panting as they inched their way down the precipitous steps while Peter, Elvira and Roberto stood at the bottom of the incline, laughing their heads off at the teenagers' plight and the poodle's dilemma.

"*Nitwitted ninepins*, ma, don't laugh," Gaspar admonished Elvira in the spirit of *Captain Haddock* while Peugeot barked to second the motion. "It's as steep as *slubberdegullions*. I'd like to see you try it, Peter. At least you have long legs. I'm just a *puny, puking, pint-sized four-foot eleven-inch pribling*," Gaspar reminded his stepfather, hoping for sympathy "and Peugeot's is even smaller!"

"Come on, darlin," Peter cajoled his bride, offering her his hand. "Let's show the *short-stop* how it's done." Peter laughed as he and Elvira proceeded to climb the pyramid on all fours just like the boys had done, while Gaspar and Alex howled with laughter after them.

Before Roberto started the climb to catch up with Peter and Elvira, he gave the kids some tips. "This temple is the most important structure on the site. Every year on the spring equinox, when the sun rises … it shines directly through one window of the temple and out the other," he told the boys, pointing upwards. "This is a similar event to the descending snake of Chichén Itzá. You probably noticed when you were up on top that this temple is connected to the rest of the site by a sacbé, or "white road", so-called because when the Maya built them, they were originally filled with stone-and-rubble before being coated with white limestone."

"What else should we explore while you guys are climbing the Seven Dolls?" Gaspar asked the guide.

"Besides this temple, the other major feature of Dzibilchaltún is the cenote.

"What's a cenote?" Alex asked, with a look of confusion on his face.

It's called Cenote Xlakah, and it's located around the center of the city's ruins … over there," Roberto said pointing off to his right. "It's thought that the availability of this source of clean drinking water influenced the choice of this location to build the city."

"Oh, you mean it's a well," Gaspar offered helpfully.

"Well it's more than a well. It's more like a cistern or a lake. The water comes from underground. Archaeological findings retrieved from the Cenote

Xlakah by divers indicate that it was also the center of a religious cult."

"A swimmin' hole," Alex shouted, "Gasp, a swimmin' hole."

"Well, yes," Roberto confessed. "These days the cenote is used for swimming by local residents and tourists year-round, but from the looks of things, you'll probably have it all to yourselves," Roberto assured them. "There's also the ruin of a sixteenth-century Spanish church built after the conquest. It's over there," Roberto said pointing to his left.

"Tell you what, Roberto," Gaspar lowered his voice conspiratorially, "Al and I are going for a swim. You take the old folks to the church and we'll meet you back at the car in about an hour."

"Very well, Señor Gaspar. I understand completely. I used to swim there a lot when I was your age," Roberto smiled knowingly. "Better than meeting us at the car, Dzibilchaltún has a great archaeological visitor center with maps, restrooms and gift shops. It's right near where we parked the car. There's also a museum there housing Mayan artifacts. I'll take your parents there. I think they will like it, so when you are ready, just meet us at the museum.

"It's a deal," Gaspar waved as he and Alex sped into the jungle in the direction of the Cenote Xlakah with Peugeot running behind them barking his approval.

When the boys reached the cenote, they found it

deserted. "Come on, Al. It's all ours," Gaspar rejoiced, as he stripped off his t-shirt and shorts.

Before a minute had passed the two boys were splashing and diving in the cool, clear fresh water while Peugeot ran back and forth along the edge, barking furiously before jumping in to join them.

After their refreshing swim, they got out and used their hands like squeegees to remove the water from their limbs while Peugeot shook himself dry. Still wet, but not dripping, the boys donned their discarded clothes and started back down the path with Peugeot at their side, heading in the direction of the church.

"We may as well check out the church as long as we're here," Gaspar drawled with a trace of boredom in his voice. "Far be it from me to miss seeing another religious structure ... heaven forbid," he joked to Alex who was even less interested in seeing more churches and cathedrals than his pal.

Entering the sixteenth-century Spanish sanctuary was reminiscent of entering St. Anna's back on Perdido Isle because both edifices were built in the middle of nowhere, surrounded by jungle.

"This is amazing, Al," Gaspar noted. "I've heard that the Conquistadors would build their churches right over the Maya, Aztec or Inca's most sacred temples. They'd raze the pagan temples to the ground, then build their structures right on top of the original native foundations. The Spanish were even rude enough to use the same old stones for their new structures. From the looks of this place, I think that's the case here. You're the architect, Al. What do you think?"

"I think you're spot on, Gasp," Alex rejoined. "Look at the floors and the lower three feet of wall. They are not at all like the later church. Definitely Maya. Look here … see … pagan carving here and again over there … see … right along the base."

"I've read that in some ancient civilizations they would connect all of their structures with underground passages and secret ceremonial rooms. I wonder if the Maya … " before Gaspar could finish his thought, they were startled by a sharp, grating sound coming from behind the altar as Peugeot let out a low growl.

"Gasp, we're not alone," Alex whispered.

Gaspar put a finger to his lips to silence his friend, grabbed Peugeot and muzzled him using his hand, while guiding Alex over to the side of the church behind a column. Together they watched a pair of men wearing filthy khaki garments emerge from behind the altar. They were both carrying dirty burlap gunnysacks, which were bulging with something that made a metallic clanking sound when they walked. It took all Gaspar's strength to muzzle Peugeot while the pup squirmed in his arms wanting to get free.

"That's enough shopping for today, Joe," the taller of the two men chuckled to the other.

"Yeah, Mike," the other man answered, looking at

his watch. "The tour buses will start arriving soon. We better hightail it out of here and come back for the rest tomorrow," Joe answered.

"Better yet, Joe, let's come back tonight, after the park's closed," Mike suggested. There's still a great haul down there for us to get out and the more loot we can offer the Jaguar, the more he'll pay us."

"Are you crazy? If the Jaguar isn't impressed with what we have right here, then we shouldn't be workin' for him. Instead we should find someone else who can better appreciate our talents."

"Pipe down, Joe. Save it for later. We'll finish up tonight, right after closing time, and we can bring a couple of the gang with us to help too."

Quickly the two men scurried out the side door of the church and headed into the jungle. Gaspar, with Peugeot still muzzled in his arms, and Alex followed them as far as the open doorway and stopped. They could just see the men's retreating backsides disappearing into the jungle.

"Come on, Al," Gaspar coaxed his friend. "Let's see what those guys have been up to." He insisted, placing Peugeot on the ground and letting him loose to sniff around.

"One thing for sure, Gasp, those guys sure weren't just taking out the trash," Alex noted.

Heading around the back of the altar they looked and looked all around the floor to find a secret trap door or a loose paving stone. There had to be some way to get underground, but their search and Peugeot's sniffing was to no avail. The carved marble altar was solid and the floor around it impossible to penetrate.

"*Aardvark*, Al. Where in the *abecedarians* did those two *hairy-headed highwaymen* appear from?" Gaspar queried.

Although the boys had given up, Peugeot was still sniffing and scratching around the altar, finally letting out a couple of barks to get Gaspar's attention. Gaspar took the hint and went over to where the pup was pawing the side of the altar. Trying one more time, poking and prodding, Gaspar finally stumbled upon a secret button, by accidentally pushing one of the protruding cabochons on the intricately decorated *churrigueresque* altar piece. With the grating sound of stone upon stone, Gaspar was able to push open the two-foot by three-foot panel in the center of the altar's side. What he saw in there was pitch black, but promising. Before he could stop him, Peugeot sprang through the opening and disappeared.

"*A thousand million times gun ports*, Al. Quick, grab a couple of candles from over there, you know, the ones you're supposed to pay for before you light them. Okay, light them. They have matches right there, that's it ... bring them over here, pronto, Peugeot's just darted inside the altar ... hurry!"

Alex returned with the lighted votives and handed one to Gaspar. "Follow me," was all Gaspar instructed, before he slipped feet first through the open panel, disappearing inside of the altar's pitch black interior, calling … "Peugeot, come back, come here Peugeot, come on boy, come back!"

What they found inside was a steep staircase leading down, down, down. The only way to navigate it was on their butts, just like their descent from the pyramid. The staircase led to a cavernous room with passages branching out in four different directions.

"Peugeot, where are you?" Gaspar called anxiously.

"I think I see him, he's gone this way," Alex insisted, running into the tunnel directly in front of them.

"Peugeot, wait for us, come back Peugeot." Gaspar hollered to his mischievous pup, as he followed Alex down the tunnel in the direction of the main temple and the cenote.

Continuing in hot pursuit of Peugeot, the boys took a short passage leading off to the left which delivered them into a huge room which was obviously the interior of a large pyramid.

"This must be the Temple of the Seven Dolls where those archaeologists found the golden idols in the 1950s that Roberto told us about," Gaspar told Alex. The room was empty. Except for ancient carvings on the stone walls, there was no treasure to speak of, or nothing easily transportable, that's for sure. "Now which way did Peugeot go?"

"We must have taken a wrong turn back there. Let's go back where we turned left and then keep going the way we started," Alex suggested.

The two boys doubled back, made a sharp turn right and headed straight ahead. They reached the end where a small mountain of dirt barely hid an opening in the wall and crawled over it, not giving it another thought. After a while, in the dim light of their votive candles they ran face-first into a black wall of dirt.

"*Pachyrhizus*," Gaspar cursed, wiping the dirt off of his face. "Dead end!"

"There must be another passage along here, somewhere," Alex whined. "Listen, that's Peugeot barking … come on Gasp."

Turning around, they scampered back down the passage, the way they'd come as the dogs barking became louder and louder. Hitting the pile of dirt in the middle of the tunnel, Alex tripped, and his candle flew out of his hand. To the boys' surprise, it went flying to Alex's right … right through the black dirt wall and out into space.

"*Zapotecs*, Al. You found it. You found the other passage," Gaspar congratulated his pal. "Look, all this dirt has been recently excavated. Those guys must have just dug this passage. Listen, Peugeot is barking just on the other side. Come on, grab your candle, it's over there in the dirt. Let's find Peugeot and check this place out."

Gaspar was beside himself with worry for his pup and filled with anticipation on what they might find in the next cavern. Together the teenagers explored the newly excavated tunnel. It was narrow and low, causing them to crawl along on their hands and knees.

"No wonder those guys were so filthy," Gaspar commented, spitting out inhaled dirt and grime. When they reached the end, Peugeot stuck his head through and started slobbering their faces by way of greeting.

Pushing Peugeot aside while wriggling through the opening, the dark tunnel soon opened up into a huge underground cavern. As they crept forward with Peugeot happily prancing about as if he were showing them his discovery, the boys suddenly realized that the grotto ended on the banks of an underground lake. Even more thrilling for the adventurers was seeing that the shore of the lake was massed with golden objects, thousands of them.

"This is incredible, Al! All this water must be draining into here from the cenote or maybe it's the other way around," Gaspar wondered out loud. "There must be an underwater tunnel leading to the cenote from here. I wonder how really far underground we are. It's obvious that the Maya used this subterranean area for making offerings to their gods. Check it out, Al. There's an awful lot of gold stuff down here! Come on, we need to report this to the authorities," Gaspar finished breathlessly. "Good work, Peugeot … you gorgeous hound. You single-handedly found the golden horde that those crooks have been stealing from." He complimented his pooch, scratching the pup's ears with appreciation.

Quickly the three adventurers retraced their steps,

finding their way back up the stairs, and into the church. As two filthy black gods and a four-footed black creature from Hell appeared out of nowhere from behind the altar, a startled old German lady let out a blood-curdling scream, scaring Gaspar, Peugeot and Alex half to death. The woman's scream reverberated throughout the lofty church causing fifty German tourists to turn towards the teenagers with eyes wide and mouths agape to see what the commotion was all about. Gaspar and Alex looked at each in disbelief and yelped, jumping back from each other when they saw how fiendishly evil, they now looked. Both boys were black with grime, looking like ghouls from *Tales of the Crypt*, scaring the living scrap out of each other before turning on their heels and running out the side door before anyone could stop them. Peugeot, playing the *Hound from Hell*, ran after them snapping and snarling, to the distress of the horrified group. It wasn't until they disappeared into the undergrowth that they stopped running and began laughing hyster-ically, realizing what they looked like appearing out of nowhere from behind the altar. After they got control of themselves, they hightailed it to the museum in search of the adults. Gaspar reached the museum first with Alex coming in a close third after Peugeot, just as Roberto and the newlyweds were leaving the building.

"What on earth," Elvira expostulated. "Where have you three been and what have you been up to? You're filthy!"

"Listen, ma, Peter, Roberto." Gaspar wheezed, out of breath. "We need your help. We saw these two guys coming up out of the ground behind the altar of the church. They were just as filthy as us, and they were carrying gunny sacks full of metal objects. We found out where they'd come from. You see, there's a secret passage under the altar that leads to a cavern full of golden treasure. We also heard them say that they would return tonight to get the rest of the loot. So, we thought we'd better tell you about it so you can call the Federales or museum police or someone," Gaspar blurted out, trying to catch his breath.

"Take a breath, Gaspar," Peter implored. "Can you take us there and show us?"

"Sure, Peter. No problem, but don't you think we should also show someone in authority."

"I'll get Señor de Montijo. He is the head curator here. He is the man in charge of all antiquities for this site," Roberto assured them.

Within the hour, Gaspar, Peugeot and Alex were leading Señor de Montijo, two of his guards and Elvira, Peter and Roberto through the panel in the side of the altar and down into the cavern full of golden idols.

"This could very well be the most stupendous archaeological find of the twenty-first century," Señor de Montijo told them with conviction. "Of course, we knew about the secret stairway under the altar. That is how my colleagues found the seven dolls under the temple, but we had no idea about this side cavern. It will take further investigation to discover how the Maya accessed this area. Perhaps over there where the cave-in has occurred, must have been the original entrance," the museum curator guessed. "An army of archaeologists will descend on this site tomorrow morning; of that you can be sure. But for tonight, we must lay a trap for the thieves. There's no telling what they may have already purloined from this site," he lamented.

Roberto made the suggestion that they have lunch in the restaurant attached to the gift shop before planning their next step. Gaspar and Alex promised to meet them there in fifteen minutes, during which time they returned to the cenote with Peugeot and jumped in fully clothed, hoping to wash off the grime they'd accumulated.

"I've always thought it would be a good idea to wash my laundry and myself at the same time," Gaspar confessed to Alex, as he helped Peugeot get the grime out of his curly coat. "This has been quite a morning, Al. What more could happen to us on this trip," Gaspar wondered as he lifted Peugeot out of the water.

"Adventure seems to find you, Gasp!" Alex complimented his pal.

"Yeah, well I want to hang around for the big capture tonight. I hope Roberto's not making plans to take us away from here, not before the big arrest," Gaspar worried.

"Yeah, let's get back and get something to eat. I'm

starved," Alex lamented. "Then when we're all together we can form a plan of attack," he spoke wisely.

Back at the cafe the adults were already eating tacos, beans and rice when the boys and the pooch came in, still wet but not dripping. More plates of tacos materialized instantly from the kitchen as well as a dish of carne asada and a bowl of water for Peugeot and two bottles of ice-cold Coke and a couple of glasses for the boys. It wasn't until the ordering and food presentation was completed and everyone was settled down enjoying their meals, that the conversation began in earnest about the teenagers' big discovery.

To Gaspar's delight, Señor de Montijo suggested that they stay the night at the guest house located on the property, which was usually reserved for important visiting dignitaries and world-renowned archaeologists. "That way you can be on the scene for the arrest," the kindly old man suggested. "After all," he said, "Señors Gaspar and Alejandro are the only witnesses who saw the men leave the church with the loot."

"And Peugeot, Señor, don't forget Peugeot. Your suggestion makes sense to me, Señor de Montijo. How about you, mom and dad?" Gaspar asked solicitously of his parents.

"Thank you for putting us up Señor de Montijo. We know there's nothing we could say or do that could keep Gaspar and Alex and Peugeot away from here tonight. Far be it for us to suggest moving on. Elvira and I will go to the guest house while the boys look around the museum," Peter suggested. "Only one thing, Gasp … please, promise me, you won't attempt to capture any more criminals until tonight!" Peter begged his stepson wearily.

This was the first time that Peter had asserted his parental authority, and his wife and stepson, Gaspar seemed happy that he had. "Dad, do me a favor and take Peugeot with you, I think it's his siesta time," Gaspar suggested.

After Gaspar and Alex had looked around the small museum, which Gaspar had no doubt would soon be expanding its exhibition space to accommodate the new discoveries, Roberto found them and asked them to come with him to the guest house. When the boys got there, they found Elvira and Peter in conversation with Señor de Montijo and an army major, in full uniform, while Peugeot snoozed quietly in the corner.

Major Portillo was in charge of the Federales who secured all the important archaeological sites and museums in the Mexican state of Yucatán. Portillo congratulated Gaspar and Alex on their bravery and sense of adventure in finding the magnificent artifacts. He wanted to interview the boys, find out what they knew about the crooks and discuss the operation for that evening.

"Can you describe the two men?" the major asked.

"Joe was taller than Mike," Gaspar explained. "Joe had very dirty sandy blonde hair and bright blue eyes.

He wore glasses with black frames and had a dark blue and white bandanna tied around his throat. His sidekick, Mike, was shorter and heavier. He had dark, curly black hair, a mustache and a goatee. He had a big stainless-steel chronometer on his left wrist, and a big red cut on his left hand which was caked with dirt. I can't say that he had a limp, but when he walked quickly, he seemed to skip, like maybe he'd hurt his knee."

"Yeah," Alex agreed, not wanting to be left out. "And the guy called Mike had a really high- pitched voice, and beady little black pig-eyes. By the way he was talking, I think Joe was the boss, you know, the guy who called the shots, the kingpin. Do you agree, Gasp?" he turned to his friend for corroboration.

"That's right, major. Also, Joe talked about someone called the Jaguar, and how 'the Jaguar would be happy with what they'd found'. Mike said that if 'the Jaguar wasn't pleased; they should find someone else to work for … who would appreciate their skills." Gaspar informed Major Portillo.

"The Jaguar," Major Portillo yelped. "The Jaguar is the most notorious antiquities thief in the world. The Jaguar is wanted by Interpol in Greece, Peru, Rome, and even in China. If the Jaguar's involved, we better bring in reinforcements. The Jaguar is a ruthless devil … he's even wanted for piracy on the high seas … " Major Portillo fretted.

"Major, something tells me, The Jaguar won't be

present tonight. These guys want to get as much loot on their own, and as soon as possible and after they're satisfied with their haul, then they'll reunite with the Jaguar and sell it all to him for as much money as possible. Anyway, that's what I think, major." Gaspar spoke his mind and then added a codicil. "Rather than arresting these guys tonight, why not let them take what they want and then follow them to the Jaguar's hideout … that way you could arrest the entire gang at one time."

"Clever thinking, Señor Gaspar, but much too dangerous. If by chance the thieves get away with the treasure … it would be a disaster for Mexico to lose such an extraordinary patrimony."

"We have a few hours, major. Why not get the good stuff out now, and seed the place with fakes? I saw enough golden idols in the gift shop to sink a ship. If we hurry, we can beat these guys at their own game!" Gaspar enthused.

"That sounds like a plan that could work." Major Portillo was impressed by Gaspar's prescience. "Let's get busy and do it. Señor de Montijo, please gather up as many fabulous fakes as you can muster. I have six men with me now and will call for reinforcements. Gaspar, you and Alejandro, take me and my men to the church and show us the way to the treasure. Señor de Montijo, you meet us there as soon as possible with the phony gold-plated decoys. Let's get moving, time is of the essence, amigos!" Major Portillo urged them on enthusiastically.

By closing time, the treasure cavern had been quickly

photographed before being emptied of its most valuable pieces. Fabulous fakes now replaced the real McCoy instead and the floor of the cavern had been swept with a palm frond to disguise the fact that many busy feet had recently trod there. As the sun hung low in the sky, Major Portillo spread his men out, taking up positions to better watch and follow the perpetrators. The federales had earlier found the tire tracks in the jungle where the crooks' vehicle had recently been driven in and out of the area. The police were now in wait for them with unmarked cars hidden along the road, north and south of where their tracks left the undergrowth. Major Portillo had stationed Gaspar, Alex, Peter and Señor de Montijo up in the choir loft of the church and had placed several of his men within the church, hiding behind pillars and pews. When the park closed the major instructed the regular guard to do whatever he did every night at closing and with that instruction, the man closed and locked the entry gates as well as the doors to the museum, gift shop and church for the evening.

The major and his men didn't have long to wait before the criminals returned to the archaeological park. Tonight, four men, dressed in black, arrived in two vans and parked under cover of the thick jungle. Leaving their vehicles, they walked silently through the jungle, arriving at the side door of the church. Using a key as if he were returning home from a party Joe, the obvious leader of the group, unlocked the door and breezily led his henchmen inside. Without looking left or right, Joe pushed the cabochon stone that sprang the lock of the altar's secret panel and feet first began the procession of four men who slipped into the dark. As they went into the secret passage, each man flipped on a miner's lamp attached to a hard hat, as well as a handheld high-powered flashlight. From the choir loft Gaspar saw the bright glow emanating from the side of the marble altar and watched it grow fainter as the men proceeded down the stairs and through the underground tunnel.

Like clockwork the four men made short shrift of their work and soon returned with their gunny sacks bulging and clanking. Joe closed the panel tightly shut with a grinding sound and followed the men out of the building. Gaspar could hear a loud click as Joe turned the key in the door's lock. Nobody moved inside the church for what seemed to Gaspar, like an eternity. Finally, the night watchmen unlocked the side door to the church and stepped inside. Simultaneously, the Federales stepped out from behind columns and pews, and the man who had been watching from the bell tower climbed down the old ladder to join them. The men, who had been in hiding on the grounds stepped forward from out of the jungle and entered the church too while Gaspar, Alex, Peter and Señor de Montijo scurried down from the choir loft to join the Federales, as they regrouped.

"That's that," Major Portillo addressed his crew matter-of-factly. "Now it's up to Garcia and his men to keep a tail on those characters. Señor de Montijo, Señor Cawthorne, Gaspar and Alex, I will be in touch with you by cell phone. You also have my number … if you hear or see anything else suspicious while you're on your tour of the Yucatán, please don't hesitate to call me. As for the real treasure, what we have of it at least, we will keep the news of its discovery under our hats for now until we capture this gang of thieves. Buenos noches, señors," the major saluted Gaspar, Alex and Peter along with the rest of his crew. "Hombres, vamanos," he commanded his men, before walking out of the church towards where his car was hidden in the jungle.

Señor de Montijo drove Gaspar, Alex and Peter back to the guest house where Elvira and Peugeot awaited their return. Peter informed Elvira of all the excitement or lack of excitement that had taken place, while Gaspar and Alex were up all night, talking about the different angles of the case and the adventure they'd stumbled into.

ON THE ROAD AGAIN

THE NEXT MORNING, AFTER BREAKFAST WITH SEÑOR DE
MONTIJO, THE TRAVELERS GOT BACK ON THE ROAD,
for the twenty-five mile trip from Dzibilchaltún to
ake. "Ake is an important Maya site. It's located in the
municipality of Tixkokob, just east of here." Roberto
informed them while driving. "Aké means the place of
reeds, in Yucatec Maya. The most interesting thing about
Ake," he told them as he pulled into the parking area a
half hour later, "are the sacbé raised roads that connect
it with other pre-Columbian sites and Maya settlements.
The ruins were only discovered and written about in
the 1840s. You'll soon realize," Roberto continued, "that
these ruins all sit within the walls of a nineteenth-century
henequén estate."

"What's henequén?" Alex asked.

"Al, it's what rope was made out of before they invented synthetic fibers." Gaspar informed his pal. "This part of the world was really important during World War I because they made rope here and a lot of people who lived here got rich from its production. Armies all over the world needed rope for their ships and planes, tents and trucks, you name it, rope was king," Gaspar informed his traveling companions what he'd learned when he researched the trip before making their travel plans. "They made rope from henequén and they made henequén from agave plants. Look over there. You can see the agaves growing … see … those great big blue-grey plants. That's the plant that the rope fibers were made from. Henequén is not as high quality as sisal, but it's cheap, easy to grow and it works," Gaspar expounded on the history of henequén.

"How do you know all this stuff, Gaspar?" his mom asked, impressed.

"I read it in National Geographic, Ma. I gave each of you photocopies of the article when we were on board *Floridablanca*," he said with just a little exasperation in his voice. "You gotta read if ya wanna know about stuff," he added, more to Al than to his parents.

"They also make Licor de Henequén down here," Peter chimed in. "Let's order some tonight El, and let the kids have a taste," he suggested to his bride.

Once the car was parked, they all tumbled out and stretched their legs.

"Where to first?" Gaspar asked Roberto.

"Follow me. We have just a short way to hike," their driver and guide told them, as Peugeot romped ahead.

Reaching their destination, Roberto expounded on the site. "As you can see, the core is this large square plaza surrounded by tall buildings. The palace is over there," Roberto pointed out the sight's special features as he walked them over to the structure. "Most Maya pyramids are built steep with many narrow steps, like the one you climbed at Dzibilchaltún, but as you can see this palace is built on top of a gradual incline."

For Gaspar the palace was the site's most impressive feature. Peugeot ran ahead, leading the way to the top terrace of the palace. From the top they could look out over the remains of the ancient raised pedestrian causeway, or sacbé, which the Maya built in order to connect the cities of Aké and Izamal. Roberto told them that the sacbé was part of a road system running from the site of Ti'ho at modern Mérida all the way to the Caribbean Sea. After hearing that, Gaspar was even more impressed by the engineering skills of the ancient Maya.

Having explored the compact archaeological site, Roberto efficiently herded them back into the car for the quick trip to Ek Balam. "You are in for a rare treat," Roberto informed them. "Ek Balam is a jewel of an archaeological site. Wait until you see the oval palace and the acropolis. It's just a short distance from Aké and only thirty-two miles further to Chichén Itzá. From the

79

pre-classic through the post-classic periods, Ek Balam was the capital city of the Mayan Kingdom."

Reaching Ek Balam, Roberto escorted them through the city's ceremonial layout. First, they entered inside the defensive walls, which ended on both sides of an unsurpassable very steep and very deep sinkhole. Passing through the entrance arch, constructed over the road leading into the city, Gaspar wondered if his companions felt like he did? For Gaspar, just walking in the footsteps of the Mayans, made him feel as if he were part of an ancient ceremonial procession. Directly in front of them loomed the oval palace, which Roberto told them was placed so that it aligned cosmologically with the stars, for certain secret ceremonies. When they heard this, both Gaspar and Alex nudged each other. Alex, because he loved the importance of architectural alignment and Gaspar, because he loved anything with hidden meaning or purpose.

After seeing the oval palace, they moved onto a pair of buildings with mirror-image temples standing atop, which they inspected and admired. Next came what Roberto called *the chapel*, and further on was a carved stela depicting the ruler of Ek Balam, Ukit Kan Le'k Tok'. Gaspar and Alex were particularly pleased to see the ancient Maya ballcourt, which Roberto told them dated to 841. Next to the ballcourt was the ancient steam bath, which Gaspar, Alex and Peter thought made a lot of sense after a tough day on the field. Next came a huge main plaza with a temple built into its corner, along with an even larger unexcavated platform that bordered the main plaza.

"This is the Acropolis," Roberto told them, extending his arms as if he were unveiling a rare work of art. "It is the largest structure at Ek Balam and is believed to contain the tomb of Ukit Kan Le'k Tok', whose stela we saw earlier. Excavations here began in 1998 when it was just a mound. And this," he said with another flourish, "is the temple in which Ukit Kan Le'k Tok', is supposedly buried. This building is called El Trono, or the throne. Notice the doorway in the shape of a monster-like mouth which depicts the mouth of a *jaguar*."

With those words the two boys jumped back, as a tall man with sandy blonde hair, black rimmed glasses and a dark blue and white bandanna tied around his neck stepped out onto the plaza and without acknowledging the group, walked back towards the entrance arch they had just come from.

"Did you see that?" Gaspar whispered to Alex. "That was Joe, the thief from Dzibilchaltún. Peter, Roberto, mom, that's him. That's Joe, the ringleader of the antiquity thieves," Gaspar whispered tersely to the others, while pointing in the direction of the departing man. Gaspar whipped out his cell phone and called Major Portillo. "Major," the others heard Gaspar's one-sided conversation. "We're touring at Ek Balam. We're in front of El Trono and you won't believe who just stepped out onto the terrace, Joe … yeah, the ringleader. I see, um humm, okay. I see … yes major, okay, goodbye." Gaspar pushed *end* and reported to his friends. "Major Portillo says they lost Joe. He gave them the slip somewhere back in Mérida. He *doesn't* want us to follow him, but if we could watch him until he leaves the site and report to the major what kind of a car, he's in, it would help. He's got his men heading this direction right now. He doesn't want to pick him up. He wants Joe to lead them to the Jaguar, " Gaspar finished.

"Okay, listen guys. You all stay here and continue your tour. I'll follow Joe and get in touch with the major, and I'll either meet you back here or at the car," Peter said, taking off in the direction of the departing thief.

"What's inside?" Gaspar asked Roberto, pointing to El Trono, as Peter walked briskly away after the mysterious man.

"Inside are rooms with wall paintings consisting of texts. Amongst these, the 'Mural of the Ninety-six Glyphs', is a masterwork of calligraphy comparable to the 'Tablet of the Ninety-six Glyphs' from Palenque. Another wall painting of the Acropolis features a mythological scene with a hunted deer, which scholars believe represents the origin of death. A series of vault capstones depict the lightning deity, a specific decoration also known from other Yucatec sites which has been prominently used here," Roberto reported.

"Come on, Al. Let's take a look," Gaspar urged his

pal. Together with Elvira, Peugeot and Roberto in tow, the two boys led the way into the dark space. Gaspar had a pocket flashlight with him. Having learned his lesson back in Dzibilchaltún, he swore never to leave home without one, especially where ruins were concerned. He'd told Alex to do the same and was pleased when his pal switched his on too. Once inside, Roberto and Elvira gave the place a cursory once over, but Gaspar, Peugeot and Alex gave it a thorough observation, from the dusty footprints on the soft ground to the cracks between the huge stones. They searched for something, anything suspicious, although neither boy nor Peugeot had any idea what that might be.

"What can you tell us about these paintings, Roberto?" Gaspar asked their guide. "Is it alright for me to take pictures?"

"Yes, Gaspar, take all the pictures you like. Archaeologists are still trying to decipher these images," Roberto answered Gaspar's first question last.

"What about all the amazing temples that are depicted in these murals?" Alex asked, between taking photographs of his own. "Have the archaeologists found them all, or are some of these still a mystery?"

"Many of these are known, like El Castillo at Chichén Itzá, or the observatory at Tulúm, this one and this one," Roberto pointed them out. "But others have yet to be found, like this one, the Temple of Chac Mool. That's, a mystery that everyone in the international archaeological community would like to solve. Look at how it's placed in the painting, perfectly situated with the sea right in front, but so far no one has been able to find out exactly where it is. And look, it has no civilization depicted around it, strictly a sacred place," Roberto said, shaking his head in the negative as he led Elvira out of the dark space.

While not really knowing what they were looking for and not finding any visible clues as to what Joe may have been up to, the boys decided to take photographs of the interior before rejoining Elvira and Roberto who were waiting for them outside.

"Well, amigos," Roberto trilled, "we are in the center of the sacred compound and this completes our visit to Ek Balam. As you have discovered it is approximately a twenty-three-acre site. But as you have seen, only the center of Ek Balam has been excavated. From where we're standing you can see the four sacbé roads stemming from here, in the four cardinal directions, north, south, east and west. These sacbé were built by the Maya as an architectural allusion to the idea of a four-part cosmos. The roads are thought by historians to have been sacred to the Maya."

"It's interesting, Roberto, that this site was discovered so recently," Gaspar pondered out loud. "There must be a lot of information here, not previously known. The kind of information that might be of interest to treasure hunters or thieves, I would imagine," Gaspar fished.

"You make a good point, Señor Gaspar," Roberto

concurred. "Ek Balam was discovered and explored first by the influential archaeologist Désiré Charnay in the late 1800s, but extensive excavation did not take place until almost a century later. This is a huge archaeological dig and the work here will take years and years to complete," Roberto reported as they walked back to the car.

When they got to the parking area, Peter was waiting for them. "How'd it go, Peter?" Gaspar asked his stepfather.

"Not so well, Gasp," Peter lamented. "The crook gave me the slip too. One minute he was right in front of me, and the next thing I knew he'd vanished. I didn't know if he was just hiding behind a tree and watching me, and I didn't want to look like I was startled or desperate to find him, so I just played it cool and walked back to the car as if everything was normal." Peter shrugged. "What else could I do? I called Major Portillo and told him what happened. He's asked us to wait for his men to show up before we leave. This must be them coming now," he exhaled, pointing to a black car heading into the parking area. The car stopped in a cloud of dust and four of Major Portillo's men bounded out. Gaspar recognized two of the men from the stakeout at the church.

"Please show us where the crook disappeared while you were tailing him."

"It's just over there, follow me and I'll show you the exact spot." Peter promised the federale.

"Can you show us the place where the crook called

Joe emerged from El Trono?" another federale asked Gaspar.

"Of course." Gaspar answered, "Come on Al, come on Peugeot, let's show them. Follow us." Peugeot led the way back to El Trono.

"Here we are," Gaspar extended his arm towards El Trono. "Joe came out of the building, right here," Gaspar insisted, pointing at the opening into the building before leading the officer inside.

It was on this second visit inside the excavated palace that Gaspar got an inkling of what the mystery of El Trono might be. He wasn't ready to say anything to Alex yet, or to the federales either, but instead formulated his thoughts and filed them away for future consideration.

Back at the car, Elvira and Roberto were waiting patiently. Gaspar, Peugeot and Alex had come upon Peter walking along the road and together they told the assembled officers that they were moving on to Valladolid and would be available by cell phone if they needed them. That was the uneventful end of their visit to Ek Balam, for now at least.

CHAPTER 9

VALLADOLID

It was late afternoon when the travelers pulled into the bustling city of Valladolid. The second largest city in the state of Yucatán, Valladolid was full of charm and lots of activity. The sidewalks were so crowded that it seemed to Gaspar that all forty-five-thousand of its inhabitants were out for a walk and those that weren't walking were probably driving as the traffic on the main drag had crawled to a standstill.

While stuck in traffic, Roberto informed them that "Valladolid was named after the capital of Spain at the time of its founding. The original city had been established by the Spanish conquistador Francisco de Montijo's nephew. The original city had been at some distance from this current town, on the edge of a lagoon called Chouac-Ha in the municipality of Tizimin. The early Spanish settlers complained so much about the mosquitos and humidity at the original location, that the government moved the city further inland ... to its present location ... right here!" Roberto chuckled. "They built the new Valladolid atop an existing Maya town called Zaci-Val. The Maya buildings were dismantled, and the stones re-used to build the Spanish colonial town which we are driving through now. Even today, when people are building houses here, they often find Maya gold and other artefacts when excavating their new foundations." Roberto informed them with enthusiasm.

Gaspar found the history of the founding of Valladolid and the discovery of Maya artefacts during modern construction amazing. He nudged Alex, giving him a knowing look with a nod, which Alex responded to with raised eyebrows and a nod of his own.

While the traffic crept forward, Roberto continued his history lesson. "In 1847 the native population rioted, killing some eighty Spanish and sacking their houses. After one of the native leaders was shot by a Spanish firing squad, the riot became a general uprising which the Spanish called the 'Caste War.'"

Roberto was really on a roll with his history lesson while cars honked behind him urging him to pay more attention to the traffic. "This city was the scene of intense fighting and the Latino forces ultimately had to abandon Valladolid. Half the Spanish were ambushed and killed during their retreat to Mérida. Valladolid was sacked by the native rebels before being recaptured again by the Spanish later in the war. At the time of the 'Caste War', Valladolid was the third largest city of the Yucatán peninsula, and even more important than Mérida and Campeche, because of its sizable well-to-do Criollo population." Roberto's tone of voice revealed his admiration for the town. "Tomorrow, I'll take you to see a number of Spanish colonial mansions in the old city." Roberto promised before adding with pride … "Because of its exotic beauty, Valladolid has always been widely known throughout the world by its nickname, *'The Sultana of the East'*."

Enduring another twenty minutes of bumper to bumper traffic, the car finally pulled up in front of the Hotel Tia Micha. From the exterior appearance of the rundown old hostelry, Gaspar thought Roberto had made a mistake. He thought they might have been better off staying back at the Doctor's House … but he kept his thoughts to himself.

"Is this our hotel, Roberto?" Gaspar asked with less than enthusiasm in his voice.

"Si, Señor. I know it looks simple but wait until you see the inside. It is owned by my friend, Tia Micha, and it is ranked number one of the top ten hotels in Valladolid. Please follow me inside to meet the owner," Roberto urged his clients.

Once through the doorway, Gaspar and his family were instantly enchanted. The hotel was made from a charming old house set in a beautiful garden with terraces and cool vine-covered patios which Mr. Peugeot instantly christened and claimed for himself. The deep windows all held balconies with garden views and the large comfortable public rooms were full of authentic Valladolid charm. Boys in starched white uniforms carried their luggage upstairs and deposited them in their rooms while Tia Micha welcomed her American guests into her establishment with enthusiasm, showing them around the public rooms, before showing them to their quarters.

"Let's wash up and meet downstairs before going out to dinner," Elvira suggested.

"We'll see you boys in the bar at 7:30," Peter chimed in, before closing the door to the bridal suite.

Gaspar and Alex were happy to share another big suite down the hall and quickly laid out their clothes for dinner before washing up. "I'll take the tub," Gaspar announced, knowing Alex always preferred a shower. While the boys headed to the bathroom, Peugeot sprawled out on Gaspar's bed and waited.

Gaspar plugged the drain and started running the hot water. While the tub was filling, he and Alex gabbed about all they'd seen today, and wondered to each other what mischief 'that crook Joe' had been up to at the ruins. Finding a bottle of bath salts, Gaspar poured way too much into the tub before undressing. As Gaspar slipped under the foamy surface, Alex jumped into the shower, through a cloud of steam.

Ahh … relaxation … Gaspar had learned the joys of soaking in a hot tub those first days at La Rinconada when Uncle Charlie's ghost had appeared to him and told him about Gasparilla's treasure. How he missed Uncle Charlie now. He knew the old ghost wouldn't appear to him in front of others and being on this trip with Alex and his parents, he hadn't had a moment to himself since they'd left Perdido Isle.

"Uncle Charlie," he whispered hoping that Alex couldn't hear him above the roar of the pelting shower. "Uncle Charlie," he called again a little louder.

"Over here, fella," came the familiar booming voice.

"Shhhhh, not so loud, Uncle," Gaspar warned him. "I need to talk to you. Could we set up a time to talk after everyone's asleep"

"Tonight, in the garden. I'll meet you at midnight by the fountain. It's private there," said the old boy who was wearing a Mexican charro outfit in black and white embroidered cotton with a huge black, white and silver spangled sombrero on his head.

"Nice get-up, Uncle Charlie," was the only compliment Gaspar could muster for the ghost's gaudy Mexican attire.

"Pretty nifty, huh," Charlie squealed with glee. "I got it off a mariachi guy down at the plaza. You don't know it, but I've been tailing you all the way down here. Nice work with those crooks by the way. Nasty characters. I'd watch your step, Gasp, before you find yourself in big trouble."

"Okay, uncle. I'll meet you at midnight. Alex should be snoring by then."

Before Uncle Charlie could leave the room, Alex stepped out of the shower, grabbed a towel and wrapped it around his waist. He turned and saw the mariachi man in the charro costume with the big sombrero heading out the door.

"Who was that?" he asked Gaspar, pulling the towel closer.

"Room service," was all Gaspar said, before starting to scrub himself with a soapy washcloth.

When the boys and Mr. Peugeot got downstairs, Elvira and Peter were waiting in the bar sipping margaritas.

"Would you boys like a drink?" Peter asked.

"Coke, please," Gaspar told the man behind the bar, "and a bowl of water for my pal Peugeot."

"For me too, please," Alex mimicked him, "Coke, not a water bowl," he specified in fear that his request be lost in translation.

"Roberto has made a special dinner reservation for us at the *Taberna de los Frailes*, which I've read wonderful things about. It's set in a garden under a wonderful thatched palapa. The food there should be amazing," Elvira promised.

"That was a wonderful visit today," Peter declared. "I especially liked the last place … Ek Balam … What a layout."

"Me, too," Alex threw in. "The placement of all those amazing buildings. I can just see it alive with Mayans covered in gold and feathers and animal skins," Alex romanced.

"This looks like a good town for sightseeing too," Gaspar enthused. "Thanks to Roberto, we certainly are seeing the sights in style. He's really been a Godsend."

On that note, Roberto popped into the lounge just as they were finishing their drinks.

"Come and join us, Roberto. Would you like a refreshment?" Gaspar asked.

"No, thank you, Señor Gaspar. It's time to go now … dinnertime," he smiled charmingly.

A short drive later, they arrived at the Taberna de los Frailes, where they were greeted royally and shown to one of the best tables in the house. Roberto ordered the dinner for them, which turned out to be a repast of local specialties. Peugeot was not left out and enjoyed a plateful of shredded chicken from his place on the banquette right next to Gaspar. After consuming a mouth-watering dinner of *lechon al horno* and *bistek de cazuela* with *relleno negro*, which turned out to be turkey cooked with a paste of charred chilies, they couldn't believe it when the waiter brought them vegetables mixed with bits of hard-boiled eggs too. Roberto had also ordered another typical dish of the region for them to try. "*Lomitos de Valladolid*", a pork dish with fresh tomato sauce served with traditional Yucateca-style beans and rice. Roberto insisted that they top off the feast with a tasting of traditional ice creams made with regional ingredients such as coconut or corn as well as fruits of the region such as guanabana, soursop, mamey, pouteria sapota as well as other flavors made with honey and nuts. The guanabana ice cream was Peugeot's favorite and Gaspar made sure the pup enjoyed a bowl full just like the rest of them.

After dinner, Roberto took them for a late-night ride through town. The proud driver went to great lengths to point out the sights by night that they'd be visiting again in the morning. One of these was the Convent of San Bernardino de Siena and Roberto also pointed out the towering Cathedral of San Gervasio located on the main square of the city. Driving a couple of blocks farther they passed the Cenote Zaci, a landscaped freshwater cenote or underground sinkhole which Roberto told them 'was open daily for exploration.'

"Maybe we should go for a swim there tomorrow, Gasp," Alex suggested hopefully, as the site flashed by the car window.

The cenote siting was followed by a drive-by look at the Casa de la Cultura, Casa de los Venados, Mercado Municipal, and the Park de Santa Lucía. On the way back to the hotel they took a cursory drive through the San Juan neighborhood with a stop in front of the Church de San Juan de Dios and then once around the block which held the adjacent Park de San Juan de Dios, before arriving back at their hotel.

Midnight couldn't come a moment too soon for Gaspar. Back in their room, Gaspar and Alex tumbled into their beds and before Gaspar knew it, Al was snoring like a buzz saw. The best thing about having Alex as a best friend was that his habits were so highly predictable.

Crawling out of bed, Gaspar pulled on some jeans and a thin sweater and crept out the door, taking the key with him. Quietly he made his way to the fountain in the garden, and there just like clockwork sat Uncle Charlie. Charlie wasn't dressed as a mariachi this time, instead he was all duded up like a roper or rider in a rodeo. What the heck? Unlike Alex, Uncle Charlie was highly unpredictable. Gosh he was happy to see him.

"Uncle, good golly, I've missed you, " Gaspar exploded in a low but enthusiastic whisper.

"How's it hang-in, Gasp?" Uncle Charlie joked, his voice low and gurgling with laughter.

"Well, I guess you know what I've been up to." Gaspar assumed before continuing, "The Doctor's House was a bit of a disappointment. Don't get me wrong, uncle. I like the place, but the rest of the gang refused to stay there. Let's face facts, the beds haven't been changed since old Dr. Mendoza y Mendoza went down on the Titanic more than a hundred years ago!"

"Yeah, kid. I should have thought of that. But to tell the truth, this is the first time I've been back myself. The last time I was there was in 1911. The Titanic tragedy happened in 1912. I picked up Eugenia in New

York, poor little orphan, and took her with me around the world. But we never went back to Celestún. It was a beautiful place to grow up in, and old Dr. Mendoza y Mendoza did save my life, so my memories of Yucatan are sweet and bittersweet too. I kept the hacienda for Eugenia Floride, but she never went back there. I had the library of rare books sent to La Rinconada, and although I thought about the old place a lot, I never went back either. It's a shame, but that's that. What more can I say.

"How about the antiquity thieves we've run into," Gaspar changed the subject. "Can you give me any insight on the Jaguar, or his henchmen, uncle?"

"That, I cannot. I can ask around, but these modern-day thugs are a little out of my league."

"Uncle, as long as you're here … in Mexico I mean … could you do me a favor and keep an eye out for us. Something tells me that this trip's not going to be all easy sailing … not until we're back in safe harbor at La Rinconada anyway." Gaspar stumbled over his uncomfortable thoughts.

"Don't worry, Gasp. I've got your back, and your mother's too."

"And Peter's, Alex's, Angela's and Felix's and Peugeot's, too, I hope." Gaspar reminded him.

"Of course, my boy. Young Peter Cawthorne has certainly turned out to be *a bit of all right*. You really like him, don't you?" Not waiting for an answer, Uncle Charlie continued. "And Alex, he's got your back too, and you his. That's the kind of best friend to have. Someone who's true blue, like me or Peugeot. You're really a lucky guy, Gasp."

"You're telling me, uncle. I'm the luckiest guy in the world, and I like to think the happiest too. Thanks for making all of this happen for me. I'll make you proud of me one way or the other. Tell me … how's the progress on The Doctor's House coming?"

"Splendid, splendid … the house has good bones. It's just like you joked … the place 'just needs some fresh paint, some throw pillows, a few flowers' and it will be just fine." Uncle Charlie chuckled. "I just wonder, what you're going to do with the place once you fix it up? Do you really think you'll ever come back here, Gasp?" the old ghost asked curiously.

"Time will tell, uncle. In the meantime I've got several ideas on the subject which I will keep to myself for now, although I'm not at all sure that you aren't the one who put them into my mind while I was sleeping." Gaspar wondered.

"Me, do a dirty underhanded thing like that!" Uncle Charlie chuckled. "Not to you, dear boy," he insisted, before disappearing for the night.

CHAPTER 10

CHICHÉN ITZÁ

Two days in Valladolid were taken up with shopping and eating, sightseeing and just being lazy around Tia Micha's pool, surrounded by her lush flowering gardens, swaying palms and splashing fountains. This morning the happy travelers would head for Chichén Itzá, the long-awaited mother lode of Mayan archaeological ruins. As they made the short drive to their destination, Roberto explained that …

"Chichén Itzá in ancient Maya meant *at the mouth of the well of the Itza*. Chichén Itzá was one of the largest Maya cities and very likely one of the mythical great cities, or Tollans, referred to in later Mesoamerican literature. Some historians think that the city may have had the most diverse population in the Maya world, which would account for the great variety of architectural styles that we're going to see there."

"Sounds like Chichén Itzá is gonna be full of amazing things to see, Roberto," Gaspar spoke up.

Roberto directed his next bit of trivia towards his young employer. "The ruins of Chichén Itzá are federal property, but what you might not know Señor Gaspar is that the land under the monuments had been privately owned until 2010, after which it was purchased by the state of Yucatán."

Gaspar did find this revelation by Roberto to be particularly interesting. As a major landowner himself, not only in Florida but also in the Yucatán, he was interested in all aspects of real estate law and ownership.

"When I first started planning this trip, I read a book I found in my great-uncle Charlie's library back home. It was all about the Spanish conquest of the Yucatán and more importantly Chichén Itzá, According to the author, the conquistador Francisco de Montijo, a veteran of the Grijalva and Cortés expeditions, successfully petitioned the King of Spain for a charter to conquer the Yucatán. His first campaign covered much of the Yucatán peninsula. That campaign managed to decimate his forces but ended with the establishment of a small fort at Xaman Ha', south of what today we call Cancún. From what I read, Montijo returned to Yucatán with reinforcements and established his main base on the west coast, near Celestún where we landed last week, where The Doctor's House is. He later sent his son, Francisco Montijo the younger, to conquer the interior of the Yucatán peninsula from the north, but the objective from the beginning was to get to Chichén Itzá and establish a Spanish capital there. Are you guys with me?" Gaspar asked his fellow travelers.

Since nobody objected, he went on with what he had learned.

"Montijo the Younger eventually arrived at Chichén Itzá, which he renamed *Ciudad Real*. At first, he encountered no resistance from the Maya and set about dividing the lands around the city, awarding them to his loyal soldiers. Over time the Maya became hostile and eventually laid siege to the Spanish, cutting off their supply line to the coast and forcing them to barricade themselves among the ruins of the ancient city of Chichén Itzá. Months passed but reinforcements never arrived. Montijo the Younger attempted an all-out assault against the Maya and lost. He was forced to abandon Chichén Itzá, stealing away under cover of darkness. Ultimately all of the Spaniards were driven off the Yucatán peninsula."

"Very good, Señor Gaspar," Roberto congratulated the kid on his knowledge of the Spanish Conquest and loss of the Yucatán. "Do you remember what happened next and how the Spanish regained control of the Yucatán peninsula?"

"Well, the book I read said that Montijo eventually returned to Yucatán and recruited Maya from Campeche and Champoton, building a large Indio-Spanish army that ultimately conquered back the peninsula for the Spanish. The Spanish crown later issued him a land grant that included Chichén Itzá, which he turned into a working cattle ranch. What I'm wondering, Roberto, is if it was owned by the same de Montijo family as our Señor de Montijo, the curator at Dzibilchaltún? Do you think he's descended from the same family as the famous conquistador?"

"I'm not sure, Gaspar, but you can surely ask him and find out." Roberto assured him. "Everyone in Mexico is very aware and very proud of their illustrious ancestors. Señor de Montijo would be honored if you asked him. If he is related, he will be proud to tell you … and if he isn't … he will be happy that you thought he might be." Roberto explained the Latin protocol regarding genealogy.

"Roberto, do you remember the name of the family who sold Chichén Itzá to the National Institute of Anthropology and History? Was it still owned by the de Montijo's at that time?" Gaspar was curious.

"In 1894 the United States consul to Yucatán, Edward Herbert Thompson purchased the Hacienda Chichén, which included the ruins of Chichén Itzá from the de Montijo family. For thirty years, Thompson explored the ancient city. His discoveries included the earliest dated Maya glyphs which he found carved upon a lintel in the Temple of the Initial Series. Thompson was also responsible for the excavation of several graves in the

Osario or High Priest's Temple. Thompson is most famous for dredging the Cenote Sagrado, where he recovered artifacts of gold, copper and carved jade, as well as the first-ever examples of what were believed to be pre-Columbian Maya cloth and wooden weapons. Thompson shipped the bulk of those artifacts to the Peabody Museum at Harvard University."

"We've got to go to the Peabody Museum and check that out, Al," Gaspar made a note to his pal.

"In 1926 the Mexican government charged Edward Thompson with theft, claiming he stole the artifacts from the Cenote Sagrado and smuggled them out of the country." Roberto continued, "Because of these accusations, the government seized the Hacienda Chichén. Thompson, who was in the United States at the time of the seizure, never returned to Yucatán. He wrote about his research and investigations of the Maya culture in a book, *People of the Serpent*, which was published in 1932. He died in New Jersey in 1935. It was not until 1944 that the Mexican Supreme Court ruled that Thompson had broken no laws and returned Chichén Itzá to his heirs."

"Justice," Gaspar enthused, "I'm glad that Mexico recognized Thompson's private property rights." He smiled to himself with satisfaction.

After the court decision in their favor, Thompson's heirs sold the hacienda as quickly as possible in case the government might change its mind and want it back."

"Who ended up buying the place?" Alex asked.

"It was sold to a Mexican tourism pioneer named Fernando Barbachano Peon." Roberto answered, as he turned the car into the entrance to the archaeological site and parked in the shade. "Well amigos, as you can see, we have arrived. Look at all the cars and buses here, and it's still early in the morning." Roberto prepared them for the worst. "Chichén Itzá is one of the most visited archaeological sites in Mexico. Over a million tourists visit the ruins every year. In a few minutes you'll understand why. Just look over there," Roberto extolled, pointing straight ahead past the windshield at the massive pyramid that rose high above the jungle canopy. "That is the famous temple, El Castillo. If you thought the temple at Aké was steep my friends, wait until you climb this one. Going up is tough. Coming down, nearly impossible," Roberto warned them ominously from the rear-view mirror with a big smile on his face and a twinkle in his eye.

Gaspar and Alex followed by Peugeot on a leash. jumped out of the car the minute it was parked and took off running in the direction of El Castillo. "See you later, guys," Gaspar called over his shoulder to Elvira, Peter and Roberto. "Last one to the top's a rotten egg."

The two boys raced each other to the bottom of the pyramid's massive stone steps and stopped short, mouths open wide as they looked up at the formidable structure.

"Okay, buddy. This is it. After you, Al," Gaspar and Peugeot stepped aside to let his friend go first.

"No, no, Gasp, you guys go first," Alex insisted

making a musical comedy bow towards his pal and his pooch.

There was no putting off the inevitable, so Gaspar and Peugeot took the first step in unison. It was excruciating. Each riser was at least a foot tall, and each tread only six inches wide, exactly the opposite plus a lot more than any building inspector in America would have allowed for a safe human ratio. Once again getting down on all fours like Peugeot, the two boys raced each other to the top following Peugeots lead. They moved very slowly, Gaspar making the mistake of looking down and Alex making the mistake of looking to see what Gaspar was looking at. The sheer drop from the precipitous staircase froze both boys with fear. Finally reaching the top, they had no desire to ever go down, not because the view was so superb but because the idea of even attempting a descent terrified them.

El Castillo dominated Chichén Itzá, as it was the Temple of Kukulkan, a Maya feathered serpent-deity similar to the Aztec Quetzalcoatl. Reaching the top, Gaspar guessed that the pyramid had to be over eighty feet high. From his vantage point Gaspar was able to count a series of nine square terraces leading up to the top, each approximately eight and a half feet high, and the pavilion at the summit that he was standing under, was at least an additional twenty feet higher than its platform. He could see that the four faces of the pyramid had protruding stairways rising at an angle of at least forty-five degrees. Gaspar would later learn that the talud walls of each terrace actually slanted at an angle of between seventy-two and seventy-four degrees. What he loved best about this particular temple were the sinister heads of a serpent which had been carved at the base of the balustrades of the northeastern staircase.

Gaspar had been wildly excited to learn in the reading materials he'd compiled that many Mesoamerican cultures periodically superimposed larger structures over older ones, and El Castillo which he was now standing at the top of, was another such example, just like the one he'd explored at Dzibilchaltún. He'd read that in the mid-1930s the Mexican government sponsored an excavation of El Castillo and that after several false starts, the archaeologists discovered a staircase under the north side of the pyramid. By digging from the top, they found another temple buried below the current one. Inside the covered over-temple chamber, they found a Chac Mool statue and a throne in the shape of a *jaguar*. The throne was painted red decorated with green spots made of inlaid jade. The Mexican government also excavated a tunnel from the base of the north staircase, up the earlier pyramid's stairway leading to the hidden temple of Chac Mool. That entrance had been opened to tourists until 2006 when National Institute of Anthropology and History permanently closed the hidden throne room to the public. Now that he was on site, Gaspar wondered if his pal Señor Montijo or maybe even his guide, Roberto, might have sufficient clout with the authorities to get the door open for him and his family ... so that they could crawl inside and have a look at Chac Mool, and the jade inlaid jaguar throne.

Having seen their fill of the view from the top-most vantage point of El Castillo and having studied every inch of the temple that the Maya had placed there ... Gaspar, Peugeot and Alex decided to make their way back down the stairs, very slowly, sliding step by step ... on their butts. Gaspar clutched Peugeot to his chest, with the pup's paws over his shoulders, and Peugeot looking back in disbelief and distress, placing his entire canine faith in his master's hands. It was a dizzying experience and one that they couldn't figure out how the ancient Maya had put up with for all those years. Finally reaching the ground the teenagers and the relieved French poodle found Peter and Elvira standing with Roberto, just looking up at the immense structure ... awe-struck.

"I dare you, mom," Gaspar giggled. "I dare you too, Peter, and you, Roberto." Go on, guys. Give it a try, I dare you to climb to the top." he challenged them, giving his mother a push towards the steep staircase. "While you all are heading up, Peugeot, Alex and I will go over and check out the Temple of Warriors and the great Ballcourt too." Gaspar pointed out into the distance as he spoke. "When you reach the top, we'll holler and wave at you from over there," Gaspar motioned again in the direction of the Temple of Warriors. Keep an eye out for us and wave back too, okay?" he insisted, nudging Alex to get a move on, in the direction of their new destination. "And Roberto, I know you have pull around here. Do you think you can get us in to see the Jaguar Throne? I know we need special permission, but perhaps if you call Señor de Montijo, he could get it for us." Gaspar begged over his shoulder as Peugeot pulled him forward.

"I'll do my best, Gaspar, if I ever get back down from up there," Roberto joked, pointing heavenward.

The Temple of the Warriors complex consisted of a large stepped pyramid fronted and flanked by rows of carved columns depicting fierce warriors prepared for battle. When Gaspar, Peugeot and Alex stood in front of these, all they could feel was awe. At the top of the stairway, placed at the pyramid's summit and leading towards the entrance to the pyramid's temple sat a statue of *Chac Mool*. Gaspar knew from reading his compiled notes that, like El Castillo, The Temple of the Warriors also encased or entombed a former structure called The Temple Chac Mool. Gaspar pulled his papers out of his pocket and read the history of the statue to Alex from his notes.

"Nineteenth-century explorers Augustus Le Plongeon and his wife Alice Dixon Le Plongeon visited Chichén, and excavated a statue of a figure on its back, knees drawn up, upper torso raised on its elbows with a plate on its stomach. Augustus Le Plongeon called it *Chac Mool*, which has been the term to describe all types of this statuary found in Mesoamerica." Gaspar read the facts to his pal.

As they walked along the south wall of the Temple of the Warriors, Alex pointed out a series of exposed, free-standing columns, positioned proudly in a row. "These would have supported a roof way back when," Alex informed his pal. "Look, Gasp, how the columns are in three distinct sections. There's a west group that extends the lines of the front of the temple, a north group with pillars that have carvings depicting soldiers in bas-relief and over here on the south and northeast elevations even more decorated pillars. I bet those must have formed an entire other temple attached at the southeast corner of the Temple of the Warriors."

Gaspar loved that Alex not only wanted to be an architect but that he could figure these things out for himself and even use a lot of architectural terminology that Gaspar still needed to learn about.

Alex ran over to The Temple of the Warriors and ran inside, with Gaspar and Peugeot close on his heels. After their eyes adjusted to the darkened room, Alex called out to his pal, "come over here and look at this, Gasp. There's a rectangular room in here decorated with carvings of people and gods, and animals and serpents. Come check it out, man." When Gaspar and Peugeot arrived on the scene, Alex continued his enthusiastic narration. "Look, it's really a marvel of ancient engineering. Take a look at that channel. It was built to funnel out all the rainwater from the complex. And look over here, Gasp." Alex said reading the information off the placard near the structure while tracing the map attached with his finger. "It says here that the channel goes all the way over there to a *rejollada*, made out of a former cenote."

"What's a rejollada?" Gaspar had never heard the term.

"It's like a cistern to collect rainwater. The Mayans were very clever about saving water and using it wisely." Alex insisted.

"That's what I like about you, Al. You're a veritable little architect, like I wanted to be but never will be. You on the other hand understand all this stuff, and how it works, or like in the case of some of these ruins, the way it's supposed to be. I on the other hand can appreciate it, but only on the surface. Your appreciation goes right down to the foundations. I've got to hand it to you, buddy. You've got a gift," Gaspar complimented his friend.

Continuing on their tour of the complex, they moved south of the group of a thousand columns to a group of three smaller, interconnected buildings. The Temple of the Carved Columns, a smaller more elegant building that consisted of a front gallery with an inner corridor, which led to an altar with another statue of Chac Mool. Many of the columns in this building had been decorated with rich bas-relief carvings of individual personages, Alex counted forty in all. Gaspar on the other hand was more intrigued by a section of the upper facade which had an interesting carved motif of x's and o's displayed in front of the structure.

"It's like a giant game of tic-tac-toe," Alex joked when he saw the unusual decoration.

"They call this area El Mercado," Gaspar informed Alex, reading from the plaque placed next to the square structure. "It says here that it's called the Mercado because of this shelf of stone that surrounds the gallery and patio. Apparently early explorers theorized that this place was used to display wares like in a marketplace, but some archaeologists believe that its purpose was more ceremonial than commercial," Gaspar finished reading the information presented on the plaque.

Moving on to the Temple of the Small Tables, the boys and Peugeot gave the sight short shrift as it was nothing but an unrestored mound of dirt. There was a plaque calling it The Thompson's Temple, which was also referred to in Gaspar's guidebook as The Palace of Ahau Balam Kauil. The so-called palace was nothing more than a small building with two levels that had friezes depicting jaguars, as well as glyphs of the Maya god Kahuil.

Look, it says here that Balam in Maya means jaguar." Gaspar informed his pal. "Balam is a good new word for us to turn into one of our own special Captain Haddock curses," he enthused. We could come up with a lot of new ones like … '*Balam you boorish–brontozori! Or how bout … balam you bawdy, basecourt, baggage!*' I can't wait to try out some new curses on you, Al!" Gaspar laughed.

Suddenly, Alex shouted, "Look over there, it's the great ballcourt … " turning Gaspar around by the shoulders to face him in the right direction.

"Over where … *balam, you bawdy, ballcourt, baggage!*" Gaspar blurted, this time turning Alex back to face the right direction.

"Ballcourt, what? Come on, let's go," Alex shouted, running towards the grass-covered playing field.

"*Ballcourt is even better than basecourt,*" don't you think?" Gaspar asked, pleased with himself and his new turn of phrase.

When they got there and were actually standing on the ground where ancient Maya athletes had competed, the boys were humbled by the magnitude of the stadium and the history it represented.

"I read somewhere that there are actually twelve more of these stadiums around here somewhere," Gaspar informed Alex. "But this is *The Great Ballcourt*. It measures 551 by 230 feet overall, and supposedly it's by far the most impressive one, architecturally in all of Yucatan. In case you're wondering, Al, it's also the largest and best preserved ballcourt in all of ancient Mesoamerica," Gaspar finished reciting the stadiums specifics which he read from his notes. "Come on, Peugeot, I'm going to unleash you so you can run around like a Mayan ball player." Gaspar trilled, letting the poodle go.

"Gasp, look at the symmetry of the parallel platforms flanking the main playing area. They must each be at least 300 feet long," Alex summed up the architecture in a sentence. "Look at the walls of these platforms. They've got to be at least twenty-five-feet high." Alex marveled, while reverentially placing the palm of his hand on the impressive carved stone wall.

"Yeah and look at those rings set high up in the center of each of the walls," Gaspar pointed. "They're carved out of solid rock with designs of intertwined feathered serpents. So cool, man."

"You think that's cool … check this out," Alex insisted, dragging Gaspar over to the side. "Look, Gasp. See how the Maya carved benches on the walls along with carved panels depicting teams of ball players. Look at that dude in the middle." Alex pointed. He's been decapitated, and oh yuck, the wound is spewing rivers of blood in the form of wriggling snakes!"

"That's sick, Al," Gaspar commented.

"That's cool, Gasp," Alex corrected him.

The two pals walked from one end of the ballcourt to the other. At the north end they found the appropriately named, North Temple, also known as the Temple of the Bearded Man, "*Templo del Hombre Barbado*," Alex told Gaspar in his best Spanish.

The small masonry building had detailed bas-relief carving on the inner walls, including a central figure with carving under his chin that resembled facial hair. When the two friends walked back to the south end of the field, they called for Peugeot, who came bounding down the playing field towards them at full blast. "Stick with us, Peugeot." Gaspar admonished his pet, "We're going to look at these other temples now."

The temples built into the east wall were even more impressive to Gaspar and Alex. These were the temples dedicated to the jaguar. The Upper Temple of the Jaguar overlooked the ballcourt and had an entrance guarded by two large columns carved in 'the feathered-serpent motif'. Inside they saw a large mural, depicting a bloody battle scene which Peugeot acknowledged with a loud sharp bark.

Entering the Lower Temple of the Jaguar, they saw columns and walls covered with elaborate bas-relief carvings, which even though neither teenager had any idea what their symbolism meant, they both commented on them to each other with enthusiasm. There was also a well-worn jaguar throne inside, missing its inlaid jade decorations. Peugeot jumped up onto the throne and gave it a whirl before jumping down, barking with approval.

The day was almost half over and there was still so much to see in this extensive archaeological site. "Something tells me we've got to come back tomorrow and do all of this over again," Al insisted.

"That would be fine with me, Al," Gaspar agreed. "I think we could stay here a week and not get tired of it. We'd probably discover something new every day. According to my notes, Al, we still have to see the Skull

Platform, the Platform of the Eagles and Jaguars, the Platform of Venus, the Steam Baths, Sacbé Number One, and the Cenote Sagrado. Then after all that … we have the entire Osario group to explore and that includes the pyramid of the same name as well as the Temple of Xtoloc. Then there's the central group which includes the Caracol, Las Monjas and Akab Dzib," Gaspar informed his friend, knowing that he was mutilating the crazy names of the historical Maya ruins.

"That does it, Gasp. You got me. Let's quit and get some lunch." Alex gave up. "If we're lucky we'll find your folks around here somewhere and hopefully we can talk them into having something to eat. After we accomplish that, then let's talk about all the other ruins we have yet to see," Alex begged.

Gaspar took out his cell phone and dialed Elvira. "We're near the foot of El Castillo," she told him.

Heading back toward El Castillo, they found Elvira, Peter and Roberto, discussing the intricacies of the carved feathered serpents flanking the main staircase.

"Clap your hands," they heard Roberto command.

"Clap, clap, clap," Elvira obeyed the guide.

"Chirp, chirp, chirp," came the resounding echo.

"Did you hear it?" asked Roberto. "The acoustics of Chichén Itzá are one of the wonders here. Thompson discovered that a hand clap in front of this staircase is followed by an echo that resembles the chirp of a quetzal. What do you think, is it true?"

"I heard it," Elvira agreed.

"Cool," Gaspar and Alex exhaled in unison.

"If you come back at the time of the spring equinox, you can see the light-and-shadow effect on the Temple of Kukulcan in which the feathered serpent god can be seen crawling down the side of the pyramid. It's quite a sight," Roberto assured his incredulous companions.

"Cool," Gaspar and Alex's echo came back as a double comment to what Roberto had told them.

"How'd you do, boys?" Elvira greeted the teenagers cheerfully.

"We've been all over the place," Gaspar informed his mother. "We're starved."

"There's a great place for lunch nearby," Roberto told them. "It's in the Hacienda Chichén Hotel, which I've booked us into for our time here. Let's go there, check in, have lunch and come back and see more of these ruins later."

"Sounds like a plan, Roberto," Peter agreed.

Lunch at Hacienda Chichén was superb. Roberto wasn't kidding when he said he knew a good place to eat nearby. The hacienda was on the grounds of the ruins, which they could see looming in the distance from the restaurant's covered terrace. Roberto, knowing his companions taste by now, suggested Hacienda Chichén's main restaurant *Chilam Balam*, which turned out to be a fine culinary destination offering a charming ambiance under the elegant arches of its colonial architecture. Lunching on the arcaded terrace with the dramatic backdrop of the great pyramid was an extra plus as far as Gaspar was concerned. Completely satiated, they quickly checked into their rooms before enthusiastically returning to the ruins for another look around. Once back inside the archaeological park, Gaspar and Alex went off on their own, leaving the old folks to enjoy a more leisurely stroll through the ruins.

Waving goodbye, Gaspar, Peugeot and Alex headed off in the direction of the Tzompantli, or Skull Platform, *Plataforma de los Cráneos*. Gaspar was a little taken aback by the depiction of skulls impaled vertically rather than horizontally like in the pictures Gaspar had seen in books about the Aztec city of Tenochtitlan, now the site of modern day Mexico City.

"It's interesting, Al, how the two cultures, Maya and Aztec used the same symbolism. But here they've stuck the pikes through the skulls vertically," Gaspar brought the difference to his friend's attention.

"Leave it to you, Gasp, to notice such a gory detail as that," Alex teased his friend.

When they were finished exploring the Skull Platform, they turned their attention to the Platform of the Eagles and Jaguars, *Plataforma de Águilas y Jaguares*, which was immediately to the east of The Great Ballcourt, they'd visited before lunch. "The platform is built in a combination of Maya and Toltec styles," Gaspar read to Alex from the plaque in front of one of the staircases, which ascended the temples facade. "Check this out, Al. The panels on each side of the platform are decorated with depictions of eagles and jaguars consuming human hearts … see!" Gaspar pointed to one of the grisly, stone carvings.

"Yuck, Gasp! It's a little too soon after lunch for such gross graphic art," Alex complained.

"Yeah, it's kinda turning me into an instant vegetarian … if you know what I mean?" Gaspar joked, giving his pal a shove.

When the boys and their pooch had gone up one side and down the other of the ceremonial platform, checking out all the gory details they finally headed off to visit the next site on their list, the Platform of Venus dedicated by the Maya to the planet Venus.

"Sorry, Gasp, but for me, this platform of Venus is sort of a non-event." Alex complained after looking around the site.

"I hear ya, Al. Let's move on … our next stop is the Cenote Sagrado." Gaspar reminded his pal.

To get there the boys took sacbé number one, the raised Maya causeway which Peugeot had fun running up and down on in front of them after Gaspar unleashed the enthusiastic hound. Sacbé number one led directly to the Cenote Sagrado. The "white road" was 890 feet long and thrity-feet wide and was by far the largest and most elaborate sacbé at Chichén Itzá.

Following in Peugeot's footsteps along the ancient

Maya highway, the boys could look over the landscape and see that the city had been built on an arid limestone plain without the benefit of any rivers or streams. Roberto had told them earlier that the rivers in the interior of Yucatán for the most part ran underground. He'd also told them that the entire region was pockmarked with natural sinkholes, or cenotes, which exposed the water table to the surface. They had already gone swimming in one at Aké, but the cenote at Chichén Itzá was even more famous because it was sacred to the ancient Maya. The Cenote Sagrado, they soon found out was also more impressive because it was two hundred feet in diameter with sheer cliffs dropping eighty-nine feet to the water below.

"Golly, Gasp. Look how deep it is." Alex gulped. "I thought we were going to be able to take a dip ... wha-da-ya-think?"

"I say, let's check the place out and decide later." Gaspar wanted a swim and wasn't going to give up a chance to cool off without a good look around first.

"Al, it says here in my notes that the Cenote Sagrado is one of two large sinkholes that provided plentiful water year-round to Chichén. It was this sacred water which made the location so attractive to the Maya for settlement. Of the two, the Cenote Sagrado is the most famous in all of Yucatan," Gaspar informed him.

"According to both Maya and Spanish, post-conquest sources, the pre-Columbian Maya sacrificed objects and human beings into the cenote during times of drought as a form of worship to the Maya rain god Chaac. Archaeological investigations support this as thousands of precious objects have been removed from the bottom of the cenote." Alex continued the history lesson, now reading from the plaque. "Edward Herbert Thompson, the former U.S. Ambassador to Mexico, remember Gasp, he's the dude that owned the Hacienda Chichén Itzá, and all these ruins, was the guy who dredged the Cenote Sagrado recovering artifacts of gold, carved jade, coral, pottery, flint, obsidian, shell, wood, rubber and cloth."

"Yeah, and don't forget, he also found human remains of children and men too." Gaspar reminded his pal. "You'd know that if you'd read the notes I provided to you on board *Floridablanca* ... and by the way, Al ... those remains all had wounds consistent with human sacrifice too ... Yuck!" Gaspar finished up.

Having explored around the Cenote Sagrado, the boys' dreams of taking a swim in the sacred waters were finally dashed. The cenote was too deep to easily climb in and out of and too public to use as a swimmin' hole as a steady stream of tourists came and went from the place during the time they stood there. If they were going to cool off from the hot Mexican sun, they'd have to find a better swimmin' hole to jump into. With a tinge of regret Gaspar, Peugeot and Alex moved on to the Temple of the Large Tables. This structure was at the northernmost of the series of buildings situated to the east of El Castillo.

According to the plaque at its entrance, its name came from a series of altars at the top of the structure that were supported by small carved figures of men with upraised arms, called *Atlantes*.

"Do you think the Maya came from Atlantis?" Alex asked Gaspar after hearing what the statues were called.

"Probably," was Gaspar's absent-minded answer. He had other things on his mind, for just then he saw a familiar figure entering the next building over. "Mike," he said.

"Who's that?" Alex asked.

"Mike, the thief of Dzibilchaltún," Gaspar whispered. "He just went into that building over there."

Stealthily the two boys with Peugeot on his leash approached the building, which the plaque at its entrance announced, 'The Steam Bath'. Cautiously they crept into the shadowed interior of the stone structure. Gaspar could see at once that it was a unique building compared to all the rest of the temples and platforms that they had recently visited. Entering the first room, they learned from the plaque there that it was a waiting gallery. A floor plan printed there showed two other rooms as part of the layout. A water bath and a steam chamber that the plaque said was operated by means of heated stones in ancient times.

"Just act like a tourist," Gaspar whispered to Alex, while pulling Peugeot up close.

When they entered the room that would have been

the water bath, Gaspar and Alex could hear voices in the next chamber, echoing back into the room where they now stood.

"We've got *nothing*, Joe." Mike's disembodied voice complained.

"Well we better get *something* and quick, Mike, if we want to survive this job." a second angry voice which had to be Joe's answered.

"Somehow we were tricked into picking up that mountain of fake gold drek." Mike was furious.

"Yeah, well, whoever did this to us is gonna pay, mark my words!" Joe's voice was threatening.

"But where are we ever going to find another haul as rich as the one at *Drizzlecreek*?" Mike whined.

"Drizzlecreek? It's pronounced Dzibilchaltún, you idiot." Joe corrected his henchman.

"Whatever." Mike was definitely not a linguist nor from the tone of his voice did he care to be.

"Your guess is as good as mine. Let's get going. Follow me," Joe's angry voice ordered.

The angry command caused Gaspar, Peugeot and Alex to hightail it outside where they hid behind a pile of rocks, waiting for Mike and his compatriot to appear. After about seven minutes, without any sign of their prey, Gaspar got up and handed Peugeot on his leash to Alex.

"You and Peugeot stay put, Al. I'm going back inside to see what's up," Gaspar instructed his pal.

When Gaspar inspected the three interior chambers,

he couldn't believe that they were all empty. Try as he might, using his pocket flashlight, he couldn't find any sign of the two men nor how they could have possibly left the building, without him and Alex seeing them. Baffled, he ran back outside to where Alex was waiting.

"You're not going to believe this," Gaspar told his pal. "They've disappeared! The only thing to do is to call Major Portillo and report the sighting. It seems silly to just say that they vanished into thin air, but that seems to be the way of it around these Maya ruins."

Dutifully Gaspar dialed the major and told him what they had seen and heard. The major thanked him and promised to investigate. He also told Gaspar that he need not wait for the major's men to arrive at the scene. It was getting late and the sun was low in the sky causing the pyramids to cast long shadows across the ground. It had been a rich full day. To start exploring the Osario group or any more of the ruins this late in the afternoon seemed like a hopeless idea to Gaspar.

"Let's quit for today," Gaspar suggested. "Let's find mom, Peter and Roberto and see if they want to go back to the hotel."

"Good idea," agreed Alex. "Besides," Alex reminded him, "we're coming back tonight for the sound and light show, so we should head back now … even if just to get our sweaters.

"I'll call mom now and see where they are," Gaspar decided.

Picking up on the first ring, his mother told him, "We're just heading back to the car."

"Wait for us," Gaspar begged. "We're on our way."

Soon they were back in their rooms at the Hacienda Chichén. The old hacienda had been converted into one of the best resort hotels in Mexico years ago and was favored by tourists in the know. Roberto had planned all their travel details and had made sure that the four travelers were happily ensconced in a beautiful two-bedroom suite with an elegant sitting room between them. Better yet, the suite came with its own covered terrace sporting head-on views of the ruins, to sit out on. While Elvira and Peter sipped margaritas, and Alex sketched the view, Gaspar immersed himself in a book on the ethnography of Chichén Itzá that Roberto had found for him in the hacienda's ample library.

Reading every word and studying the cryptograms carefully, he thought he had discovered the secret of what he had only guessed at earlier in the day when visiting the Jaguar platform.

After the sun had set, a hearty Mexican dinner was served on their private terrace by the hacienda's uniformed staff. After dinner, they bundled up with coats and sweaters for the much-anticipated sound and light show and headed back to the ruins. While the others were engrossed in the magic of the performance, complete with booming voices, Mayan music, costumed dancers, computerized theatrical lighting and exploding pyrotechnics, Gaspar silently slunk off to do a little investigating on his own.

Retracing his steps to the steam bath building which he and Alex had visited earlier in the day, Gaspar took out his pocket flashlight and ducked inside. Slowly he traced his flashlight around each of the three rooms until he finally found what he was looking for. He thought he'd seen it earlier in the day but wasn't sure. Now he was certain. A large stone in the corner near the water bath had a chink in it, and on the ground, covered by dusty footprints, a paving stone also seemed off kilter. Stepping on the paver with all of the weight of his measly ninety pounds, Gaspar activated an ancient mechanism that moved the stone forward exposing a passageway with stairs leading down. Passing through the opening, Gaspar started down the steep stairs. The room that he discovered there had to be the ancient furnace where the rocks would have been heated to warm the water for the pool above and to create the steam for the ancient sauna. Gaspar surmised that slaves had to have fed the furnaces and had to have had a way to get in and out of the area. The beam from his flashlight revealed several passageways leading away from the furnace room and Gaspar chose the one leading in what he hoped was the direction of the Eagle and Jaguar Platform. He made the right choice, as the passage led into a series of highly decorated rooms directly under the platform itself and the decorations he found there were actually the murals which he had been studying in the book back at the hotel. One of the murals depicted a seacoast with a massive pyramid just inland from a crescent bay, like the mural that had attracted his attention at El Trono at Ek Balam. *The Lost Temple of Chac Mool*, Gaspar mouthed silently. Another mural showed what Gaspar considered could only be Chichén Itzá, based on his knowledge of what he had explored earlier that day. There was another mural depicting the palace complex at Aké, and another showing some of the buildings they'd visited at Ek Balam. Combined, the murals were a literal map of the ancient Maya empire. *An ancient Mayan GPS system*, he thought and laughed to himself. Shining his flashlight beam from depiction to depiction he could discern other monuments in other panels, which he knew he would be seeing in the coming days when they finally got to Tulúm, Cobá, Muyil, Labna, Xlapak, Sayil and Edzna. Of all the monuments pictured the only one he didn't recognize from his study of the guidebooks, was the huge pyramid near the sea. It had to be the same one that Roberto had pointed out back at El Trono. He took a photo of the mural depicting *The Lost Temple of Chac Mool*, using the camera on his phone. Scanning the room one more time he saw what he thought might be a way out, and shortly found the ancient mechanism that unlatched the spring that slid a stone open for him to pass through. When he got outside, he could hear the noise and pyrotechnic booms issuing from the sound and light show. He also came face-to-face with a federale in uniform who grabbed him by his shirt collar and dragged him off in the direction of the performance without speaking a word. Gaspar knew he'd have some explaining to do. To the terrified teenager's relief, he was dragged right in front of Major Portillo himself, who laughed out loud when he saw Gaspar dragged before him in the clutches of the big guard.

"So, we meet again, Gaspar Brown. What have you been up to, running around the ruins in the dead of night?" Portillo asked jovially.

"I found the secret way out of the steam baths. There's dozens of tunnels down there, with probably a dozen ways out."

"Tell us about it, Gaspar. We have maps of all the secret passages or at least most of them. The one you found leads down to the ancient furnaces and from there the tunnels branch out all over Chichén Itzá like a spider's web. It was a way for slaves to get from place to place without being seen, and also a way for the ancient priests to appear and disappear as if by magic, which was a great way to impress the masses who they controlled through superstition and magic."

"And I thought I'd made a major archaeological discovery," Gaspar moaned with embarrassment. "Am I under arrest, major?" he asked in all seriousness.

"Not at all. But I would appreciate it if you would leave the investigation of *the jaguar* and his gang of thieves to me and my men. I don't want you getting yourself hurt … or worse. Don't worry, Gaspar. We'll find those guys and they'll lead us to the Jaguar himself. Now do me a favor and go back and watch the show. You'll like it … it's a lot of fun."

Gaspar shook Portillo's hand and walked sheepishly away in the direction of the sound and light show. When he got there, the performance was just ending.

"Where've ya been?" Alex asked wide-eyed.

"Had to take a leak," was Gaspar's quick response.

Back at the hotel, many of the guests who'd attended the show gathered in the lobby for coffee, liqueurs and a selection of desserts including French pastries, ice creams and cakes. The hotel visitors were a jolly group, friendly and interested in the history of the area. They were a mixture of Europeans, Americans and well-heeled Mexicans. One large man sat holding court in a corner of the room. He was surrounded by several beautiful women and every now and then one or two of the men present in the room would walk over to pay their respects.

"Who's the old buddha in the corner?" Gaspar asked Señor Gutierrez, the hotel manager.

"That is Señor Balam, one of Mexico's richest men, an amateur archaeologist and an important collector of Pre-Columbian art."

"Balam," Gaspar repeated. "Is that a typical name in Mexico, Señor Gutierrez?"

"No, Señor Gaspar. It is not a typical name. I'm not

even sure if it is not his nickname or a made- up name, but it is the name he goes under and the name he has registered under here at the hotel, year after year. Would you like to meet him? I'd be happy to introduce you to him."

"That would be very nice," Gaspar answered in the affirmative. "I'll follow you."

With that the hotel manager got up and escorted Gaspar over to the large man holding court. "Señor Balam, may I present our distinguished guest from America, Señor Gaspar Brown."

"Gaspar Brown? The boy billionaire?" the old buddha spoke with disbelief at his good fortune. "I am very pleased to make your acquaintance, young man. Come sit next to me," he insisted, shooing away Mr. Gutierrez as well as the three pretty girls who had draped themselves around him. "Besides the ruins, what brings you to Yucatán?" he asked pointedly.

"I own property in Celestún. The Hacienda Huayrocondo." Gaspar answered honestly.

"Celestún, why would anyone want to own property in that *backwater*?" Balam harumphed snidely.

"Not a backwater at all, Señor … a veritable *paradise*." Gaspar corrected him.

"Oh, I can imagine. Forgive me, my boy, but I am only interested in antiquities, the beauties of nature and real estate evade me. As you probably know, Celestún is bereft of anything Maya. So, if the Maya had no use for the place, then I don't either."

"Pity," Gaspar responded. "I have a lot of land there, and I'm planning to develop it into a major destination resort," Gaspar let his imagination run away with him.

"That does sound promising, but real estate development has never interested me. Collecting is my game, that and other business ventures which have proven to be lucrative," the Mexican relayed.

"What exactly is your business, Señor Balam? Your reputation *doesn't* proceed you, but I always like to know not only how people spend their fortunes, but also how they've acquired them."

"*Papa* and *mama* left me a *little* something, but I have managed to transform their *pittance* into a rather sizeable fortune, a network of businesses here in Mexico, which many of my colleagues find indispensable to their well-being. It is much too complicated to go into here, but perhaps one day if your development plans prove successful, you may want to take advantage of some of the financial services I have to offer."

"Thank you, señor. I'll make sure my people get in touch with your people when the time comes."

"You do that, sonny," came the fat man's second snide remark, as he dismissed Gaspar summarily from having any further conversation with him.

"It's been a pleasure meeting you, Señor Balam," Gaspar said without extending his hand, before turning his back on the older man, and walking briskly away.

"What was that all about?" Peter asked as Gaspar rejoined the group.

"That is Señor Balam, a very interesting character and someone worth watching," Gaspar replied.

"Balam, you mean the richest man in Mexico." Peter was impressed, looking back at the fat man.

"That would be *him*," Gaspar agreed.

"Let's turn in, boys," Elvira suggested. "We still have a big day of exploration tomorrow."

•••

The next morning, Gaspar and Alex were up early, ready to enter the archaeological park the minute the gates opened. Elvira and Peter sent word to go on without them. 'They would catch up later.' Gaspar decided to leave Peugeot behind under the watchful eyes of his parents as he felt the sleepy pup would be happier staying in this morning.

Roberto took the boys over to the site and walked around with them, showing them the important points of interest. "I know you guys have been all over this place," Roberto cajoled them, "so just tell me … what haven't you seen yet that I can still show you?"

"This morning we want to see the Osario group," Gaspar insisted with conviction. "Tell us all you can about the Osario structures, Roberto. We're all ears," the teenager trilled as they walked swiftly along the path.

"Well, to start, the Osario group includes the pyramid known as the Temple of Xtoloc, and the central group includes the Caracol, Las Monjas, and Akab Dzib. The Osario itself, like El Castillo, is a step-pyramid with a temple dominating its platform. Like its larger neighbor, it has four sides with staircases on each side. But unlike El Castillo, there is an opening into the pyramid at the center which leads to a natural cave thirty-nine feet below. Edward H. Thompson, the former owner of the site, excavated this cave in the late nineteenth century, and because he found several skeletons and artifacts such as jade beads there ... he named the structure the High Priests' Temple. Archaeologists today believe the structure was neither a tomb nor that the personages buried in it were high priests either.

The High Priests' Temple was the first of the impressive structures Gaspar and Alex would see under the watchful eye of their knowledgeable guide. Together the three men climbed to the top of the structure and then climbed down to the center in order to enter the cave, which was spooky, but exhilarating to see.

Moving along they came to the recently restored Temple of Xtoloc, named after the Maya word for iguana. The impressive temple was built just outside the Osario platform and it overlooked the other large cenote at Chichén Itzá, also called 'Xtoloc'. Roberto showed them the series of pilasters inside the temple that were carved with images of people as well as representations of plants, birds and scenes from Maya mythology. Gaspar took pictures with his phone, while Alex sketched furiously the various decorative motifs found inside.

Roberto then pointed out the several aligned structures which had been built between the Xtoloc temple and the Osario. These he told them included the Platform of Venus which was similar in design to the structure of the same name that they'd explored yesterday. They walked quickly past The Platform of the Tombs which Roberto dismissed as insignificant and a small round structure that Roberto told them was still unnamed. These three less important structures were constructed in a row extending straight from the Osario. Beyond them the Osario platform terminated in a wall, which contained an opening to a sacbé that ran several hundred feet back to the Xtoloc temple. Both Gaspar and Alex marveled at the planning and the formal layout of the ceremonial structures they'd just visited.

Walking further south of the Osario, they came upon two small buildings that Roberto told them archaeologists believed were residences for important personages. "These," Roberto told Gaspar and Alex, "are named the House of the Metates and the House of the Mestizas."

Gaspar and Alex gave each other a look of total confusion and just nodded in consent, neither of them wanting to reveal their ignorance, not having a clue as to what a metate was, although they both had a pretty good idea what a mestiza was.

As they continued walking trying to catch up with Roberto. who was still babbling on about the ancient Maya, several steps ahead of them ... Gaspar whispered to Alex," remind me to Google metate tonight when we get back to the hotel."

Continuing on, they came to a smaller platform holding many important structures, several of which were oriented toward the Xtoloc cenote. "These buildings are called the *Casa Colorada* group." Roberto told them. "These structures are amongst the oldest in Chichén Itzá." Roberto educated his clients. "The Casa Colorada is Spanish for Red House," Roberto informed them. "This is one of the best- preserved buildings at Chichén Itzá. Its Maya name is *Chichanchob*, which means small holes."

Entering the first chamber they saw extensive hiero-glyphs carved into the stone walls. Roberto told them that the glyphs mentioned various rulers of Chichén Itzá, as well as rulers of the nearby city of Ek Balam. To further prove his point, he showed the boys an inscription containing a Maya date which correlated to 869 BC.

"It is one of the oldest dates found in all of the Yucatán," he told the teenagers solemnly. "When we go around the outside, you'll see a small ballcourt adjoining the back wall of the house which the Mexican Instituto Nacional de Antropología e Historia restored in 2009," he told them proudly. "While the Casa Colorada is in a good state of preservation, you can see that the other buildings in the group, with one exception, are just decrepit mounds," Roberto told his companions, almost apologetically. "One building, right over there is still half-standing," he noted, pointing to his left. "Its name is Casa del Venado, or House of the Deer. The origin of the name is unknown, as there are no representations of deer or other animals on the building. But it is a romantic name, don't you think?" Roberto asked no one in particular. "Follow me boys, our next stop is La Iglesias, it's in the Las Monjas complex. Wait until you see it. The entire building is magnificently decorated with elaborate carved stone masks."

Coming upon the extensively decorated structure, Alex blurted. "Gaspar has an iglesia at La Rinconada. That's the name of his house in Florida. You should see it, Roberto. It's actually bigger than this iglesia … it doesn't have all those carved stone masks on its facade, but it's equally impressive."

"Yeah, no masks, and definitely not as old, or as important as this one," Gaspar blushed, embarrassed by the spotlight his pal had just turned on him.

"I'd like to see your church and house one day, if you invite me." Roberto told Gaspar graciously.

"Of course, you're invited," Gaspar enthused. "*Mi casa es su casa, amigo*," the teenager insisted, putting an arm around Roberto's shoulders. "What's that?" Gaspar asked pointing to a nearby structure, hoping to change the subject.

"El Caracol," was all Roberto had to say by way of

introducing one of Chichén Itzá's and the Yucatán's most celebrated Maya structures.

"It looks like an observatory," Alex commented.

"It's called *El Caracol* which means … *The Snail* … because of its round shape and because of the spiral staircase carved in stone on the inside," Gaspar informed his pal. "Archaeologists have theorized El Caracol to have been a proto-observatory with doors and windows aligned to astronomical events, specifically around the path of Venus as it traverses the heavens." Gaspar finished spouting what little he could remember from all the notes that he'd read in preparation for seeing the real thing.

"It *is* an observatory/temple," Roberto qualified his answer. "This area is called *Las Monjas* and *El Caracol* is one of the more notable structures anywhere in Chichén Itzá. The whole area is a complex of terminal classic buildings constructed in the Puuc architectural style. The Spanish named this complex Las Monjas, The Nuns or The Nunnery, but it was actually a governmental palace. You can see that the Las Monjas group is distinguished by its concentration of hieroglyphic texts dating to the late to terminal classic periods. These texts frequently mention a ruler by the name of Kakupakal. This is his name right here," Roberto showed them, pointing to a mish mash of carved characters carved on the wall.

"Whoever carved this, writes just like you, Al," Gaspar joked. "It looks like a bunch of chicken scratch."

"That's pronounced *Chichén scratch*," Alex joked.

"Now we come to the most mysterious structure at Chichén Itzá." Roberto told them cryptically. It's known as *Akab Dzib*," Roberto spoke the name with a shudder. "In Yucatec Mayan the name means, "dark, in the most *mysterious* sense," he told them ominously. "An earlier name of the building, according to a translation of glyphs in the Casa Colorada, is *Wak wak Puh Ak Na* which means *the flat house with the excessive number of chambers*. This was the home of the administrator of Chichén Itzá, *Kokom Yahawal Cho' K'ak'*. The Instituto Nacional de Antropología e Historia completed a restoration of the building in 2007. You can see that in comparison to the other structures around here this one is relatively short, only twenty feet high, and one hundred and sixty feet in length by forty-nine feet in width. The long, western-facing facade has seven doorways, but the eastern facade has only four. These are broken by a large staircase that leads to the roof. This is the front of the structure," Roberto gesticulated towards the façade with the staircase. "See how it looks out over what is today a steep, but dry cenote. The southern end of the building has only one entrance. The door opens into a small chamber and on the opposite wall is another doorway, above which on the lintel are intricately carved glyphs. Let's go inside now and I'll show them to you." Entering the dark interior, it took a moment for their eyes to become accustomed to the gloom. Taking out their flashlights Roberto continued the tour. "Notice over here the *mysterious* writing that gives the building its name today," he told them, flashing his light onto the glyphs carved over the doorway. "And look over here," the guide insisted, shining his torch under the lintel of another door jamb exposing a carved panel of a seated figure surrounded by more mysterious glyphs. Continuing inside one of the chambers, he shined his light up to the ceiling to show the boys a painted handprint there before leading them back out into the sunlight.

"Wow, Roberto. That was terrific. We're so glad you came with us today. If you hadn't been here, we would have missed all those cool details … especially that handprint. Imagine that Gasp … a million-year-old painted handprint." Alex enthused.

"Not quite a million years old, Al … but ancient nonetheless." Gaspar set his friend straight.

So far, the day had gone great and the visit to these special sites with Roberto's keen knowledge of what they were seeing, had been a plus for Gaspar and Alex. Although it was getting close to noon, none of them seemed anxious to break for lunch, although Gaspar did wonder if his mother and stepfather would ever join them. Putting the thought aside, he asked Roberto, "where to next?"

"*Old Chichén* or *Chichén Viejo* in Spanish. There's no other way to describe the next group of structures over here," Roberto told them as he led them to the south of the central site. "This is where most of the Puuc style architecture of the city is concentrated," Roberto informed them. "I'll show you the Phallic Temple, the Platform of the Great Turtle, the Temple of the Owls and the Temple of the Monkeys."

"Sounds very educational," Gaspar winked at Alex. "Be sure and point out the Phallic Temple to Al. It's something he needs to learn about," Gaspar chuckled catching the twinkle in Roberto's eye.

"Si, Señor," Roberto agreed. "I'll make sure he gets a good look at it."

"What are you guys talking about?" Alex grilled them. "What are you up to?"

"Besides the Phallic Temple," Gaspar giggled, "are there any other important structures to see before lunch, Roberto?"

"Chichén Itzá has a lot of great sites packed into its ceremonial center, but we'll be doing well to get the ones I just mentioned out of the way before heading back to the hotel for lunch." Roberto insisted.

"Lead on, Roberto, the Phallic Temple awaits," Gaspar chuckled, to Alex's continued perplexity.

It was just before one o'clock when the three musketeers returned to the hotel having polished off the Platform of the Great Turtle, the Temple of the Owls and the Temple of the Monkeys. Gaspar had made Roberto save The Phallic Temple for last, both of them causing Alex all kinds of discomfort in the telling of the history of the place, with Gaspar making up all kinds of horrific tales of what kind of rituals had taken place there, mostly involving teenage rites of passage into manhood. Gaspar and Roberto howled with laughter when they realized that Alex believed every tall tale they'd just made up! At least Gaspar's *were* tall tales, but now he wondered if some of what Roberto had reported on the Maya goings- on there might not actually have been the truth. The thought caused a sensation like a lightning bolt to course through his body from the tip of his toes to the top of his head.

Back at the hotel, Roberto headed to the restaurant while the boys went straight to the suite where they found Gaspar's parents lounging in their robes. Even Peugeot barely raised his head to receive them, that's how lethargic the boys found the atmosphere inside the suite.

"Mom," Gaspar cajoled Elvira, "it's past one and we're starving. Don't you want to go downstairs and get some lunch?"

"Oh, darling," his mother protested, "we're just so tired. Peter and I have decided to stay in all day. You two run along and have lunch and take Mr. Peugeot with you," she urged.

"But you're missing the ruins," Gaspar protested. "Roberto has shown us the most amazing things. Wait till you see the Phallic Temple. It will blow you away."

"See it. I've been worshipping at it all morning," Elvira said in an inaudible mumble, that only Peter, who was sitting at her side could hear.

Gaspar didn't hear her aside and sailed on with his argument. "Okay, but if you get the gumption you should really try and join us this afternoon. Roberto's promised to get us inside El Castillo to see the Jaguar throne, and he's also going to take us to the Caves of Balamka'anche'!" Gaspar thought that if anything could get the honeymooners out of the suite, the Caves of Balamka'anche' would be the irresistible carrot to dangle in front of them.

"That's nice, darling," was the most excitement his mother could muster. "You and Alex go with Roberto and you can tell us about everything tonight at dinner. We ought to be feeling rested by dinner time," she drawled, looking at Peter for concurrence.

Entering the hotel restaurant, the maître de took them directly to their favorite table out on the terrace, where Roberto was waiting for them. To get there Gaspar, Peugeot and Alex had to pass by the dreadful Señor Balam, who sat stuffing his fat face, while a pretty Señorita pawed him on his left and another stunner on his right wiped bits of lunch from his quivering jowls. As they passed by the unattractive man, the fat oaf scowled at Gaspar as if just having seen something inedible that turned his stomach. Gaspar just stared back as he walked past the unappetizing scene. He hoped that a look of mild amusement mixed with disgust was successfully spread across his face, but without a mirror to look into and never having practiced such a look, he feared he may not have gotten his message across to the *yeasty, weather-bitten Mexican wagtail*. To the teenagers' delight, Mr. Peugeot let loose an unrehearsed growl as he passed Balam's table. Gaspar was happy for the small gesture from his helpful hound.

Sitting down by the balustrade under the arched arcade of the old hacienda, Gaspar started his usual game of Sixty-five questions. "Who is Balam, Roberto, and why is he so toxic?"

"Oh, Señor Gaspar, that is going to be a very long story … " Roberto started, "but I'll tell you all I know. Balam is the son of a Lebanese immigrant who came to Mexico during World War II. His family was, stopped at the Tijuana border because the quota for Lebanese into the United States, had been filled, so they were turned away, trapped in Mexico, so to speak. Like most immigrants in difficult situations, the family, their actual name was Balaian, stayed in Tijuana and opened a grocery store. The store prospered and grew into an incredible chain of supermarkets. The Balaian now have stores in every city and town in Mexico. After their huge success in super-mercados they branched out into imports and exports and prospered mightily, doubling and tripling their initial fortune."

"Sounds like a good, clean, straight-forward business," Gaspar stated.

"Yes, but that was his grandfather. His father and

uncles worked for the company, branching out all over Mexico, opening banks and gasoline stations, restaurants and hotels. Today it is a huge privately held conglomerate. All the members of the family have become rich and are accepted by the Mexican grandees and the socially powerful ... all but Señor Balam that is. Señor Balam lives a life apart from his family. He has set himself up as a collector and connoisseur. He does not attend high society affairs and surrounds himself with luxury and beautiful, but not necessarily nice women. He has a wife, the product of an early arranged marriage that his parents insisted on. Carla Balaian has had a tragic existence according to the gossip columns. Her only joy in life these days seems to be jewelry and she's covered in it. From the reports and the endless photographs published to prove their point, the papers say that she's never been seen in the same piece twice. Those in the know say that when she buys a suite of jewelry at Verdura or David Webb or Tony Duquette, that she'll order the same suite in every color ... ruby, sapphire, emerald, diamond ... get the picture?" Roberto chuckled.

"Got it," Gaspar laughed. The one thing Gaspar understood loud and clear was jewelry. What would Roberto, Alex and even Balam or Balaian think if they knew he had Gasparilla's legendary horde of gold and jewels hidden in the basement at La Rinconada. He smiled to himself.

"So, what's his reputation? What are the rumors

printed about him?" Gaspar dug a little deeper.

"Oh, the usual gossip about Mafia connections, people paying protection to him or to his gang. He's a rough character, hangs with a rough crowd, loose women, angry men. They say he'll stop at nothing to get what he wants, and what he wants most is Maya, Aztec and Inca gold. Several robberies from some of the national museums throughout the America's have been linked to him by rumor and innuendo, and there have also been thefts from important private collections around the world which he's visited, which have mysteriously gone unsolved."

"Where there's smoke, there's fire," Alex threw in wisely.

"Well he definitely seems to be up to something unsavory here at Chichén Itzá," Gaspar pondered. "I wonder what his game is, and I wonder if he could also be on the tail of Joe and Mike, our thug friends from Dzibilchaltún?" Gaspar tried to put two and two together.

"Let's order lunch, Gasp," Alex begged. "I'm about ready to give up the ghost."

Roberto summoned the waiter and hearty lunches were ordered all around.

"Roberto, you're such a font of knowledge. Tell us how you came to learn so much about the Maya and Aztec cultures, and tell us about your own life," Gaspar urged their companion to enlighten them.

"I was born in Yucatán. My father worked for the

Instituto Nacional de Antropología e Historia, and he taught me everything he knew about the ancient cultures. I also went to the University of Mexico, in Mexico City. Someday, my friends, you must visit the capital. It's full of beautiful architecture and amazing museums. I studied there and got a job at the Museo Nacional de Antropologia. It is the most amazing museum. Wait until you see the collections there. Everything that is not on site here, is there. Trust me, it is a treasure trove."

"I've read about the museum in Mexico City. It's famous," Gaspar sang. "Why would you ever leave it?"

"Well, that's a good question," Roberto replied, without a tinge of regret in his voice. "After five years as one of the top curators, I woke up and realized that I actually didn't like working indoors. Apparently, all I ever wanted to do while I was there was get out. It just took me a while to actually listen to my inner voice and act on it. You see ... I really wanted to be on the job, here, in the Yucatán, and I'm so happy now and only wish I'd acted on my feelings earlier. I was never an archaeologist. That too would have proven to be boring work for me. I am restless, adventurous, a people person. I love meeting new friends, like yourselves and showing them the marvels of the Maya right here, on the spot, out in the open air and sunshine. Let's just say, I'm doing what I do best, and I'm loving it," Roberto finished his statement with a big smile.

"To your own self, be true," Gaspar recited. "Good for you, Roberto. If more people followed their hearts and listened to their inner voices, the world would certainly be a happier and better place." Gaspar applauded the guide.

"What's with the inner voice scrap?" Alex chided his friend, using their favorite curse word. "Where do you come up with all this stuff, Gasp?"

"I *read*, Al. You've seen my library. It's full of books on metaphysical things as well as art, architecture and science. Someday you've got to join me in there and open up some volumes. There's nothing but hours and hours of pleasure on those shelves," Gaspar told his friend with conviction. "Take you for example, Al. You want to be an architect. You've been spending hours and hours of happy time, sketching the ruins we've been visiting. Think how miserable you'd be if you'd been forced to spend your time doing plumbing or carpentry or laying bricks. We all have to feed our souls and the only way to do that is to listen to our inner voice, really listen and hear it, and then act on what we hear."

"Precisely," Roberto chimed in. "That is precisely what I did, and I have never regretted a day of my life since leaving that amazing museum."

"What sign are you, Roberto?" Gaspar asked.

"Sagittarius."

"Ah, the Archer … you shoot straight for what you want and get it! Well done," Gaspar complimented the man.

"And you, Señor, what sign are you?" Roberto asked.

"Gemini."

"The twins. Some days you want to be a prince in a castle, and other days you want to be a starving artist in a garret." Roberto summed up Gaspar's personality, in a nutshell. "I shall henceforth think of you as the *Prince of Paradox*," Roberto laughed.

"I'm a Libra," Alex offered.

"Always weighing everything," Roberto said.

"Can't decide if you want this or that," Gaspar chuckled.

"Give me a break, guys," Alex begged, as the waiter brought their lunch.

While they ate their delicious repast, Roberto told them more tales of Chichén Itzá and some of its more recent history.

"Chichén Itzá is hands down the most-visited archae-ological site in Mexico. Tourism has been a major factor here for more than a century. It all started in the late 1800s when John Lloyd Stephens wrote his book *Incidents of Travel in Yucatán*. That book single-handedly inspired many to make the pilgrimage to Chichén Itzá. Even before the book was published, Benjamin Norman and Baron Emanuel von Friedrichsthal traveled to Chichén after meeting Stephens, and they both published the results of what they found. Friedrichsthal was the first to photograph Chichén Itzá, using the recently invented daguerreotype. You need to see those beautiful photo-graphs. They are amazing," Roberto insisted.

"I've seen a lot of them in books, but I'd love to see the real thing. They're all at the museum in Mexico City, aren't they?" Gaspar asked.

"Yes, you'll find them there. But if they're not on exhibit, I can help you get special permission to see them. Just let me know," Roberto assured him, before continuing with his history lesson. "After Edward Thompson purchased the Hacienda Chichén in 1894, which as you know included the entire archaeological site of Chichén Itzá, he received a constant stream of visitors. He had considered constructing a hotel on his property around 1910 but abandoned those plans, probably because of the Mexican Revolution. This was his house, and ironically it is now a hotel," Roberto chuckled, gesticulating around the house and towards the grounds which surrounded them.

"Do you think he's looking down in approval at all this or do you think he'd be angry that his house has become a hostel open to the public?" Alex wondered.

"I don't think he's looking down," Roberto said. "There's a lot of talk that he is here on the premises, or at least that his ghost is here on the premises, protecting Chichén Itzá. Guests and workers have seen and heard him roaming through the ruins, still throwing his weight around."

Gaspar immediately thought of Uncle Charlie before Alex broke into his reverie.

"What a story," Alex blurted. "Imagine owning all of

this, the remains of a lost civilization. It's amazing. What would you do, Gasp, if you discovered a Maya temple full of gold at La Rinconada?" Alex romanced.

"I don't know. The idea is mind-boggling, the possibilities endless. Let me get back to you, Al, after I give it a little bit of thought," Gaspar joked.

The waiter came by the table, as the busboy took away the lunch plates. "May I offer you dessert, gentlemen?" he asked politely.

"Of course!" both boys answered in unison.

After dessert orders were placed," Roberto asked, "shall I tell you more?"

"By all means," Gaspar commanded.

"Since Thompson's banishment, there have been two additional expeditions to recover artifacts from the Cenote Sagrado. The first was sponsored by the National Geographic Society. The second was sponsored by private interests. Both projects were supervised by our National Institute of Anthropology and History which continues its ongoing efforts to excavate and restore other monuments in the archaeological zone including the Osario, Akab D'zib and several buildings in Chichén Viejo too. More recently archaeologists, under the direction of Rafael Cobos, have made excavations adjacent to El Castillo to investigate constructions that predate even that ancient building."

"It must have been a difficult trek to get out here way back in the early part of the century when the ruins were first being investigated," Alex wondered. "I guess they had to pack in on mules or horses."

"Your right, Alex," Roberto chimed in. "It wasn't until the early 1920s, that a group of Yucatecans, led by writer/photographer Francisco Gomez Rul, began working toward expanding tourism here. It was because of their constant badgering that the government finally built the roads leading to and connecting the more famous monuments, including Chichén Itzá and that was way back in 1923. It was Gomez Rul who published one of the first guidebooks to Yucatán using photographs he'd taken of the ruins."

"What an opportunity to be on the ground floor of what would become a booming tourist business," Gaspar voiced his thoughts. "An opportunity of a lifetime considering how many millions of dollars or pesos are pouring into the Yucatán now because of it."

"It was Gomez Rul's son-in-law Fernando Barbachano Peon, a grand-nephew of former Yucatán Governor Miguel Barbachano, who actually started Yucatán's first official tourism business in the early 1920s. He began by meeting passengers that arrived by steamship in the town of Progreso, which is just south of Celestún where The Doctor's House is, and the most important port city north of Mérida. He personally persuaded the passengers to disembark and spend a week with him in Yucatán, after which they could catch the next steamship to their scheduled destinations. In his first year Barbachano Peon reportedly was only able to convince seven passengers to leave the ship and join his tour. In the mid-1920s Barbachano Peon persuaded Edward Thompson to sell him 5 acres next to Chichén so that he could build a small hotel. In 1930 the Mayaland Hotel opened, just north of the Hacienda Chichén, which at that time had been taken over by the Carnegie Institute for their own expeditions."

"Did the Carnegie Institute own the hacienda?" Alex asked.

"No, they just leased it from Mr. Thompson, but in 1944 Barbachano Peon purchased all of the Hacienda Chichén, including the ruins of Chichén Itzá from the heirs of Edward Thompson. By that time, the Carnegie Institute had completed its work and had abandoned the hacienda, which gave Barbachano the opportunity to turn this magnificent old house into another seasonal hotel."

"And what a hotel," Gaspar enthused looking around him.

"In 1972, Mexico enacted the *Ley Federal Sobre Monumentos y Zonas Arqueológicas, Artísticas e Históricas*, a federal law created to place jurisdictions over monuments and archaeological, artistic and historic sites. That put all the nation's pre-Columbian monuments, including those at Chichén Itzá, under federal ownership. Chichén Itzá is now a UNESCO World Heritage Site, and the second-most visited of Mexico's archaeological treasures. El Castillo was even named one of the new Seven

Wonders of the World after a worldwide vote." Roberto reported proudly.

"Cool," Alex interjected.

"The ensuing publicity over the new designation reignited debate in Mexico over the ownership of the site. This culminated in 2010, when the state of Yucatán purchased the land upon which the most recognized monuments rested from then owner Hans Juergen Thies Barbachano."

"I was wondering about that," Gaspar jumped in. "I hope he got a fair price for the real estate," the private-property-rights loving teenager added with concern.

"I assure you the family was well-compensated," Roberto assuaged Gaspar's deep-rooted capitalist fears and continued the telling of the site's history. "Over the past several years the Instituto Nacional de Antropología e Historia, which manages the site, has been closing monuments to public access. While visitors can walk around them, they can no longer climb some of them or go inside some of their chambers. The most recent was El Castillo, which was closed after a San Diego, California woman fell to her death in 2006. But as you have experienced with me as your guide, as a fellow of the instituto, I can get you inside almost all of the most interesting structures.

"Yeah, and because their security is so lax here, me and Gaspar have been able to get in and look around all kinds of places. And so, have those criminals Joe and

Mike, who we've seen hanging around here, no doubt …
looking for trouble," Alex informed Roberto airily.

"Listen, guys. If we're going to see the Jaguar Throne
and the Caves of Balamka'anche' today, we better hit
the road," Roberto cajoled them to get a move-on and
finish their desserts.

•••

Jumping into Roberto's SUV, they drove a couple of miles
southeast of Chichén Itzá and parked at the base of a hill
where the sacred caves of Balamka'anche' were hidden
amidst the rocks. Roberto explained that in Yucatec
Maya, "Balamka'anche' meant *The Jaguar Caves.*" For the
first time, Gaspar's ears perked up … *Balamka'anche'* …
*Jaguar. He had missed the tie-in all these days, Ek Balam …
The Palace of Ahau Balam Kauil … the name of the hotel's
restaurant, Chilam Balam … Señor Balam … Mr. Jaguar
… THE JAGUAR!* Gaspar's mind reeled with possibilities,
but he silently kept his suspicions to himself. Coming
back to reality, he heard Roberto telling them "inside the
caves you can still see a large selection of ancient pottery
and idols which are still in the positions where they were
discovered, just as they were left in pre-Columbian times."

Following a well-marked and well-worn path, they
hiked up to the caves' entrance with Mr. Peugeot as
usual, leading the pack. Once inside, the air was cool
and still. Roberto kept up his invaluable lesson as they

walked inside. "The caves were discovered by Edward Thompson and Alfred Tozzer around 1905. Professor Pearse and a team of biologists explored the caves in 1932 and again in 1936. E. Wyllys Andrews IV also explored the caves in the 1930s, and Edwin Shook and R.E. Smith explored the caves on behalf of the Carnegie Institute in 1954. Between them they dug several trenches to recover potsherds and other artifacts. All of these men of science independently determined that the caves had been inhabited from the pre-classic to the post-conquest era and that they were, indeed, sacred to the Maya," Roberto concluded.

"The big discoveries here came in 1959 when José Humberto Gómez, a local guide, uncovered a false wall within the cave. Behind it he found an extended network of caves with significant quantities of undisturbed archaeological remains including pottery, stone-carved censers, stone implements and some exquisite jewelry. Later the Instituto Nacional de Antropología e Historia converted the caves into an underground museum and the objects, after being catalogued, were returned to their original places so visitors can see them in situ," Roberto told his captive audience before leading Gaspar, Peugeot and Alex down through the tunnels and into the lower caverns.

"Don't be fooled, boys," Roberto warned them, "just because it's a museum now doesn't mean that these caves aren't treacherous, or even dangerous. If you stray off the marked path, you can get lost within the maze of tunnels.

Stay close and don't wander off please. Your parents won't appreciate it if I lose you after all these days."

Taking Roberto's words to heart, Gaspar pulled Peugeot's leash tight bringing his pup up close before entering the main cavern. Once inside Roberto pointed out the limestone column in the center of the large space, which had been carved into the shape of the Maya world tree, the shape so important to the ancient civilization's mythological belief systems. Poking around, Gaspar and Alex took note of the various artifacts that surrounded them. That's when Gaspar saw something he couldn't believe. The thieves of Dzibilchaltún, Joe and Mike, had just strolled into the main cavern and without looking at any of the artifacts walked straight to a tunnel across the cavern from where Gaspar was standing, and right through the opening as if they owned the joint.

"Al, Roberto, quick," Gaspar roused his two companions with an urgent whisper. "The thieves of Dzibilchaltún, Joe and Mike. They're here! They just walked down that tunnel," he whispered tersely, pointing in the direction the two men had taken. "They walked in looking like they owned the place. Come on, let's follow them and see what they're up to." Gaspar insisted pulling Peugeot forward.

Without waiting for concurrence from his companions, Gaspar darted through the opening of the tunnel with Peugeot trotting by his side in hot pursuit of the two criminals. Alex and Roberto couldn't stop them, so they silently sped after them. In the dim light, Gaspar could barely make out the departing men but creeping as fast as he and Peugeot could, without making any noise or being seen, they tailed the crooks to a fork in the tunnel. Together Gaspar and Peugeot followed the crooks to the right and down another tunnel that opened up into a large cavern. Hiding near the opening to the cavern, they watched Joe and Mike stroll across the open, high-ceilinged space and disappear down another tunnel, just as Alex and Roberto caught up to them.

"They went *that-a-way*," Gaspar informed his friends in a stage whisper, using the well-known line from his favorite old westerns, while pointing to the tunnel opposite.

"We really should call the federales," Roberto told them.

"No time, and no satellite reception down here," Gaspar told him. "Tell you what, Roberto. Take Peugeot and go back and call the cops. Al and I will keep an eye on the goons and see what they're up to."

While Roberto and Peugeot went back to the entrance in order to phone the authorities, Gaspar with Alex on his heels, sped across the cavern and disappeared down the tunnel opposite in hot pursuit of the Dzibilchaltún thieves. Catching sight of Joe and Mike again, Gaspar slowed his pace until he could better hear their voices. Slowly he led Alex forward until they were at the mouth of yet another cavern.

"All we have is junk, Joe!" they heard Mike complain.

"What I can't figure out is what happened to all the real gold relics?" Joe worried back.

"It doesn't make any sense. Someone took out the real stuff and exchanged it for this tourist crap," came Mike's reply.

"Yeah, but Diego says that Señor de Montijo doesn't have the good stuff either. Diego says that the old boy is completely distraught over the loss and he's blaming the federales for stealing the rest of what should have been our loot. I don't see how we'll ever get our hands on what should have been ours ever again." Joe continued his complaint.

"Well, if the federales have the gold, you're right … we'll never be able to get it back from them to sell to the Jaguar … not in a million years," Mike agreed with his crooked cohort.

"The only thing for us to do is to get out of Mexico … *pronto*. Once the Jaguar finds out that we can't deliver, we're as good as dead. That devil doesn't fool around. I had a pal who crossed him once and he was found a little while later, dead on the beach. The federales said his wounds were from a shark attack and dismissed the case. But I ask you, what kind-of-a-shark fires twelve bullets into a body before hacking it apart with a machete!" Joe related his worst fears.

"Oh, come on man … you've already told me that story … did you have to tell me about it again? How many times do I have to hear about the Jaguar's ability to commit a gruesome revenge? Cut me some slack, will ya. I'm at the breaking point here." Mike fretted.

"Let's grab what we can from here and scram. Hurry up, we haven't a minute to lose." Joe wailed like a banshee. With reality setting in, the ringleader was all worked up and starting to panic.

Gaspar and Alex held their collective breaths as the two crooks' nerves started to unravel. Gaspar carefully peeked his head around the opening of the tunnel where they were hiding and saw the two men, working feverishly to fill two gunnysacks full of golden idols and other ancient objects. The thieves had stepped into a low alcove, which had been covered by a large rock and were too busy packing up to notice anything else going on around them. Slowly Gaspar entered the room and motioned to Alex to follow him, holding a finger to his lips to insure silence. Together the two boys slinked around the outside edge of the cavern, and coming up to where the big rock had been shoved back, together they rolled the rock back over the entrance to the alcove, entrapping the thieves in their own secret hiding place. Screams and shouts coming from the hysterical men inside the low cramped space could barely be heard as Gaspar and Alex pushed hard against the big boulder which could only be moved left or right in order to insure that the men inside couldn't budge it.

Just in the nick of time, Roberto and Peugeot

returned with two security guards in tow, only to find his young friends pushing with all their might on the big slab of rock. The startled guards had their guns drawn and for a minute thought that Gaspar and Alex were the banditos.

"Roberto, tell those men to put their guns down … they need to come and help us. We've got the two crooks holed up inside here … and they have the gold from the first haul at Dzibilchaltún with them," Gaspar informed the guide.

Roberto, with Peugeot barking his head off, finally set the guards straight insuring them that Gaspar and Alex were indeed the good guys and that they'd trapped the bad guys, *los ladrones*, in an alcove behind the rock. Instead of holstering their pistols to relieve the teenagers from rock duty, the two simple men took a ready-for-action Charlie's Angels kind-of-stance and pointed their guns at the rounded slab of rock.

"Let her rip, Al," Gaspar commanded. Together the boys heaved the big stone away from the opening, freeing the robbers, who were caught red-handed with all the real gold loot from their haul from under the church at Dzibilchaltún. Amusingly they also had all the tourist reproductions with them too. "Señor de Montijo will be glad to get all this stuff back," Gaspar assured the two crooks. "Especially the tourist reproductions," he chuckled, seeing the diversity of precious treasure mixed with junk. He sells this fake stuff for a lot of money in the gift shop and that helps pay for all the upkeep at the Dzibilchaltún archaeological site." Gaspar explained to the dumbfounded crooks who looked on, mouths agape at being caught by a pair of teenaged American tourists. For good measure, Peugeot continued to bare his teeth at the robbers, growling menacingly until the federales had the crooks in handcuffs.

With a great deal of scuffling and not a lot of confusion, a squad of federales came running into the cavern like the Keystone Cops on holiday. Major Portillo followed behind them, making a grand entrance at the end of his troops comedic foray.

"I see you've done our job for us again," Portillo applauded the boys, but Gaspar couldn't tell by his tone if Major Portillo was happy or actually angry with him this time.

"Major, here are Joe and Mike. Here are the valuable antiquities that they took from Dzibilchaltún the first time we saw them coming out from under the altar. They have all the tourist drek with them, tying them to the second robbery as well." Gaspar logically laid out the facts for the major.

"Very thorough, I must say," Portillo complimented the amateur teenaged sleuths, snidely. "In the future I would appreciate it if you and Mr. Mendoza would leave all police business to the authorities, Señor Brown." The federale made his anger more than clear this time, taking the wind out of Gaspar's sails.

"We were only going to keep an eye on them for you, major. We overheard them talking and when we heard them say they were going to take the loot and leave Mexico forever, and double cross the Jaguar at the same time. It seemed to curtail their escape sooner, was the logical thing to do … lest they get away … yet again. I'm sorry if I've done something to offend you, sir," Gaspar apologized, feeling humiliated that he'd been forced to abase himself to the unappreciative Major Portillo.

"Let's get out of here, Al," Gaspar urged his pal. Come on Roberto, time to go home."

"Don't you want me to take you inside El Castillo to see the Jaguar Throne?" Roberto asked, crestfallen.

"Not today, Roberto," Gaspar sulked. "I think I've had enough of anything to do with jaguars for today."

Without further ado, the three companions with Mr. Peugeot on his leash slunk out of the Caves of Balamka'anche' and headed for the hotel in silence.

When they got back, Gaspar asked Roberto to join them in their suite. Entering the drawing room, they found Elvira and Peter, dressed for dinner, sipping cocktails.

"That was a long day, boys," Peter said by way of greeting. "We thought we'd never see you again."

"Where'd you go Gaspar and what took you so long?" his mother asked lovingly.

"After lunch, I took them to the Caves of Balamka'anche'," Roberto informed her. "We had a very adventurous time there, señora. I'm happy to tell you that Gaspar and Alex captured the thieves of Dzibilchaltún single-handedly. My only role in the entire operation was to call the federales. I must say, señora, that Major Portillo was less than appreciative or even enthusiastic that Gaspar and Alex had saved the day, bringing in not only the thieves, but a lot of stolen artifacts as well."

"That's very odd," commented Peter. "He should have been thrilled with the capture."

"Yeah," broke in Gaspar, "especially since Al and I overheard them saying that they were going to grab the loot, double cross the Jaguar and get out of Mexico tonight, if it was the last thing they did."

"Yeah," Alex started in, "we also heard them say that Señor de Montijo had lost most or all of the valuable treasure that we helped him remove from the cave under the altar, you know the real gold antiquities stuff we replaced with the fabulous fakes. The crooks heard this from a compatriot of theirs called Diego. They even said something about the real gold treasure had probably been stolen by the federales."

"Well listen, kids," Peter said gently, ignoring what Alex had just told him. "Major Portillo probably has a lot of trouble on his plate considering all the valuable archaeological digs they have around here. I think for now at least, we should cut the guy a little slack. Besides, Gaspar, your mother and I are throwing a little party tonight. Why don't the three of you, that means you too,

Roberto, get washed up, put on some party clothes and join us downstairs in forty-five minutes. That's when we have our reservation in the restaurant for dinner.

"What's the occasion?" Gaspar asked.

"Nothing special, just a celebration. You know, happy to be here, happy to be together, happy to be happy … do we need any other reasons, darling," Elvira chirped.

"Sounds good to me," Gaspar smiled for the first time since leaving the caves.

"Me too," chimed in Alex.

"Me too," laughed Roberto, "thank you for including me, señors."

Forty-five minutes later the travelers walked into the dining room, where a table for ten awaited them.

"Who else is invited?" Gaspar wondered out loud.

"Let's see, besides us … Señor de Montijo, the owners of the hotel Mr. and Mrs. Hans Thies Barbachano, and Mr. and Mrs. Balam Balaian," Peter informed his son.

"Mrs. Balaian. I didn't know that dirty old man had a wife!" Alex blurted out before he realized what he was saying.

"But mom, Peter …˙ Balam … you don't understand … Balam is …

"*Here,*" Peter said, in no uncertain terms. "Balam is *here*. Hello, Balam. So glad you could join us, and this must be your lovely wife, Carla. Encantado, Señora," Peter said, bowing over the lady's hand. "Darling, this is Balam's wife, Carla. Señora Balaian, this is my wife, Elvira."

"Con mucho gusto," Elvira sang, kissing Mrs. Balaian on each cheek. "I'm so pleased to meet you. May I present my son Gaspar," Elvira insisted, pulling Gaspar into the circle. "Gaspar, this is Señora Balaian, and I think you already know Señor Balaian," his mother trilled sweetly.

"Yes," Gaspar said coldly, "we've met." Then to Mrs. Balaian he said, "I'm very pleased to meet you, ma'am. This is my friend Alexander Mendoza, and this is another friend, Roberto Ortiz."

The Balaians gave both Alexander and Roberto short shrift along with a couple of weird smirks, before turning their attention back to the newlyweds, Peter and Elvira. The next to arrive were Mr. and Mrs. Thies Barbachano who had Señor de Montijo, the distinguished director of the Dzibilchaltún archaeology site, in tow. Introductions were made all around before the assembled group sat down to dinner. Elvira had arranged the place cards at the table earlier, seating it clockwise starting with Peter then Mrs. Barbachano, Mr. de Montijo, Gaspar, Mr. Balaian, Elvira, Mr. Barbachano, Roberto Ortiz, Alex Mendoza, and finally Mrs. Balaian, who was, seated on the other side of Peter.

Drink orders were taken, and menus presented all around. Pleasantries were exchanged and then interrupted, when the waiter took their orders for dinner.

After all the fuss of ordering dinner was over, the conversations started up again in earnest. Gaspar watched as Peter schmoozed the two ladies on his left and right, paying a bit more attention to Señora Balaian than to Señora Barbachano. Elvira seemed to be pulling her weight with Balam Balaian, and Mr. Barbachano. Gaspar paid attention to Señor de Montijo, who he was particularly happy to sit next to because he had a lot of questions he wanted to ask the distinguished older gentleman. Meanwhile, Roberto made conversation with Alex as Mrs. Balaian seemed less interested in a *joven* or mere teenager than in her handsome host, Peter Cawthorne. Gaspar wondered what this dinner was about but decided to make the most of what he considered a bad situation.

"Señor de Montijo," Gaspar started the conversational ball rolling, "tell me the news from Dzibilchaltún? I've heard rumors that everything didn't go so well that night when we cheated the looters out of their treasure."

"Oh, Gaspar, bad news does travel fast. It's a mystery, but the actual golden treasure trove of antiquities that we replaced with fake tourist gimcracks somehow disappeared that night. Sometime between its removal from under the church altar and when it was brought to my offices for safekeeping, the actual artifacts were also replaced with fakes similar to the ones we placed in the cavern for the thieves to find."

"I can't believe it," Gaspar was shocked.

"It's true, Gaspar. It could only have been switched en route between the church and my office. It could only have been done, by one of the federales. I didn't discover the switch until after you left the next morning.

I've tried to keep the theft a secret from my colleagues at the Instituto, hoping that Major Portillo would be able to discover the culprit within his ranks and return the hoard before the loss was discovered. How did you hear about it?"

"Just this afternoon, señor. Alex and I were visiting the Caves of Balamka'anche' and we ran into the two thieves, Joe and Mike, who stole the first group of items from you. We overheard them talking and they said that Diego, whoever he is, had told them about the switch."

"Diego, Diego, *quen es Diego*?" The old man asked out loud, shaking his head in the negative.

"He must be one of Portillo's men, a federale. Are you sure no one on your staff is named Diego?" Gaspar asked.

"Diego … I will find out who this Diego is … as God is my witness. Whoever this person is, he is certainly part of the plot to switch the artifacts. I will be sure to find out … as God is my witness," the old man stammered again, under his breath.

"What are you whispering about so mysteriously?" came the oily sing-song voice of Balam Balaian's heavily accented English.

"Oh, nothing important," Gaspar lied. "Señor de Montijo was just telling me about his plans to exhibit some newly-recovered artifacts in his museum at Dzibilchaltún."

"Oh, Montijo, so you've discovered some new artifacts at Dzibilchaltún. Anything in gold? Anything I'd be interested in?" The fat man asked obnoxiously.

"Nothing of the caliber of your own personal collection, Señor Balaian. Nothing worthy of your interest, of that I can assure you, señor," Montijo replied graciously, although Gaspar knew he was lying.

"I like *gold*," Balam hissed into Gaspar's ear. *"Maya gold, Aztec gold and Inca gold*, that is what I like. I'll do anything I have to ... whether I have to beg, borrow or steal it, I always get the gold objects that I want," he said in a tone of voice that sounded more like a threat than a statement of fact.

Gaspar was taken aback by the greedy insistence of the ugly man's tenor. He couldn't believe the obsession he'd just detected in the evil man's voice, not to mention the tone of avarice which emanated from the complicated demeanor of the unattractive character sitting next to him. "I'm sure most of the great artifacts from around here have already been found and are safely ensconced in museums in this country and around the world," Gaspar shot back.

"What you say is true, sonny, all except for the word *safely*," Balam chuckled sardonically.

Gaspar couldn't stand the man. He was definitely evil, and for the life of him he couldn't figure out why Elvira and Peter would have invited the creep and his sleazy wife for dinner.

The evening wore on and finally ... blessedly came to an end. Poor Alex never even elicited a nod, let alone a word from the overbearing, overdressed and over-jeweled Señora Balaian.

Back in their room, Alex asked Gaspar, "what was that all about?"

But Gaspar was unable to give him a straight answer. "What a nightmare," was all Gaspar had to say to sum up the evening. And that went for the entire afternoon at the *Caves of Balamka'anche'* too, he thought to himself.

CHAPTER 11

COBÁ

THE NEXT MORNING THE TOUR CONTINUED AGAIN IN EARNEST AS THE FOUR TRAVELERS PILED INTO Roberto's SUV for the ride to Cobá, Muyil and Tulúm. Once at Tulúm, Gaspar's plan was to once again board their yacht, *Floridablanca*, which Craig Cadawalader hopefully would have waiting for them offshore.

"Do we have a long drive ahead of us?" Elvira asked, as she settled into her seat.

"We'll only be driving about ninety kilometers," Roberto announced, as the car headed out of the Hacienda Chichén grounds towards the road to Cobá.

"What will we see there?" Alex prodded. "More of the same?"

"You'll find that Cobá is a large ruined city located in the state of Quintana Roo. There is a large temple there, two ballcourts and two groups of ruined structures. The city was only recently discovered, and still hasn't been completely excavated or for that matter, even surveyed. From Coba we'll visit Muyil and from there it is only another forty kilometers to the Caribbean Sea where *Floridablanca* will meet you at Tulúm."

Gaspar wanted to give a cheer at the mention of his precious yacht but held himself in check.

"While we're driving, Roberto, tell us a little more about the site so we'll know what to expect when we get there," Gaspar suggested.

"Cobá was built around two lagoons with an entire network of sacbé, you remember, the typical Maya raised roads which radiate out from the central site to various smaller sites nearby. Some of these causeways run all the way to the Caribbean coast, and the longest runs over sixty-two miles to the site of Yaxuna, which we will also see today. Coba contains several large pyramids. The tallest one is called Nohoch Mul and is 138 feet in height."

"That's taller than El Castillo at Chichén Itzá," Alex exhaled in awe.

"You are absolutely correct, Alex. Nohoch Mul *is* the *tallest* pyramid discovered so far on the Yucatán peninsula. There are archaeologists who insist that there is evidence in the hieroglyphics and murals, of even taller structures which have not as yet been discovered."

Gaspar found that hard to believe and challenged Roberto. "You mean with all the people living in the

Yucatán, and all the tourism and interest from the World Monuments Fund and other cultural institutions, that the entire place hasn't been mapped and surveyed using Lydar technology to find additional sites yet?"

"That's correct, Gaspar. What I've already told you about here in Cobá is true all over the Yucatán and Central America. Besides, the big prize is still *The Lost Temple of Chac Mool*. When that's finally found and unearthed, it will no doubt set the world on its ear."

"With all of the people around here and all the interest in ancient civilizations it just doesn't make sense that there are still massive monuments to be discovered," Gaspar argued.

"Believe it or not, the entire Yucatan isn't even inhabited today by as many people as used to live here during the reign of the Maya, and that includes all the tourists. Cobá alone is estimated to have had some fifty-thousand inhabitants at its peak, and the built-up area of the city extended over eighty kilometers."

"When was the city constructed?" Peter wanted to know.

"Archaeological evidence indicates that Cobá was first settled between 100 BC and 100 AD. At that time, there was a town with buildings made of wood and palm fronds. The only archaeological evidence of those early times are fragments of pottery which have been found there. After 100 AD the area around Cobá evidenced strong population growth, and with it an increase in its social and political status among Maya city states, ultimately, Cobá would become one of the biggest and most powerful city states in the northern Yucatán area. The bulk of Cobá's major construction was done in the middle and late Classic periods, with most of the hieroglyphic inscriptions dating from the seventh century. Interestingly Cobá remained an important site in the post-Classic era when new temples were built and old ones kept in repair until at least the fourteenth century, and possibly as late as the arrival of the Spanish. Because they were close to the sea, Cobá traded extensively with other Mayan communities, particularly the ones further south along the Caribbean coast in what is now Belize and Honduras."

"What were their seaports?" Gaspar wanted to know.

"The people here utilized the ports of Xcaret, Xel-Há, Tankah, Muyil, and Tulúm. They also did a lot of trading by crossing overland," Roberto informed him.

"Are you telling us that the people of Cobá were even more powerful than the people of Chichén Itzá?" Alex asked in disbelief.

"The people of Cobá and the people of Chichén were bitter enemies," Roberto assured him. Between 200 and 600 AD Cobá dominated a vast area including the lands north of the state of Quintana Roo and areas in the east of the state of Yucatán. Their power resided in their control of large swaths of farmland, control over trading routes and more importantly, control over ample water resources. Fresh water for drinking and farming was the most critical of the Maya's commodities. Besides the wealth of water, the trading routes that Cobá controlled were without parallel in the Yucatán at the time. Through sea trade from their port of Xel Há, Cobá maintained close contacts with the large city states of Guatemala as well as those south of Campeche like Tikal, Dzibanché and Calakmul."

"When did it all come crashing down?" Peter asked.

Here, after 600 AD, the emergence of powerful city states of the Puuc culture and the emergence of Chichén Itzá as a stronger foe altered the political spectrum in the Yucatán peninsula and began eroding the dominance of Cobá. Beginning around 900 or 1000 AD Cobá began a lengthy power struggle with Chichén Itzá. In the end Chichén Itzá ended up dominating Cobá, as it gained control of Yaxuná, one of Cobá's key cities. After 1000 AD Cobá lost much of its political weight among the city states, although it still maintained some symbolic and religious importance for its neighbors. This previous prestige allowed Cobá to maintain or recover some of its tarnished status. This is evidenced by the new buildings built in the typical Eastern coastal style which date to between 1200-1500 AD. By this time however, power centers and trading routes had moved to the coast, forcing cities like Cobá into a secondary status, although somewhat more successful than its more ephemeral enemy Chichén Itzá. By the time the Spanish conquered the peninsula in 1550, Cobá had been abandoned."

"Look over there," Gaspar shouted, pointing off to the left where a huge structure jutted out above the jungle.

"That's Nohoch Mul," Roberto announced. "We have arrived."

After Roberto parked the car, the group started out together to explore the ruins, as Roberto continued to relay important details of the site.

"Knowledge of this expansive site was never completely lost," he told them. "John Lloyd Stephens mentioned hearing reports of Cobá in 1841, but this site was so distant from any known road or village that he decided the difficulty in trying to get here was too daunting. During the nineteenth century due to the Caste War of Yucatán, the area could not be safely visited by outsiders. Even so, the intrepid explorer Teoberto Maler paid a short visit to Cobá in 1893 and took at least one photograph of the site. Unfortunately, he didn't publish it at the time and so the site remained unknown to the archaeological community at large until the 1920s. It's hard to believe that no scholars ever visited here before that," Roberto recounted to his friends' amazement. "In 1926 Dr. Thomas Gann, an amateur explorer, was brought to the site by some local big game hunters. It was Gann who published the very first description of the ruins later that same year. Gann also gave a short description to the archaeologists at the

Carnegie Institute working at Chichén Itzá, and they sent out an expedition under Eric Thompson to check Cobá out. Thompson's initial report of a surprisingly large site with many inscriptions prompted his colleague Sylvanus Morley to mount a more thorough examination. Eric Thompson also made a number of return visits to Cobá, and in 1932 he published his own detailed description of what he found here," Roberto concluded.

"It's hard to believe the world was so large and places like Yucatán so remote just a century ago," Gaspar exclaimed naively. "Today if we want to go someplace it seems like it's just a hop, skip and a jump to get there."

"The first modern road to Cobá wasn't built until the early 1970s. That was when Cancún was planned as a major resort. The government and the developers realized that clearing and restoring some of this large site would make it an important tourist attraction and they were right," Roberto told them.

"Take it from us *old folks*, Gasp, it's still not as easy to get around in certain parts of the world as you think. Not for everyone, that is," Peter reminded him.

"I understand, Peter. For Alex and me it seems like the twentieth century was like ancient times. I know you and mom had cars and telephones and airplanes to fly in but compared to what Roberto is telling us about Yucatán, just a hundred years ago seems prehistoric!"

"Yeah, Gaspar. Well you'll soon learn how time flies. Before you know it, you'll be showing your own kids around one day and you'll be telling them about the good old days and your visit to the Yucatán. They'll be wanting to go someplace by spaceship, telling you how *ancient* your childhood seems to them."

"Okay, Peter, I'll cut you *old folk from the last century* some slack, but I was just saying ... " Gaspar gave up and decided to change the subject. "Besides wars and trade with their neighbors, Roberto, how did the people here in Cobá establish and maintain their influence?" Gaspar moved forward.

"Military alliances and arranged marriages among the elite were the easiest ways for the people to establish authority and gain influence, both inside Cobá and also with their neighbors."

"I get it," Gaspar said. "Same old, same old, the world just keeps on spinning."

"Because the people here were exposed to other cultures, I will be able to point out traces of Teotihuacan architecture to you, like the platform in the paintings group that was excavated in 1999. These would attest to the existence of contacts with the central Mexican cultures and the powerful cities of the early Classic epoch."

"It's exciting that they're still excavating the city, finding new structures and artifacts, Roberto," Elvira chimed in.

"Work and progress on this site have continued since the early 1970s, señora. The Mexican National Institute of Anthropology & History began new archaeological excavations in 1972 directed by my friend Professor Carlos Navarrete, who has successfully consolidated a couple of buildings. If he's on site today, we shall surely meet him and ask him to take us around a little. Besides all the archaeological finds, in 1980 another paved road to Cobá was opened, allowing tour buses to visit here more frequently. Cobá has really become a major international tourist destination in a short matter of time with many tourists visiting the site on day trips from Cancún and Riviera Maya. Even now, several decades later, only a small portion of the site has been cleared from the jungle. Look around. Can you believe that we're surrounded by an entire ancient city here? What we are about to see is just the tip of the icebox." Roberto enthused.

Gaspar didn't laugh. He'd heard *tip of the iceberg* called *tip of the icebox* before, and that had been by Alex's dad, Felix. What is it with these Mexicans that they say icebox instead of iceberg, he wondered to himself, smiling? After all the buildup, Gaspar had to admit that he was unimpressed. He was sure that what Roberto said was true. He just wished the archaeologists would step on it and uncover the rest of the city. After a lot of endless walking they finally arrived at Nohoch Mul, which was a very, very tall, *tall temple*. Reaching its base, Gaspar, Peugeot and Alex immediately scrambled up on all fours, all the while taunting Elvira, Peter and Roberto to *hurry up*. After surveying their surroundings from on high, they descended on their butts, slowly creeping down the pyramid's steep stairs with Peugeot hanging onto Gaspar's shoulders for dear life, until they finally touched terra firma.

Following one of the many sacbés, which they had seen fanning out in all directions from their vantage point at the top of Nohoch Mul, they arrived at Chumuc Mul, one of the two ballcourts at Cobá, which Gaspar found not at all as impressive as the one he, Alex and Peugeot had explored at Chichén Itzá. From the ballcourt, they entered a group of ruins nestled between the two lakes, Lago Cobá and Lago Macaxoc.

Just another rock pile, was the unenthusiastic first impression which ran through Gaspar's mind.

"This is the largest concentration of buildings in all of Cobá, comprising forty-three structures. You'll also notice that six *sacbé* roads branch out from this group," Roberto enthused, twirling around while pointing in each of six different directions. With great enthusiasm he proceeded to show them a grand plaza, a series of various courtyards and several structures with vaulted rooms. Here they found another ballcourt … the open kind consisting of two parallel buildings decorated with several carved stelae. Stopping in front of the building which Roberto called *La Iglesia*, or The Church, he showed them a stelae and a circular altar which the others oohed and aahed at, but which Gaspar thought was a complete waste of time after the treasures they'd seen at *Chichén Itzá*.

"Roberto, what is the significance of these carved stelae?" Peter asked.

"All of the most important, as well as the most basic events of the ruling class were registered on sculpted stone monuments such as these," Roberto told them. "Notice how the stelae is formed by nine round-cornered stones, each reaching a height of twenty-four meters. These stelae were not constructed all at once, but in various stages, each built upon the preceding one," Roberto explained. "For example, construction of this stelae began in the first early Classic period, sometime around 300 AD," Roberto explained. "The last modification, way up there at the top," he said pointing heavenward, "was made during the post Classic period, around 1000 AD."

"Wow," Alex expounded, "600 years later."

"Precisely." Roberto concurred, before leading them to the east of Lago Macanxoc, to see the Macanxoc group, an excavation where Gaspar thought the archaeologists time could have been put to better use.

By the time they reached the *Cenote de el Jaguar* they were hot and sticky. One look at the site and Gaspar and Alex both agreed that they'd seen better *swimmin' holes*, in their time. Despite the miserable heat, neither of the boys nor the parents or their guide had any desire to jump in.

As the others turned to follow Roberto to the *Conjunto Pinturas* group of ruins, Gaspar got a text message from Captain Craig Cadawalader, regarding *Floridablanca. We're anchored off Tulúm, awaiting your arrival.* was all the message said. Without thinking, Gaspar texted back, "We'll be right there," so excited was he at the prospect of being back on board his fabulous craft.

Taking Alex aside he informed him, "Al, I've just got a text from Craig. He needs me on board, pronto. I'm gonna slip away now. Take care of Peugeot for me and stay here with the others. You guys can catch up with me day after tomorrow. I don't want you to miss any of this great architecture and world-wonder stuff. Don't say anything to the parents right now. When they figure out I'm missing, tell them where I've gone. They can call me if they have any questions."

"You can count on me, Gasp." Alex insisted, taking Peugeot's leash from his pal. Take care of yourself and keep in touch," he told his pal, before turning to catch up with the others. When Alex looked back over his shoulder, Gaspar had disappeared down the path leading to the parking lot.

When Gaspar got to the car park, he found a tour bus that was heading for Tulúm and bribed the driver with a twenty-dollar bill to let him onboard. An hour and a half later, he was calling Craig to send the tender over to the beach just north of the *Castillo*, the most prominent Maya ruin in Tulúm. Climbing out of the bus with the other tourists, his heart skipped a beat when he saw the majestic *Floridablanca*, bobbing at anchor just off the coast, right in front of the ancient Mayan temple.

Gaspar separated from the tour group and ran to the beach, where as good as his word, Craig had brought the tender to pick him up.

"Afternoon, skipper."

"Good afternoon, sir," Craig responded.

"Take me to her," Gaspar commanded. Without another word, they were off, cutting through the Caribbean whitecaps, heading back to Gaspar's beloved ship.

Back at the ruins Peter, Elvira and Roberto listened to the news of Gaspar's escape with amusement. "That's our boy," Elvira chuckled to Peter. "Nothing can stop him when he gets an idea into his head. I'm just sorry he's going to miss the rest of the tour. Alex, you'll have to bring him up to speed with your sketches on what he's missing."

"After lunch," Roberto informed them, "we'll stop and see Yaxuná and Muyil where we'll spend the night. We'll meet up with Gaspar and *Floridablanca* in Tulúm tomorrow.

CHAPTER 12

FLORIDABLANCA

THE MINUTE HIS FEET HIT THE DECK; GASPAR KNEW HE
WAS HOME. *THANK GOD*, HE THOUGHT, *ALONE AT LAST
… sort of.* All he wanted to do was get something to eat and
fall asleep in the sun. He needed time alone … to think.

"Is everything all right, sir?" Captain Cadawalader
asked solicitously.

"Marvelous, captain," Gaspar smiled. "I'm just so
happy to be back on board … I can't tell you. We've
had days and days of looking at rock piles along with
plenty of adventures too. I'll tell you about everything
… at lunch. I hope you have something delicious to eat
onboard?" he asked, facetiously.

"Murray's making lunch as we speak. Something tells
me it has something to do with peanut butter, jelly and
bacon," Captain Cadawalader teased him.

"Perfect, call me when it's ready, captain. First things first, I'm going for a swim." With that simple pronouncement and without ceremony, Gaspar stripped off all his clothes and jumped overboard into the Caribbean. Paddling around *Floridablanca* brought back memories of his first days at La Rinconada, when he'd first laid eyes on the sunken yacht and swam around it and how he and Alex had successfully raised it. That had been his initial exposure to sunken treasure, but certainly not his last, not in a long shot.

"Lunch is served, sir," Murray called overboard from the rail.

"I'll be right up, Murray," Gaspar called back, swimming to the ladder and pulling himself out of the cool water.

The clothes he'd left on deck had been removed and fresh towels had been stacked on a chair nearby. Wrapping one around his waist, Gaspar sauntered over to the lunch table under the blue and white striped awning of the poop deck.

"Ask the captain to join me, please Murray."

After a moment Captain Cadawalader appeared.

"Would you like to join me for lunch, captain?" Gaspar asked.

"Thank you very much, sir," Craig answered. "I've already eaten, but I will join you with an iced coffee," he told his boss, taking the seat next to Gaspar.

Murray disappeared in the direction of the galley

and returned shortly with a tall glass of iced coffee and a napkin.

After Murray was out of earshot, Gaspar filled Craig in on all the goings-on since *Floridablanca* had left Celestún. He told Craig about the robbery at Dzibilchaltún and how he and Al had run into the looters Joe and Mike at Chichén Itzá and how they'd captured the crooks red-handed with the stolen Mayan treasure inside the Caves of Balamka'anche'. He recited how the crooks had mentioned a cohort with the name of Diego, and how the frightened men worried how brutally the Jaguar would retaliate against them for not getting him the gold idols they'd promised. Gaspar told his pal, Captain Craig what Señor de Montijo had confessed regarding the missing treasure, which the federales had presumably saved from the thieves, but which suddenly disappeared somewhere between the church and Señor de Montijo's office at *Dzibilchaltún*. He explained how one-minute Major Portillo was his friend and the next minute, the federale was sullen, mean and abusive. He even told Captain Craig about Señora Balaian and her lust for jewels, and how really awful, rude and dismissive she'd been to Alex at the dinner table. Finally Gaspar spoke the words which he had thought at the time, *"I can't, for the life of me, figure out why on earth my mom and Peter invited that motley crew for dinner in the first place."*

"That's quite an adventure, sir," Captain Cadawalader

piped up. "Next time, I'll think twice before leaving you and your party behind again."

"Not at all, captain," Gaspar corrected him. "I'm glad you were at sea. That way, if I needed you to come to the rescue, you'd be free to do so. Here's what I want you to do for me now. Call Lieutenant Carl Jacobson at the Coast Guard station on Perdido Isle and ask him if he has any pals in the Mexican Navy who we can call on in a pinch. Also ask him if he has any inside information on any of the characters, I've just told you about, especially the Jaguar, Balaian, Portillo and even de Montijo. Then do me a favor and call Captain Morgan at the police station in *Calaluna* and ask him the same questions. Ask him if he has a friend in the federales down here, and ask if he can call Interpol and find out anything juicy on my three suspects? Be sure and tell Jacobson and Morgan that antiquities smuggling, and golden idols are involved. If you need me, I'll be down in my cabin."

"Aye, aye, sir," Captain Cadawalader saluted Gaspar, before departing for the bridge to make his calls.

When Gaspar got back to his cabin, he ripped off his towel and headed for the shower. There he washed himself, navy style, like his father had taught him so many years ago … *'wet yourself all over, turn off the water and soap yourself up really good, then rinse yourself off. It's the only way to conserve fresh water while at sea,'.* That's exactly the way Gaspar taught Alex to bathe while on board. When he was done, he put on Bermuda shorts and a T-shirt, and walked back into his stateroom where he found Uncle Charlie sprawled out on the bed, wearing a boxy white linen suit, a blue and white polka-dot cravat and blue and white polka dot socks. His ever-present blue velvet carpet slippers had been tossed aside, under the desk.

"Uncle Charlie, what a pleasant surprise," Gaspar blurted, delighted to see the old ghost.

"Welcome back to *Floridablanca*, nephew," Uncle Charlie greeted Gaspar enthusiastically, while sitting up against the pillows. I've had a pleasant cruise around the coast of Yucatán, but it's been quite lonely here these past days. As you know, I haven't just been luxuriating on board all this time. I did have some fun watching you on the job in *Drizzledrazzle* or whatever you call that pile of rocks," Uncle Charlie joked.

"Dzibilchaltún, uncle. It's Maya talk."

"Maya-Shmaya, but what does it mean?"

"You've got me there," Gaspar shrugged.

"Holler, uncle!"

"Okay, '*Uncle*,' Uncle Charlie!" Gaspar laughed, happy to be with his secret friend, compatriot and protector.

"Now, Gasp, what are *we* going to do about those dirty antiquity thieves?"

"*We*, Uncle Charlie? I hope you mean that because I'm gonna need all the help I can get if *we're* gonna stop the crooks," Gaspar told him in all earnestness.

"The best I can do for you, boy, is to keep an eye out. You know I can't do anything physical to help you, but

I can certainly keep watching and see what I can learn about all these crazy characters."

"You know, Uncle Charlie, I'm not planning to do the federales' work for them. If they're in on robberies, then fat chance of solving anything, let alone getting out alive. One part of me says 'run', and the other part of me says 'help'. I keep going back to Señor de Montijo and I genuinely feel that he is one of the *good guys* in this story. He was so excited by the discovery and so joyous when he was making plans for expanding his museum and making Dzibilchaltún a more important site in the eyes of the academic world. Something tells me that Señor de Montijo is *good goods*, but I'm investigating him anyway.

"That's right, Gasp. Don't leave any stone unturned. Trust but verify. Everyone in this case including Roberto, your guide, could be in on it ... if you know what I mean."

"Roberto, now you've got to be kidding, Uncle Charlie. Roberto is harmless," Gaspar insisted.

"Is he?" Uncle Charlie asked, raising an eyebrow.

"Well, I hope so, for heaven's sake. Okay, I'll have him checked out too!" Gaspar agreed, exasperated.

"What news of the Doctor's House?" Uncle Charlie asked.

"No news is good news. I've had a couple of reports from the decorators. Charlotte, their project manager, told me that all was well and that I should be pleased when I finally get back there to see what they're doing. Felix and Angela called Alex to see how he was doing while we were in *Chichén* and he put me on the phone. They said that the transformation was amazing, and that they couldn't believe their eyes.

"Hmmm, maybe I should stop by and take a look. Perhaps I'll do that while you take your siesta." Uncle Charlie suggested.

"Do I look that tired, uncle?" Gaspar knew he felt tired but wondered if it actually showed.

"You look like you could use a really good night's sleep," the old ghost told him as he disappeared through the bulkhead.

•••

When Gaspar woke up it was six o'clock the next morning. He was still in his Bermudas and T-shirt and he was still on top of the bed where he'd passed out before Uncle Charlie disappeared yesterday afternoon. Getting up, he headed for the door to the gangway that led up to the saloon. The rest of the ship was dead asleep, but he knew that they would soon be stirring. He went up to the bridge where young Jimmy Cahill was on watch. Jimmy was a sailor and another of Craig's buddies who the captain had Shanghaied into sailing on *Floridablanca*'s maiden cruise.

"Good morning, sir," Jimmy saluted Gaspar. "You have some faxes from Perdido Isle that have come in this morning. Two are from the Coast Guard and one is from the Chief of Police," the young sailor told him with a hint of excitement, handing Gaspar several printouts.

"Thanks Jimmy. When Captain Cadawalader gets up, I'd like to see him in the saloon. And if you see Murray, please tell him to look for me there too.

Gaspar scurried back to the main saloon and spread the faxes across the desk. He read the message from the Coast Guard first. It read:

AHOY, GASPAR,

GOOD TO HEAR FROM YOU. HOPING YOU AND YOUR FAMILY ARE HAVING A GREAT CRUISE TO THE YUCATÁN AND BEYOND. IF YOU NEED ANY HELP WHILE IN MEXICAN WATERS, PLEASE CONTACT MY *HERMANO*, ADMIRAL JOSE LUIS SORZANO Y ARTIEDA. JOSE LUIS WAS MY BUDDY AT ANNOPOLIS AND A GREAT GUY. HE STUDIED THERE UNDER A FOREIGN STUDENT AGREEMENT WITH THE NAVY. I HAVE ALREADY CALLED AND TOLD HIM ABOUT YOU AND *FLORIDABLANCA* AND THAT YOU'RE SAILING IN HIS JURISDICTION. HIS DIRECT NUMBER IS 1+52 155 582 0339. HE TOLD ME TO HAVE YOU CALL HIM DAY OR NIGHT IF YOU SHOULD RUN INTO ANY TROUBLE. HAVE A GREAT TRIP AND KEEP IN TOUCH.

SINCERELY,

CARL

LIEUTENANT CARL JACOBSON

UNITED STATES COAST GUARD

PERDIDO ISLE STATION

CORAL COUNTY, FLORIDA

A second fax from Carl Jacobson had also come in. This one was handwritten and read:

Have searched the files for Balaian, Portillo and De Montijo and nothing suspicious has turned up at this end. I will continue checking with the Mexican authorities as best I can and get back to you.
Sincerely,
Jacobson

Gaspar was thankful to have such a good friend in Carl Jacobson. He also knew that Jacobson was in his debt since it was Gaspar and Alex and their pals who turned in the hated drug trafficker Unzega, when the boys caught him red-handed, smuggling contraband across La Rinconada's private property.

Without fanfare, Murray walked in and asked Gaspar what he would like for breakfast. Before Gaspar could answer, Craig Cadawalader also arrived in the saloon.

"Captain, I'm just about to order breakfast. I'd like you to join me to go over a few things," Gaspar presented his invitation.

"Delighted," replied Cadawalader. "What have you ordered?"

"I was just about to tell Murray that I'd like some bacon, buttered toast and fresh fruit, and Murray, please bring me a glass of orange juice to get started." Gaspar ordered the smiling cook.

"I'll have the same, Murray. But I'll start with coffee,

black, no juice," Craig's breakfast never varied.

"I wonder if I'll ever learn to like '*Mississippi Mud*'," Gaspar laughed, thinking of Karen and her sidekick Frank and how they referred to coffee back at Karen's Café on Perdido Isle.

Murray chuckled as he waddled out of the room … mumbling, *Mississippi Mud,* to himself.

After Murray left the saloon, Cadawalader asked, "What's up, sir?" He now gave his boss his undivided attention.

"We have some answers from our friends back home regarding your inquiries of yesterday," Gaspar handed Lieutenant Jacobson's two faxes to Craig and said, "I'm just starting to read the reply from Captain Morgan now." He held up another fax and read it silently while Craig read the ones from Jacobson.

DEAR GASPAR,

THE UNITED STATES GOVERNMENT HASN'T ANYTHING CONCRETE ON BALAIAN. HOWEVER, HIS NAME HAS COME UP IN SEVERAL INVESTIGATIONS IN NEW YORK AND LOS ANGELES OVER VARIOUS ROBBERIES INVOLVING PRE-COLUMBIAN ANTIQUITIES, ESPECIALLY THOSE OF MAYA, AZTEC OR INCA GOLD. SIMILAR INVESTIGATIONS BY INTERPOL HAVE LINKED BALAIAN TO ROBBERIES FROM PRIVATE COLLECTIONS AND MUSEUMS IN CENTRAL AND SOUTH AMERICA. HE IS ALSO WANTED FOR QUESTIONING IN SWITZERLAND, WHERE A MAJOR HEIST TOOK PLACE IN

A VILLA ON LAKE GENEVA WHILE HE WAS PRESENT AS A GUEST. AS FOR MAJOR PORTILLO, HE IS NOT WELL-LIKED BY HIS COLLEAGUES IN THE FEDERALES, AND HE HAS BEEN BROUGHT UP ON CORRUPTION CHARGES SEVERAL TIMES BUT THE AUTHORITIES HAVE NEVER BEEN ABLE TO MAKE THEM STICK. THERE DOES NOT SEEM TO BE ANY CONNECTION BETWEEN BALAIAN AND PORTILLO, AND THERE DOESN'T SEEM TO BE ANY CONNECTION BETWEEN BALAIAN, PORTILLO AND THE CRIMINAL KNOWN AS *THE JAGUAR*. HOWEVER, IT IS KNOWN THAT *THE JAGUAR* IS THE HEAD OF AN ORGANIZED RING OF CROOKS WHO LOOT ARCHAEOLOGICAL SITES, REGIONAL MUSEUMS AND NOT SO WELL-KNOWN PRIVATE COLLECTIONS. THIS GANG IS ONLY INTERESTED IN GOLD OBJECTS. TO DATE ALL OF THE LOOT THOUGHT TO HAVE BEEN STOLEN BY THE JAGUAR MOB HAS NEVER BEEN RECOVERED. SEÑOR DE MONTIJO IS CLEAN AS A WHISTLE WITH A SOLID REPUTATION IN HIS COMMUNITY. IF I LEARN MORE, I WILL CONTACT YOU IMMEDIATELY BY FAX. GIVE MY BEST WISHES TO THE NEWLYWEDS AND PLEASE DON'T GET INVOLVED IN ANYTHING DANGEROUS WHILE YOU'RE AWAY FROM HOME. IF YOU NEED HELP WHILE IN MEXICO, MAY I SUGGEST MY NEW FRIEND, MAJOR UGARTE, WHO WORKED WITH ME ON THE UNZEGA CASE. HE IS AS STRAIGHT AS AN ARROW AND IS ONE OF MY SOURCES OF INFORMATION REGARDING YOUR PAL PORTILLO'S LOW ESTEEM IN THE EYES OF HIS COLLEAGUES. YOU CAN REACH UGARTE AT 1+52 155 549 2580 HAVE A GREAT

TRIP AND I'LL SEE YOU WHEN YOU GET BACK.

SINCERELY,

CAPTAIN MORGAN

HENRY MORGAN

CHIEF OF POLICE

CALALUNA, PERDIDO ISLE

CORAL COUNTY, FLORIDA

"Here, read this one from Captain Morgan," Gaspar instructed, handing the fax from the police chief to Craig.

As Craig was reading Captain Morgan's message, Murray came in with the beginning of their breakfast, orange juice for Gaspar, and a *cup-of-joe* for Craig.

After Murray left the room again, Craig spoke up. "Well, sir, I think you have a nose for solving mysteries. If *where there's smoke, there's fire* means anything at all, then I think you're on to something here," Cadawalader assured his young boss.

"Well, it's really none of my business, but Alex and I did witness the crooks leaving the crime scene. We did discover the place where they had uncovered the artifacts and we did notify the authorities, or at least Señor de Montijo, the director of the *Dzibilchaltún* site. I feel very proprietary about that stolen gold and would at least like to get that stuff back for Señor de Montijo, · if not break the back of the Jaguar himself and his dirty gang while doing so."

"Well, sir," Craig said, taking a gulp of coffee, "no one could ever accuse you of being on the wrong side of the law. Doing what's right seems to be what you do best. Just don't get yourself hurt or worse … killed … doing it, please. These seem like ruthless characters that you don't want to tangle with." Craig shook his head.

"Well, Craig," Gaspar let down his strict navy etiquette for a moment. "I have a plan, but it's not completely formulated yet. What I want you to do is take the newlyweds, you know, mom and Peter … take them down south, go as far as Punta del Este or Buenos Aires. Stop in Colombia and Brazil if you like. Give them a great honeymoon cruise, then come back to pick up Alex and me in Celestún. And Craig, if I need you in a hurry, I'll expect you to hightail it back, *rapido!*"

"What are you up to in Celestún, sir?" Craig inquired.

"I'm not sure myself, captain, but I'll need to get back there in order to find out. The minute I do find out, I promise … you'll be the first to know."

"Are you expecting the rest of the party to arrive today, sir?"

"Yes, they should be here sometime this morning. I doubt that they'll want to visit Tulúm without me."

"And when shall we leave for Central and South America?" Cadawalader asked.

"I would imagine the day after tomorrow would be a good idea," Gaspar decided. "I'll tell them the plan. Leave that to me please," he told his trusted captain.

"Did you sleep through the entire night?" Cadawalader wondered.

"Yes, I couldn't believe it. I fell asleep right after lunch and didn't wake up until six this morning! That's the first time that's ever happened to me. I guess that's why I'm so hungry right this minute," he said taking a big bite of buttered toast. "But I'm raring to go too. I can't wait to explore those ruins over there," he said pointing out the window. "Have you ever been to Yucatán? You should join us today. I think you'll like seeing the Maya ruins."

"Thank you, sir. I'd love to join your shore excursion," Captain Cadawalader gushed.

"Have the crew stow our scuba gear in the tender … yours, mine and Al's. I think there must be some really good diving off of that beach, all kinds of underwater caves and stuff, at least that's what the guidebooks say." Gaspar smiled at the thought of scuba diving in the clear turquoise waters.

"Does Alexander know how to scuba?" Captain Cadawalader wondered.

"He can dive all right; he's just never had a chance. His dad, Felix, wouldn't give him permission to dive. But since Felix isn't around, it won't be our fault if Al falls out of the tender while trying on my extra equipment. What the heck." Gaspar chuckled conspiratorially.

Craig laughed out loud. "That's what makes you the best kind of friend any guy could ever want to have, Gaspar," he exclaimed breaking the Navy etiquette he insisted upon between captain and owner for the very first time.

After Captain Cadawalader left the saloon to take care of business, a text came through on Gaspar's cell from Peter, asking Gaspar if he'd arrived safely and if all was well onboard *Floridablanca*.

Simultaneously, another text came through from Elvira asking him how he was doing and letting him know that they would be arriving at Tulúm, around ten o'clock that morning.

An instant later a third text arrived from Alex, saying that he'd missed a terrific day of rock climbing and that they'd spent the night out in the jungle at a terrific hotel and that they'd probably be in Tulúm in an hour or so, right after breakfast.

Gaspar sent one text back, to the three of them. All it said was, *'All is well. See you when you get here. Give Peugeot a kiss from me! Best, Gasp.'* That was enough … without a minute to spare, he decided it was time to get ready to go back on shore.

TULÚM

THE TRAVELERS ARRIVED IN TULÚM AT TEN O'CLOCK IN THE MORNING JUST LIKE GASPAR PLANNED IT. In preparation for their arrival, Gaspar and Craig landed the tender on the beach and left Jimmy Cahill in charge of the motor launch, while they went up to the ruins to meet Gaspar's family and friends and more importantly, Mr. Peugeot. Roberto had already herded his three clients and the prancing French poodle into a group near the entrance to the main temple, El Castillo and was well into his spiel, when Gaspar and Craig caught up with them. There were hellos all around and plenty of admiration for *Floridablanca* bobbing at anchor, just offshore. After kissing his mom hello with cursory hellos for Peter, Alex and Roberto, Gaspar got down on his haunches and grabbed Peugeot's head between the palms of his hands and let the dog wash his face with wet kisses.

"Yuck," Alex invoked, "dog germs!" He laughed.

"Let's get going," Gaspar urged, grabbing Peugeot's leash, preparing to lead the way. "What's first, Roberto, El Castillo?" he asked the guide enthusiastically.

"Of course, El Castillo," Roberto agreed.

Peugeot led the group towards the massive structure while Roberto lectured the humans about Tulúm. "Tulúm," Roberto expounded, "was a Pre-Columbian walled city which served the Maya as a major port for Cobá. As you can see, the cliffs which the ruins are built on top of are thirty-nine feet above the Caribbean Sea. Tulúm was one of the last cities inhabited and built by the Mayans; it was at its height between the thirteenth and fifthteenth centuries and managed to survive about seventy years after the Spanish conquered Mexico. Tulúm's demise were the diseases the Spanish brought here from Europe. The first modern mention of Tulúm was written down by Juan Díaz, a member of Juan de Grijalva's Spanish expedition in 1518. It wasn't until 1843, however that the first detailed description of the ruins was published by John Lloyd Stephens and Frederick Catherwood in their book *Incidents of Travel in Yucatán*. The people here had access to trade routes from both land and sea, making Tulúm an important trade hub, especially for obsidian. From numerous depictions in murals and other works around the site, you'll soon understand that the people of Tulúm worshiped the diving or descending god. Come with me and I'll show you what I'm talking about," Roberto moved them along in the direction of El Castillo.

"What makes this architecture different than what we've seen in the other Maya sites we've already visited Roberto?" Alex asked earnestly.

"Well, Alex, Tulúm has architecture typical of Maya sites on the east coast of the Yucatán Peninsula. You can recognize this architecture by that step running around the base of the building which sits on a low substructure," Roberto said, pointing out one of the architectural features of El Castillo. "See how the walls flare," Roberto pointed this special architectural detail out to Alex and his companions. "There are typically two sets of moldings near the top like you see here. The room on top usually contains one or two small windows with an altar at the back wall, roofed by either a beam-and-rubble ceiling or they're sometimes vaulted, as the case may be."

Gaspar was pleased that Alex was happy with Roberto's answer to his question. But he wanted to keep the exploration moving. "Let's climb up, Al. Come on Craig, mom, Peter. Come on Roberto, get the lead out," he scolded his pal, taking off at full speed for the hike up and around El Castillo.

While his unruly companions and the poodle dog climbed up, on, around and inside the building, Roberto pointed out what he could, to the disjointed group. He noted to those who would listen that the building was a mere twenty-five feet tall, and that it had been built on top of a previous building that was colonnaded and had a beam and mortar roof. When they went inside, he pointed out the serpent motifs carved into the lintels in the upper rooms.

"The construction of the Castillo," Roberto revealed, "had taken place in stages." What interested Gaspar the most was the revelation that a small shrine was used to create a beacon for incoming canoes to steer towards. As the owner of a famous yacht, Gaspar fancied himself a seafaring man, and appreciated that the shrine marked a break in the barrier reef, exactly opposite the site.

"Remember that, captain," he ordered Craig. "Lest ye dash *Floridablanca* against the reef, when you heave anchor tomorrow," he said only half facetiously to Craig who had a good chuckle over the ancient information provided.

From the top of El Castillo, Roberto pointed out the cove and landing beach, which had been naturally created by a break in the sea cliffs, making it the perfect place for canoes laden with cargo to enter through. "This characteristic of the site," Roberto told them, "was one of the main reasons the Maya founded the city of Tulúm, exactly here." From their high vantage point, the group could now survey not only the entire walled city, but also *Floridablanca* bobbing at anchor on the sparkling Caribbean waters.

"This is quite a massive wall, guys!" Peter remarked,

"Constructing such a huge wall would have taken an enormous amount of energy and time."

"The wall is the proof which shows how important defense was to the Maya when they chose this site," Roberto backed up Peter's statement.

"Look at the watch towers at the corners," Peter pointed out the small structures that formed a prominent architectural feature of the monument.

"Just another important example, Peter, to show how well-defended the city was," Roberto chimed in. "There are also five narrow gateways in the wall, with two each on the north and south sides and one on the west side. Near the northern side of the wall, over there," Roberto pointed, "is a small cenote which provided the city with fresh water. But it's this impressive wall that makes Tulúm one of the most well-known fortified sites of the Maya world," Roberto concluded.

"Where to now, Roberto?" Gaspar asked.

"There are three major structures of interest here," Roberto explained. "*El Castillo*, the *Temple of the Frescoes*, and *the Temple of the Descending God*. Those are the three most famous buildings at Tulúm. The most spectacular building here is the Temple of the Frescoes. We should go there next," Roberto insisted, leading them in the direction of the structure.

"What will we find when we get there, Roberto?" Elvira asked sweetly.

"The temple is unusual because it has not only a

lower gallery but a smaller second story gallery as well."

"What was it used for?" Craig asked.

"The Temple of the Frescoes was used as an observatory for tracking the movements of the sun. You will see figurines of the Maya 'diving god' set into niches which decorate the facade of the temple.

Arriving at the Temple of the Frescoes they studied the figure of 'the diving god' preserved above the entrance on the western wall. They also admired a mural on the eastern wall that resembled what Roberto told them was a style that originated in highland Mexico, called the Mixteca-Puebla style.

From the Temple of the Frescoes they went on to see the ruin of the great palace as well as the *Templo Dios del Viento* (God of the Winds Temple) which guarded the sea entrance to Tulúm's bay.

"Have they found a lot of gold objects here in Tulum?" Gaspar asked.

"As we've learned along the way, the Maya loved to trade. Tulúm was a major port for the Maya and both coastal and land routes converged here. All three of these reasons account for Tulúm's prosperity and why archaeologists have found such a great number of significant artifacts in and around the site. The plethora of rich artifacts discovered here are evidence of the people of Tulúm's direct contact with areas all over central Mexico as well as central America. Copper artifacts from the Mexican highlands have been found in Tulúm, as well as flint artifacts, ceramics, incense burners, and yes … plenty of gold objects from all over the Yucatán. Salt and textiles were also among some of the goods brought to Tulúm by sea that would then be dispersed inland to other Maya cities.

"What would some of the typical types of exports have been going out of Tulúm?" Craig asked.

"Typical exported goods included feathers and copper objects that came from inland sources. These goods could be transported by sea to rivers such as the Río Motagua and the Río Usumacinta-Pasión by which they were brought from the highlands and the lowlands by seafaring canoes to Tulúm. The Río Motagua starts from the highlands of Guatemala and empties into the Caribbean, while the Río Usumacinta-Pasión river system also originates in the Guatemalan highlands but empties into the Gulf of Mexico. It may have been one of these seafaring canoes from Tulúm, that Christopher Columbus first encountered off the shores of Honduras. Jade and obsidian appear to be some of the more prestigious materials found here. The obsidian would have had to have traveled from as far away as Ixtepeque in northern Guatemala which is 430 miles away from Tulúm, but it got here. This huge distance coupled with the density of obsidian found at the site, show that Tulúm was a major center for the trading of obsidian."

Finally reaching The Temple of the Diving God, they'd also reached the end of their tour.

"This temple kinda makes you wanna go for a dive, don't it, Mr. Peugeot?" Gaspar turned on a funny southern accent for effect. "What a ya think, Al … shall we go divin'," he asked grabbing Peugeot's ears.

"Yeah, would you take me out with you this time, buddy? I bet there's mountains of treasure in these waters, and not too far down either," Al enthused, while Peugeot barked his approval.

"Okay, you got it man. Listen everybody, let's head back to the boat for lunch. Then anyone who wants to join Al, Craig and me for diving around the base of the Tulúm cliffs is welcome to join us. I can't wait to see what we might discover down there," Gaspar beamed.

"Sounds like a plan, guys," Peter approved, "Elvira and I and Mr. Peugeot can watch from the deck and cheer you on."

"The tender is waiting on the beach, right over there," Craig gesticulated towards the left of the ruins. "Let's get back onboard?"

"Last one to the boat's a rotten egg." Gaspar called over his shoulder as he and Mr. Peugeot led the charge for the beach, followed only by Alex, who beat him to the tender by a yard while the rest sauntered over at their leisure.

CHAPTER 14

CATCHING UP

Bᴀᴄᴋ ᴏɴ ʙᴏᴀʀᴅ *Fʟᴏʀɪᴅᴀʙʟᴀɴᴄᴀ*, ᴀ ꜰᴇꜱᴛɪᴠᴇ ʟᴜɴᴄʜ ʜᴀᴅ ʙᴇᴇɴ ꜱᴇᴛ ᴜᴘ ᴏɴ ᴛʜᴇ ᴘᴏᴏᴘᴅᴇᴄᴋ ᴜɴᴅᴇʀ ᴛʜᴇ ʙʟᴀᴄᴋ and white striped awning. Gaspar had called ahead to Murray to make sure that Roberto and Craig had places at table and there was even a chair for Peugeot. While they'd been at Tulúm, Craig's mates had ferried the travelers' belongings from the back of Roberto's SUV, over to the yacht and distributed the luggage between the travelers' various staterooms.

Lunch was a rollicking fun affair, where Gaspar caught up with all that his parents and Alex had seen, after he took off without them for Tulúm. "Tell me about Yaxuná, Al," Gaspar begged. "I was just sick to miss it," he lied.

"I've made sketches of all of it," Alex bragged. "I'll

show you my drawings and bore the heck out of you later," he promised.

"Yeah, I'm sure you will, but what did you see? What did I miss?" Gaspar kept the conversational ball rolling.

"Well … " Alex started off hesitantly. "To start, it's actually pronounced Yah-shoo-nah' in Maya and it means *The Turquoise House* … right Roberto?"

"Precisely, Alex," Roberto confirmed, proud that someone had actually listened and learned.

"Keep going, Al. You're such a good student. I want to hear everything that you got out of your visit," Gaspar urged his friend on.

The temples at Yaxuná also have other temples underneath them that are actually pre-classic style from around 400 BC."

"That old!" Gaspar marveled.

"Yeah, and those older temples weren't built by the Mayans, but by some other people … *maybe even extraterrestrials*." Alex laid it on thick.

"I never told you that, Alex." Roberto was horrified.

"No, but I came to the extraterrestrial conclusion on my own." Alex defended his theory. "It's the only thing that makes sense. Anyway, the Mayans just took them over and made themselves at home, building their temples right on top of the old existing extraterrestrial structures."

"Now you're talking, Al. Just like the Spanish conquistadors did when they took over the Maya cities here and the Inca cities in Peru, building Catholic churches over the existing pagan temples."

"Yeah, Gasp, exactly. These guys were also major farmers, and the whole site is still surrounded by corn-fields which the local people still work." Alex was really into his lesson.

"You know me, Al. Just tell me about the man-made stuff. Agriculture bores me. Remember, I've got black thumb," Gaspar joked.

"Got it. Well the sacbé in Yaxuná … you know, the raised causeway is the longest known Mayan road in existence. It extends a hundred kilometers leading directly back to Coba. And Yaxuná's temples were some of the highest and grandest pyramids of their day, built of monolithic stones. You would have loved climbing them, Gasp, and even better, watching your mom and Peter climb down them on their butts." Alex giggled.

"Cool," Gaspar laughed.

"There were lots of carvings and hieroglyphics that were so worn out, even Roberto couldn't decipher them. Several of the temples had walls of carved stones on the bottom, and rows of columns on top consistent with the Puuc style that Roberto's always telling us about. Roberto said if we want to see more examples of this type of architecture, we'll have to go to Labna, Sayil, Edzná or Uxmal."

"Now there's an idea," Gaspar said deep in thought. "Let's remember to do that someday, but I'm not sure we'll have time on this trip to take all that in. Maybe Uxmal, but we'll look at a map and see." Gaspar promised, without making a commitment.

Alex continued recounting more of the Yaxuná visit. "Most archaeologists think the structures we saw were built between 400 and 650 AD, but Roberto says that theory is still being researched. Roberto said there are still some gray areas in the history of the Maya, and different influences or styles have been noted … like Roberto told us at Coba, remember? People from as far away as Honduras, El Salvador, Guatemala and places outside the Yucatán, were constantly influencing the different Mayan styles."

"Yeah and maybe even people from Mars!" Gaspar giggled, unable to stop himself.

"I'm reading a book I got from the Yaxuná gift shop," Alex continued, ignoring his friend's silly remark. "It's all about the excavations there. It doesn´t have any photos so I'm not sure what's what, but I'm matching up my drawings with the descriptions in the book and it seems to be working out all right … I promise I'll show you tonight. It's fun for me to try and imagine what these places looked like twenty-five hundred years ago or a thousand years ago. This is one of the things I've liked most about visiting all these Maya sites, the chance to imagine the way life was … in the good old days."

"That's what I like about you, Al, your ability to visualize," Gaspar complimented his friend. "What about you, ma. What was your experience like at Yaxuná?"

"Well, Gaspar. I'm embarrassed to tell you but when we climbed the first pyramid, which was not completely excavated or maintained, I saw a snake slither by, which gave me the idea to stop climbing Maya pyramids altogether. Ever since seeing that serpent, I've been hesitant to stray too far from the beaten path and something tells me that's the way it's going to be … going forward."

"Oh, ma, you're such a chicken."

"The Chicken of Chichén Itzá," Elvira joked.

"Had you gone into the brush with us just a little farther, señora, you would have found some very interesting excavations to look at," Roberto interjected.

"What else did you learn about and see. I'm sure Captain Cadawalader would love to hear about it as much as I do," Gaspar cajoled them.

"We saw so many hieroglyphs that have the symbol of the cross, that I finally asked Roberto the significance of the symbol. He told me that in Maya the cross signifies north, south, east and west," Peter offered.

"I never knew that. Are they still excavating at Yaxuná?" Gaspar wanted to know

"The area around Yaxuná is flat," Roberto spoke up, "so any protrusions are most likely sites awaiting excavation. The history that is buried in places like Yaxuná will supply archaeologists new and useful information for years to come. According to the Diario del Yucatán newspaper, there are big plans to continue the work at

Yaxuná and other sites situated around the area, like Ek Balam, where excavations were begun years ago … but never completed.

"You wouldn't have liked the ballcourt at Yaxuná, Gasp," Alex said. "It's one of those sites that hasn't been completed yet. The one we saw at Chichén Itzá makes the one at Yaxuná look like it was hit by a bomb."

"That bad, huh," Gaspar muttered.

"You would have liked the round caracol-shaped building though," Peter enthused. It was similar to the one at Chichén Itzá, and probably used as an observatory. At least that's what Roberto told us, right professor," Peter looked to Roberto for confirmation.

"That's right, Peter," Roberto assured him, just as Murray arrived carrying dessert for the table. Peugeot barked his delight, hoping it would be a delicious treat for him to taste.

CHAPTER 15

UNDER THE SEA

LUNCH FINISHED UP AS MURRAY'S RICH DESSERT DISAP-
PEARED, AMIDST A LOT OF OOHS, AAHS AND LIP SMACKING,
before being followed by complaints of how stuffed they
all were. Even Peugeot jumped down from his seat at
table and curled up like a donut on deck before passing
out, snoring peacefully.

"Shall we join Mr. Peugeot and have a half hour
siesta, then go diving, captain? Or shall we go diving
now?" Gaspar asked.

"Let's go now," Captain Craig answered. "We won't
need wetsuits here, the water's so warm, just tanks, fins
and masks and the crew have already placed those on
board the tender."

"Okay then, let's do it." Gaspar enthused, jumping
up. "Come on, Al. Let's put on our trunks and get going."

Fifteen minutes later the three divers assembled on deck and took the yacht's exterior steps down to the waiting tender. Soon they were bobbing at anchor just inside the great Mayan barrier reef, which Craig informed them was the second largest in the world. Without wasting a minute, they strapped on their tanks and were ready to go over the tender's gunwale, eager to explore Tulúm's historic bay.

"Craig, you lead. Al, since this is your first official dive, you go next. I'll follow up and have your back, okay." Gaspar took charge.

"You got it, sir," Cadawalader replied, before going overboard, backwards.

"Okay, Al. Are you ready for your very first dive?" Gaspar asked his pal, who nodded in the affirmative. "One, two, three, over you go," Gaspar counted down. He watched as Alex went overboard backwards, mimicking Craig as well as Gaspar, whom he'd watched making the same move countless times back home.

Gaspar didn't wait a minute to follow his pal into the drink and soon all three friends were swimming in formation … deep, deep down into the turquoise waters off ancient Tulúm. Together they explored the base of the sea cliffs, as well as the barrier reef with its soft corals and colorful fish. Gaspar was hoping to find Aztec or Maya gold scattered between the rocks on the sandy bottom, but alas … there were no such souvenirs to be found. Gaspar had expected the water temperature to be a warm seventy-nine degrees Fahrenheit, but soon discovered that it was closer to eighty-four degrees near the surface, getting slightly cooler the deeper they swam. The reef soon offered up some of the most spectacular and exciting diving opportunities he had ever experienced. Gaspar figured that there must have been at least several hundred species swimming past him, and all kinds of coral including black coral, brain coral and fire coral made up the reef where seahorses galore cavorted in and out of the many nooks and crannies. Gaspar also witnessed an unbelievable non-stop parade of multi-colored iridescent tropical fish, sea turtles, barracuda, angel fish, sting rays and manta rays, as well as a bull shark and a hammerhead.

•••

After an hour underwater, with Alex swimming between Craig and Gaspar like a pro, Craig motioned to follow him upwards. Soon the three divers broke the surface near to where the tender, with Jimmy Cahill at the helm, was waiting for them.

"That was fun, Gasp," Craig exclaimed, abandoning his naval formality as they climbed into the tender. "How-bout we go diving in one of the local cenotes I've read about?"

"Great idea, Craig. Wha-da-ya think, Al, shall we do it?"

"I'm game, count me in," Alex replied in the affirmative.

"This will be a two-tank dive," Craig advised, as Jimmy headed the tender towards shore.

Hitting the beach, the trio ran smack into another American diver, a long-haired hipster, beach bum type, who'd just stepped out of the water and was discarding his gear, when he stopped them and asked where they were headed.

"We're going cenote diving." Gaspar answered, "Do you know which one is considered the best?"

"That would be Dos Ojos, amigo. I'm headed there myself, if you guys want to join me."

"Have you dived there previously?" Craig asked, suspiciously.

"Yeah man, it's awesome. Let me show it to you, dude," the diver suggested.

"We know about Dos Ojos. We've read all about it. Is it nearby?" Gaspar asked the stranger.

"Not too far," the diver was non-committal.

"It's supposed to be one of the most expansive systems of underwater caverns in Yucatán," Gaspar added breathlessly.

"It's a bitchin' place man," the hipster assured him.

"Exactly how far is it?" Craig asked, in a slightly more friendly tone.

"Fifteen minutes, man," the beach bum told him. "I've got my wheels right over there. He pointed towards a decrepit old VW van in the parking lot. When we're done, I'll drive you dudes back here if you want, no *problema* man."

"Okay," Craig agreed. "Let me just tell my man where we're headed so that he'll know when to pick us up." With that, Craig went back down to the water's edge to tell Jimmy where they were going and to go back and get Roberto to follow them over to the Dos Ojos cenote. He also asked Jimmy to follow them to the parking lot and take down a visual of the man's wheels and the license number. After all the excitement Gaspar had already gotten into with the Jaguar's antiquity thieves, Craig wasn't taking any chances with his boss's safety.

While Craig was giving instructions to Jimmy, their new dive buddy asked Gaspar "didn't I see you guys getting off that big yacht over there?"

"Yes, we did," Gaspar answered honestly. "It's called *Floridablanca*. Beautiful isn't she."

"Beautiful is an understatement," the diver exhaled. "By the way, I'm Hanuman. What's your name?"

"I'm Gaspar Brown, and this is my pal, Alex Mendoza."

"And your friend?" Hanuman asked, watching Craig and Jimmy as they sauntered back up the beach towards them.

"That's Craig Cadawalader. He's the captain of *Floridablanca*, and the guy with him is one of his crew, Jimmy Cahill," Gaspar informed the stranger. "Craig, this is Hanuman. Hanuman, this is Captain Craig

Cadawalader, and this hearty mate is Jimmy Cahill. Jimmy say hello to our new diving buddy," Gaspar made the introductions.

"Hanuman, now that's an interesting name, don't you think, Jimmy?" Craig asked his mate. "Have you a last name, Hanuman?"

"No, just Hanuman. I named myself after the Hindu monkey god, man." the new-age hipster explained.

"That's all I need to know," Craig, smiled. "Let's get going, guys. Dos Ojos awaits!"

Driving north of Tulúm for just eighteen minutes, Hanuman turned his VW to the right, off of highway 307 and parked in an almost-deserted dirt lot. Having arrived at the Dos Ojos cenote, the four divers piled out of the van, grabbing their tanks, fins, masks and whatever other paraphernalia they needed. Set for adventure, they ran over in a group to the edge of the cenote, with Hanuman leading the way. Reaching the edge of the water-filled sinkhole, they scurried down the rickety stairs to the water's edge. Reaching the landing, they strapped on their tanks, pulled on their fins and placed their masks tightly over their eyes. Without a word to the others, Hanuman was the first of the group to jump into the water.

"Follow me, Alex," Craig ordered. "We'll follow the same pattern as we did in the Caribbean. Gaspar you follow up the rear just like before. And listen guys, cave diving is completely different than diving in the open sea. Keep close, do not lose sight of me or the man in front of you. If you have any trouble, let me know by tapping me on the shoulder and we'll head back out."

"Aye, aye, captain," both boys agreed simultaneously, as Hanuman's head broke the surface of the water.

"Come on in, guys?" Hanuman sang, "The water's warm!"

Craig, then Alex, followed by Gaspar jumped into the cenote. The water was indeed warm and fresh and clear. Diving under, Gaspar couldn't believe his eyes or their good luck in running into Hanuman, who now led them through this magical underwater place. This was so much better than the Cenote Xlakah that he and Alex had swam in, back at Dzibilchaltún. Having the tanks with them and being able to dive deep through the sunken caverns was an experience that Gaspar would not soon forget. He hoped that Alex was enjoying the experience as much as he was.

On the short drive out, Hanuman explained that the cenote was named Dos Ojos because it was actually two circular cenotes that connected underground through a series of tunnels, caverns and passages. Now, experiencing the cenote firsthand, Gaspar realized right away that this was a world- famous destination, perfect for swimmers, snorkelers and scuba divers alike. As Gaspar followed his companions down into the deep, he marveled at the large system of caves below. Together they explored at least a thousand meters of the wondrous underwater world. Following Hanuman, they went from cavern to cavern, each area filled with fish and plant life and the most amazing rock formations any of them had ever seen. They passed through tunnels and passageways with ceilings made of stalactites which had formed centuries before the caves had filled with water. Following Hanuman upwards, they broke the surface in the second of the large circular cenotes that made up Dos Ojos.

"Wow, that was great, Hanuman!" Gaspar shouted the minute he removed his regulator.

"Fantastic!" followed Craig's cry of appreciation.

"Cool, man," Alex chimed in. "Do we go out here, or do we swim back for more?"

"We swim back, buddy," Hanuman notified Alex and the others. "There are even more caverns and tunnels on this side. If you're ready, follow me."

"Lead on, brother," Craig insisted. One by one, they dived back under, playing follow the leader again, through the underwater wonderland.

Swimming back through more caverns and tunnels, they made a full circle finally ending up at the cenote where they had started their tour. It had been a major swim and the boys were glad to rest, but sad that the adventure at Dos Ojos was over. Pulling themselves out of the water, they dragged their equipment up the steep staircase and back to Hanuman's car.

"What a day," Gaspar exclaimed, exhilaration in his voice.

"We need to do this more often," Craig suggested.

"That was one of the best dives of my life."

"Yeah," Alex beamed. "Thanks, Hanuman, for bringing us here!"

"I'm the lucky one," Hanuman said. "I'm glad we hooked up, guys. I love showing this place to people who've never been here before, and it's even better when it's so well appreciated.

"So, Han, what're your plans for dinner tonight?" Gaspar asked. "Would you like to join us?"

"That's a very kind invitation. I don't want to horn in, but I'd be delighted." Hanuman accepted.

"Great, that's settled then." Gaspar was pleased. "Where are you staying, Han, and where would be the most fun place for all of us to dine tonight?" Gaspar asked.

"Oh man, I thought you figured that out already. Can't you tell by just looking at my van? Sometimes I sleep on the beach, and sometimes in my van. It just depends on how fancy I want to get. Swimming in the cenotes is my best bathtub, and food is cheap in the local joints around here. There's a beach shack near the ruins that's got good barbecued shrimp and fresh fish tacos and plenty of beer, although something tells me you kids aren't old enough to guzzle beers yet ... not even in Mexico," he chuckled. "I think you'd like the crowd there. We sit on the beach. There's always some musicians, a bonfire or two, and plenty of archaeologists, historians, students ... you get the picture, it's very laid back."

"Perfect," Gaspar agreed. "Captain, let's make a party of it. Invite the crew and I'll tell mom and Peter, Mr. Peugeot and Roberto."

"You can tell Roberto now, Gasp," Craig said pointing towards the SUV parked near Hanuman's old wreck.

Gaspar didn't realize that Craig had taken the precaution of ordering Roberto to pick them up at the cenote just in case Hanuman turned out to be a flake or worse yet … trouble. "I guess we have a ride, Han. So, let's meet at the beach shack at eight. Are we dressing up?"

"Come as you are, man. It's uber casual on the beach, dude!" Hanuman laughed.

"Okay, see you at eight," Gaspar trilled as he, Craig and Alex headed towards Roberto's SUV.

That night all the crew and the sailing party onboard *Floridablanca* got shore leave to attend the big beach party Gaspar was giving on the mainland. Sitting next to Mr. Peugeot on the sand by the shack's thatch-roofed palapa under the lighted ruins of Tulúm was magical. Seeing the lights of *Floridablanca* bobbing in the distance under the full moon made Gaspar proud. The grilled fish and shrimp, and warm corn tortillas served with butter and salsa picante were enjoyed by all, as were the cold bottles of Dos Equis beer which Craig and his crew, Elvira, Peter, Roberto and Hanuman drank with gusto. Hanuman turned out to be the life of the party and a popular guy with the locals, the archaeologists, the scientists and all the pretty girls who hung out regularly at the shack.

Their new friend and amicable free spirit made a point of introducing all his pals to Gaspar and his extended family. The locals and the visitors had a jolly time exchanging tales of their adventures in the Yucatán with each other. When the music started, everyone including Mr. Peugeot danced around the bonfire, laughing and shouting while Peugeot barked with joy. Gaspar thought it was what a real Mayan tribal dance might have been like. It wasn't until midnight that the party started breaking up. Elvira and Peter made a sign that it was time to call it a night, and Craig and his crew said goodnight to the remaining revelers and headed for the tender. Before leaving with Peugeot and the rest of his party, Gaspar asked Hanuman if he would like to spend the night onboard the yacht. Gaspar was delighted when his new friend told him that he would love to sleep in a real bed, even if just for one night. Together they walked to the tender and lifted Peugeot in before hopping in themselves, to the surprise of Peter, Elvira and Craig, although all of them had the good sense not to say a word.

"Isn't it great … Hanuman's accepted my invitation to spend the night onboard. Let's give him the blue stateroom, captain, the one next to Alex and me," Gaspar suggested.

CHAPTER 16

SPLITTING UP

T HE NEXT MORNING WHEN ELVIRA AND PETER ARRIVED
ON DECK FOR BREAKFAST, THEY FOUND GASPAR SEATED
at the table on the poop deck, drinking a glass of orange
juice with Peugeot sitting up on the chair next to him
with a supercilious smile on his handsome poodle-dog
face.

"Good morning, mom, good morning, Peter," Gaspar
sang out happily. "Did you have a good night's sleep?"
he inquired solicitously.

"Oh, yes, thank you, Gaspar. We slept like Mayan
Gods," his mother assured him.

"Wasn't that a fun beach party last night?" Gaspar
asked.

"Yes," Peter answered looking over the rail towards
the ruins of Tulúm. "What the heck! What happened to

Tulúm!" Peter shouted aghast, "We've been Shanghaied."

Gaspar guffawed and Peugeot barked dismissively at Peter's distress. "That's Playa del Carmen, Peter, and that," he said pointing away from shore, "is the island of Cozumel."

"What on earth? When did this happen?" Elvira asked in amazement.

"Last night, or to be more precise, early this morning," Gaspar giggled. "Surprise!"

"What will you think of next, Gaspar?" Peter asked chuckling.

"That's what's so fun about being spontaneous." Gaspar crowed. "Like meeting Han, yesterday."

"I hope you're not planning on picking up any more strays along the way." Peter joked.

"I think we were lucky meeting up with Hanuman." Gaspar interjected. "What a character."

"Well, Gaspar, I must say your generosity knows no bounds," Peter offered cryptically. "But what do you know about him? After all, he's a total stranger. Although he's extremely nice and interesting to say the least, I'm not so sure inviting him into the lap of luxury aboard *Floridablanca* was necessarily the right thing to do." Peter's lawyer mode kicked in.

"We have enough to go around, Peter, and besides, Hanuman is a very upstanding person, full of knowledge and love of life. I learned that about him in the first fifteen minutes after I met him. He's a font of knowledge about the Yucatán and the people here. His curiosity about everything he sees is remarkable. I think you'll find him to be not only harmless but a wonderful new edition to our expedition as well as the life of the party," Gaspar enthused.

"Are you thinking of inviting him to stay on permanently?" Elvira asked, surprise in her voice.

"Well, mom, if he'd like to hang out with us, I for one wouldn't mind in the least. A more interesting, carefree, no strings attached kind of guy we may never meet again. I think Hanuman has a lot to give and to teach us. I don't think any negative influences he may have could possibly rub off on two impressionable teenagers like me and Al … just by having him around. Anyway, there's no need to get excited. I haven't asked him to stay on … yet, but like I say … if he wanted to, I for one wouldn't be opposed to it. If you have any reservations about him, talk to Craig. He's a good judge of character and if you all disapprove, then I'll act accordingly." Gaspar assured his parents.

Suddenly, Alex and Hanuman stumbled up on deck, followed by Craig, all of them chatting and laughing together. Murray came out and took orders for ham and eggs, coffee, tea, biscuits and pancakes. To Murray and Gaspar's delight, Hanuman ordered all the above and orange juice too.

"I hope you'll forgive me, but I haven't been offered food like this, or even seen food like this in probably over a year." Hanuman apologized for his gluttony, sheepishly.

"Having breakfast with you folks is like receiving *manna* from heaven," he laughed. "Do you have maple syrup?"

Murray nodded his head and blurted, "from Vermont," before heading back to the galley.

Peter and Elvira had to laugh, instantly falling in love with happy-go-lucky Hanuman.

"Hanuman, how would you describe yourself. In our day we would have called you a hippie, Elvira told him.

"Well, El," Hanuman drawled, shortening his hostess's name to the familiar, "I'm the last person on earth to pigeon-hole myself. If I had to give myself a title, I guess I'd say I'm a child of the age of Aquarius, a new age hippie! I'm not one of your run-of-the-mill flower children from the sixties. I'm more of a planet-loving pre-Raphaelite with a twist … a free spirit, unfettered and full of love for my fellow man and my mother earth. Now that's one heck of a mouthful, as far as a personal description goes. Wouldn't you say, Gasp?" Hanuman asked his generous host and new best friend with a chuckle.

"It's exactly as I would have described you myself, Hanuman, only much better stated. Tell us, Han. Where were you born? Do you have any family? How do you live, and what did you do before you set yourself free? Where do you see yourself ten years from now?" Gaspar asked his guest a list of pointed questions.

"I was born in Toledo, Ohio. My father is a banker and my mother is a small-town society matron. I have three brothers and two sisters. They all live happy middle class lives back in Toledo, all married with children and probably just as happy being stuck in the mud as I am not to be. I left home when I was sixteen with every intention of traveling the world. I have very few possessions. In fact, as of this moment none but my van, my diving equipment and a few items of clothing. I was fortunate to receive a small inheritance from my grandfather the day I was born which my father has very carefully invested and nurtured for all of my twenty-four years. Wherever I am in the world, I call my dad and ask him to wire me a small sum, just enough to keep me in food and gas. I've driven all over the United States and all over Mexico. I'm making my way very slowly all the way down to the tip of Tierra del Fuego … if I'm lucky and that old van holds out, that is. So that's my life in a nutshell. I like to read, and every now and then I pick up books at local libraries, garage sales or thrift shops. I tend to stay in places that I like for months on end. I've been hanging out in the Yucatán now for the past three months. I've made a lot of friends at the various archaeological sites and even helped with some of the digging and other grunt work, just so that I could listen in and learn about the Maya. I intend to do the same all along the isthmus. When I finally get to Peru, I hope to work at Machu Picchu. If I'm lucky also at Tiahuanaco on the Bolivian side … you know … the pre-Inca ruins along the shores of Lake Titicaca."

"Do you have a cell phone, Hanuman?" Gaspar asked.

"Yes, I do. It's my lifeline. I've made so many friends with people from all over the world that hopefully ... I'll always have someone I can call on in a pinch, no matter what country I'm in."

"Give me your number," Gaspar ordered, pulling out his phone. "I want to put you into my contacts."

The two new friends exchanged numbers as Murray served breakfast.

"Hanuman, you never told us your given name," Elvira reminded him.

"Westerbrook, El. Joel Westerbrook, to be exact. But I think people remember Hanuman, a one-name name, better than Joel Westerbrook. Which is why I've officially changed it, at least with myself and with my friends."

"Are you a practicing Hindu?" Elvira drilled a little further.

"No, not at all. In fact, I don't believe in organized religion. I believe in God, and I thank God for all the blessings he's bestowed upon me, like meeting you good people. But I'm not a practicing anything. I just liked the name Hanuman, which as I think you already know is the name of the Hindu monkey god, but mostly because, I like monkeys ... a lot!" he laughed.

"Well, Hanuman, you're a very interesting young man," Peter complimented him. "I'm glad Gaspar met you and invited you onboard. We hope to see a lot of you in the future and look forward to hearing about your adventures too."

"Thank you, Peter. I'm honored to be one of your party, even if only for one night," Hanuman said, plunging into his pancakes, which he'd smothered in maple syrup.

"Not just one night, Han," Gaspar got his attention. "You see," he said, gesticulating towards the shore and then towards the island, "we're not in Kansas anymore."

"Playa? *playa!* Oh my god! Playa … my favorite place, and Cozumel … *Cozumel … fantastico!* How did this happen?" Hanuman wondered, looking at the new scenery. "Were we set adrift?"

"Not at all, Hanuman," Captain Cadawalader spoke up. "Mr. Brown ordered me to sail the boat here early this morning, and here we are. Have you any further orders, sir?" the captain asked, turning towards Gaspar.

"Oh, just that you join us for some cool scuba diving here, captain, if you won't mind accompanying us again?" Gaspar waited for Craig's reaction.

"Not at all, sir. I would be delighted to join you in the deep," Craig smiled happily.

"Great. Then in that case, let's finish breakfast and drop anchor, captain," Gaspar commanded.

"Aye, aye, sir." Cadawalader saluted, downing his cup of coffee before heading off in the direction of the bridge.

"Mom, we're going to anchor right here. We'll dive directly off *Floridablanca*, that way if you and Peter and if you'd be so kind, Mr. Peugeot, want to take the tender in to Playa del Carmen for some shopping or looking around, it will be convenient for you getting back and forth. Just make sure you take Jimmy's cell phone number with you," Gaspar reminded her.

"Thank you, darling," Elvira cooed. "You think of everything."

"Only for you, ma, only for you," Gaspar smiled, blowing her a kiss as he headed below to get ready for the big dive.

Fifteen minutes later, the four divers met on deck, ready to hit the water. "What do we have to look forward to here, Han?" Gaspar asked his new pal, who claimed to know the neighborhood well.

Hanuman, spoke up, "Gasp, there's nothing to do here but have fun and enjoy the natural beauty. First and foremost, what you need to do is just be on vacation! That's what people do best here. When you get in the water ... wind down, relax, kick back. Get in vacation mode, dudes. The slow pace of Mexico is even slower here at Playa and Cozumel. Don't feel like you have to be doing something all the time. When you're in town just stroll around, eat good food and find something cold to drink. That should be enough excitement for this part of your vacation. Luckily mother nature provided Playa with the best possible set-up for relaxing ... the beach! The beach here is truly fantastic. Look at it. The soft white sand never gets hot, so you won't burn your feet or your buns. Up there, at that end, it's clothing optional if you're in the mood, guys," Hanuman said, punching Alex's shoulder. "The sea is warm, turquoise blue and crystal clear. Have you ever seen such a color? My advice is to chill out and let the Caribbean sun heat up your body and your mind. Just sitting in the waves on the edge of this continent is a great way to spend your time in Playa."

Gaspar decided there and then that Hanuman had the soul of a philosopher.

"Tell us about the caves and cenotes around here, Han," Alex begged.

"How can I describe the indescribable," Hanuman answered. "The only thing I can recommend is that you see them for yourselves. Are you ready? Last one in's a rotten egg!" Hanuman yelled as he climbed down the ship's brow and fell backwards off the last step, into the warm Caribbean Sea.

"He's a wild one," Gaspar marveled as Hanuman went under water. "Go on, Craig, jump in, then you Al, and I'll be the rotten egg," Gaspar laughed.

Later that day, after their dive, the friends regrouped on deck for drinks with the parents and the pup. "What a day, Gaspar enthused to Elvira, Peter and Peugeot. I hope you had as much fun as we did, mom?" he asked, picking up Peugeot and holding him close, nuzzling his head like a baby.

"Oh, we had a lot of fun, Gaspar. Playa del Carmen is a delightful town. We had a superb lunch and shopped till we dropped. I'm afraid that the hold is now full of

Mexican piñatas, colorful dishes, blue rimmed goblets, and all kinds of crazy metalwork decorations that we found irresistible," Elvira confessed.

"Where can you use that kind of stuff, Mrs. Cawthorne?" Alex asked bemused.

"In my little house in Calaluna," Elvira answered. "Peter and I are going to throw a Mexican fiesta when we get back." she announced happily.

"It sounds like fun." Alex enthused, "That old house will no doubt be very interestingly decorated with the souvenirs you've collected on this trip," Alex complimented her.

"How did you like diving today, Alex?" Elvira changed the subject.

"*Mother of pearl*," Alex cursed. "It was amazing, but don't tell my parents! My dad will have a total breakdown if he finds out that I've been swimming underwater … out in the ocean, like a fish."

"I'll cover for you," Elvira promised. "Now tell me what you saw down there," she begged.

"We saw the most beautiful corals and tropical fish. The colors here at Cozumel are like none I've ever seen." Alex was beside himself with delight.

"How-bout you, Peter?" Gaspar asked his stepdad. "Did you enjoy Playa?"

"Oh, yeah. Strolling along 5th Avenue in Playa wasn't quite the same as shopping 5th Avenue in New York. But walking along La Quinta was very pleasant indeed.

It's a pedestrian only street. You could say it's a casual esplanade lined with Playa's absolute best shops and boutiques." Peter described the landlubber scene for the water babies.

"Wait till you see all the souvenirs, clothes, handicrafts, silver and other things we found there," Elvira chimed in.

"Yeah, we also found a terrific open-air restaurant with a great ambiance where we thought we'd have dinner tonight. Of course, you're all invited to join us," Peter said. "It's right next door to the Atomic Internet Café and Pool Hall on Calle Ocho, between Avenidas Cinco y Diez, if you guys want to stay up and play pool after dinner," he added enticingly. "They have three pool tables and based on all the activity we saw there this afternoon, it also seems to be a good place to check e-mails and surf the web," Peter finished up.

"We had so much fun," Elvira jumped back in. "After lunch we took a taxi to the Aviary Xaman-Ha. It has many interesting and rare species of birds from all around the Yucatán Peninsula. Have you ever been there, Hanuman?" Elvira asked.

"No, ma'am. I'm sorry to say that I haven't. But if you recommend it … I want to see it!" Hanuman answered his hostess courteously.

"I think it's well worth a visit." Elvira insisted. "Gaspar, it may be your and Alex's only chance to see toucans and pink flamingos on this trip. Wait till you see it … there's a large *cageless* area where the birds can be observed as if they were in their natural habitats. It was a great outing for me, and Peter and Mr. Peugeot liked it. He was so well behaved, he never even barked at a bird, let alone tried to chase one. We all had such a good time there that we thought it would be fun to go back again, maybe with you boys," Elvira suggested.

"Okay, mom. If it works out timewise, let's do it." Gaspar agreed much to his mom's delight.

"Tell us about Cozumel, boys." Elvira wanted to hear about everything they'd done and seen.

"Well, for one thing," Alex offered, "it's the biggest island in Mexico, but was small enough for us guys to cover in just a day.

"Yeah," Gaspar started in. "There's a town on the island called San Miguel. I'm afraid by what you've just told us, Peter, that San Miguel lacks the charm and personality of Playa. We found a good restaurant for lunch but avoided the tourist shopping, which was from what little we saw, run-of-the-mill."

"Cruise ships stop there almost every day of the week," Hanuman informed them, "so prices can be pretty steep. The eating and drinking scene are focused on the American visitor, like Hard Rock Café and other franchise establishments. What the island really has going for it is the snorkeling and diving. Cozumel has been a diving destination since the 1960s when Jacques Cousteau made the world aware of the incredible reefs in the area," Hanuman told them.

"Did you see any interesting archaeology while you were there?" Peter asked.

"There are a few small ruins, but none of any real significance," Alex stated like a pro, dismissing what he had seen as beneath them compared to the glories of Tulúm and Chichén Itzá.

"So, are you up to a night on the town in Playa?" Peter asked. "If so, let's meet here at 7:30 and take the tender in to the al fresco joint Elvira and I have reserved for us.

"Sounds good to me," Gaspar agreed. "How about you guys?" One by one Alex, Hanuman and Craig agreed by shaking their heads, 'Yes' that dinner in town would be fun.

After refreshments were consumed, the party spread out and did whatever they wanted. Hanuman asked Alex to take him on a tour of *Floridablanca*, and Gaspar asked his mother and Peter if he could have a word with them. Sitting down in the saloon where they could be alone, he laid out his plan.

"I have an idea that I think you'll like. Alex and I want to get back to Celestún and hang out there for a while with Felix and Angela. There's still a lot of Maya sites between here and there that we could visit, and plenty of cenotes for us to dive in too. I'd like Craig to take you two on a real honeymoon, all the way down to South America if you like. Take *Floridablanca* and see

Belize and Guatemala. Go to Colombia and Brazil. Rio must be marvelous at this time of year too. If you like you can even go on to Punta del Este, and on the way … check out Buenos Aires. If you want us to meet you, we can fly down and join the ship. If you get tired or bored, you can fly back to Mérida or come back up to Celestún on the yacht. Look at a map. If you'd prefer to go to the Bahamas or Barbados, do it. *Floridablanca* is yours. Take it wherever you want and have a wonderful romantic time. Alex and I will take Roberto, and maybe Hanuman, if he wants to tag along with a couple of underage teenagers, and head back to Celestún. Hanuman is a great diver and he can take us to all the best dive spots like he did yesterday. And you know how reliable Roberto is, so you have nothing to worry about. With you in Craig's hands, I'll also know that you'll be safe and happy," Gaspar finished his pitch, hoping the adults would agree to separate from the kids for a while.

"Well, dear, it sounds like a lot of fun. If you really want to head back overland, we understand. If you change your mind, just holler and we'll stop at the nearest port with an international airport and wait for you to fly in," Elvira assured her son sweetly. "By the way, where is Roberto? Why haven't any of us seen him this morning?"

"We left him back at Tulúm. I told him last night about my plans for Playa and Cozumel. I asked him to meet us here tomorrow morning, just in case our plans changed, or Hanuman needed a ride back to his van.

"Gaspar, you never cease to amaze me," Peter complimented him. "You're always so thoughtful where your mother and I are concerned, not to mention your friends and employees. I agree with Elvira. We'll go on and see the sights and get as far south as possible. But like she says, if you change your mind, all you need to do is call us and we'll come back to Celestún or if you want, you can fly down and meet us wherever we are."

"Great," Gaspar considered it a deal. "I'll tell Craig to prepare to sail tomorrow morning, right after we disembark. We'll all have breakfast together and then see you off." Gaspar gave his mother a big kiss on the cheek. "Ma, you're the best. Thanks for trusting me, and for giving me so much freedom. You know I'll never abuse it. I'll always do the right thing and make you and Peter proud," he said, putting his arm around Peter's shoulder and giving his stepfather a big abrazo.

The next morning, after a very late-night shooting pool with the local sharks, the party assembled on the poop deck at eleven o'clock, where Murray served a hearty farewell breakfast to his very groggy guests. Roberto called in to say that he'd arrived at Playa and was standing by with the SUV, and as far as Gaspar was concerned all systems were go. Without too much ado the boys, with Hanuman in tow, disembarked by tender for the mainland. Elvira and Peter stood at the rail and waved goodbye and Gaspar, Alex and Hanuman did the same right back at them. The boys were exhilarated and couldn't wait to start their new adventure. Alex, for one, was looking forward to seeing his parents, who had been working back at The Doctor's House in Celestún these many weeks.

CHAPTER 17

THE ROAD TO CELESTÚN

ITTING THE BEACH, THE GROUP WAVED GOODBYE AGAIN, WITH MR. PEUGEOT BARKING LOUDLY, AS THE tender headed back to *Floridablanca*. Before long, Craig had unfurled the sails and the beautiful white and gold craft headed past Cozumel and out to sea. It was one of Gaspar's favorite sights, seeing his beautiful ship under full sail.

"Ahoy, Roberto … good to see you again. You remember our pal, Hanuman." Gaspar reintroduced the new member of the tour.

"Con mucho gusto." Roberto nodded towards Hanuman, as Hanuman smiled and nodded back.

"Well, men," Gaspar trilled, "where to?"

"You must tell us, señor," Roberto deferred to his employer.

"Okay, guys, I'd like to get back to Celestún in a timely fashion via a lot of Maya ruins. I'd also like to do this in a free and easy way, spontaneously, like Hanuman is accustomed to. If we have to camp out or stay in less than five-star places, that's fine with me. I'd like to eat good food, but I'm not opposed to eating with or like the natives. Does that make sense?" he asked looking for his companions' approval of his plans.

"Sounds good to me," Hanuman agreed.

"I'm in," Alex seconded.

"Whatever you say, señor," Roberto deferred.

"Great, now that we four bachelors have figured that out, let's get started. Roberto, I've mapped out a route. I want to go to Muyil, Labna, Xlapak, Sayil, Kabah, Uxmal, Okintock, and then home to Celestún. Then from Celestún we can go to Campeche and Edzna if we get bored. I also want to stop at all the cenotes and swimmin' holes we find. But only the good ones, Hanuman. We'll rely on you to point them out to us."

"You got it, Gasp," Hanuman assured him.

"Roberto, the crew should have helped you pack our tanks and scuba equipment and Peugeot's treats this morning, while we were at breakfast."

"It is all here, señor," Roberto confirmed.

"Perfect. All Alex and I are bringing are some swim trunks, towels and T-shirts. Hanuman, when we get to Tulúm, grab what you need out of your van and park it some place safe. When you're ready to go back to Tulúm,

I'll make sure you have a ride, so don't worry about that. Just make sure your van is parked safely, and don't forget your scuba stuff."

"All I need, Gasp, is right here with me," Hanuman assured his host. "When we pass through Tulúm, I'll move my van to a friend's house for safekeeping, no *problema*," Hanuman *Spanglished*.

Driving in the direction of Tulúm, their first stop would be Muyil. "We're now driving through the Municipality of Felipe Carrillo Puerto in the state of Quintana Roo," Roberto announced. "Artifacts found here date back from as early as 350 BC and to as late as 1200-1500 AD. The ruins of Muyil are an example of Peten architecture, like those found in southern Mayan sites with their steep walled pyramids similar to those found at Tikal in Guatemala. Muyil was also known by the Maya as Chunyaxché." Roberto told them. "It is one of the earliest and longest-inhabited ancient Maya sites on the eastern coast of Yucatán," he told them as he headed into the deserted parking lot.

Jumping out of the car along with his three interested passengers, Gaspar handed Roberto Peugeot's leash with Peugeot attached as the bemused guide continued his introduction to the site. "As you can see, gentlemen and *perito*" he addressed Peugeot directly, "Muyil is situated on the Sian Ka'an lagoon, a Maya name meaning 'where the sky is born'."

"Was this another Maya trading post?" Alex inquired.

"Yes indeed, Alex. Muyil was located along a trade route once accessible via a series of canals. Among the most commonly traded goods were jade, obsidian, chocolate, honey, feathers, chewing gum and salt. It is believed that throughout much of its history, Muyil had strong ties to the center of Cobá, located twenty-seven miles to the northeast."

Their visit to Muyil was short and uneventful and they were soon back in the car heading for Tulúm. Arriving at their destination they found Hanuman's van and followed him to his friend's house in town where he left his worn-out old wreck for safekeeping. The only thing Hanuman took from the van was a backpack, which he threw into the back of the SUV without ceremony. Buckled in, with Peugeot and Gaspar riding shotgun and Alex and Han spread out in back, Roberto took off, heading the car towards Labna, the second stop on the way to Celestún.

A week later ... after swimming in every cenote along the way, climbing the pyramids at Labna, camping out under the stars in Xlapak, bird watching at Sayil and joining in a local soccer match at Kabah, the young explorers finally reached Uxmal, one of the jewels of the Yucatán archaeological sites. Having taken Hanuman's philosophy of enjoying their vacation time to the fullest, the boys were feeling completely satiated from the spicy local food they'd been eating, and by their exposure to the clean, fresh air they were breathing while the brilliant Mexican sun turned their bodies nut brown. Roberto was a good sport and played along with their cross-country new age safari as if it were his idea from the beginning. Although he kept mostly to himself when Gaspar, Peugeot, Alex and Hanuman were hanging out with the new-found free-and-easy friends that they'd met along the way, Roberto seemed to be having a good time watching over the teenaged Americano's enthusiastic *Mayan Magical Mystery Tour*.

Arriving at Uxmal, they set out to see the highlights of the site, Gaspar insisting that Roberto stay close by with Peugeot in tow, so that he could pass on his special knowledge along the way. The first words out of Gaspar's mouth when he saw the place were, "we need to bring mom and Peter back here to see this, guys. Roberto, why have you saved the best for last?"

"What can I say," stuttered Roberto. "Uxmal (he pronounced it *Óoxmáal)* is an ancient Maya city of the classical period."

"What does Uxmal mean, Roberto?" Alex asked.

"The name derives from *Oxmal* meaning three times built, referring to a legend that tells how the city had to be rebuilt three times. Archaeologists have found no proof to this legend, so it's anyone's guess what Uxmal really stands for." Roberto laughed, before continuing. "Since the etymology of the name Uxmal is now disputed, another suggested possibility is *Uchmal*, which in Maya means what is to come or the future. There is also an overlapping legend which says that Uxmal is supposed to be an invisible city, built in one night through the magic of the *Maya dwarf king*," Roberto finished with a fairy tale."

"Well, so much for the science of archaeology." Gaspar laughed.

"That's quite a legend, Roberto," Hanuman applauded. "I for one believe that it was created in one night by the Maya dwarf king and refuse to believe any other explanation."

"I believe in the Maya dwarf king!" shouted Gaspar.

"And I believe in the Maya dwarf king, too," seconded Alex.

"I think you are the Maya dwarf king, Gaspar." Hanuman ribbed his host.

"All hail the Maya dwarf king," Alex proclaimed, laughing hysterically as Gaspar took a royal bow and Peugeot barked loudly, seconding the motion.

After the boys and the pup had quieted down … Roberto couldn't help reverting to his role as professor emeritus of all things Maya. "You will soon see that Uxmal is one of the most important archaeological sites of Maya culture, along with those of Xunantunich, Chichén Itzá and Tikal. This is called the Puuc region, and Uxmal is considered one of the Maya cities most representative of this region's dominant architectural style. We are only sixty-two kilometers south of Mérida, and not too far from Celestún, so if we want to come back with Mr. and Mrs. Cawthorne and your parents Alex, that will be easy." Roberto assured them. "The buildings here are noteworthy for their size and decoration. As you have seen before there are also dozens of sacbés linking Uxmal with other cities in the area such as Chichén Itzá, and some of them reach as far away as Xunantunich in Belize and Tikal in Guatemala."

"That's amazing," Alex breathed, looking around the extraordinary site.

"The buildings here are typical of the Puuc style with smooth low walls, decorated with ornate friezes based on representations of typical Maya huts. You'll also see carvings of entwined two-headed snakes, and many masks of the rain god Chaac. If you look closely, you'll see that Maya feathered serpents with alarmingly sinister looking fangs are carved everywhere. Alex, I think you will appreciate me pointing out some of the decorative influences of Nahua origin, pertaining to the cult of Quetzalcoatl and Tlaloc that were integrated here with the traditional Puuc architecture."

"I'd like that very much, Roberto. What say you, Gasp?" Alex asked.

"Lead on, Roberto," Gaspar commanded. "And don't leave any stone unturned."

"This is the Pyramid of the Magician," Roberto announced, standing in front of a monumental con-struction in an amazing state of repair. "Notice how this structure, like so many others here at Uxmal, has taken advantage of the natural terrain to gain height, thereby acquiring important volume. The Pyramid of the Magician, as you can see, is a stepped pyramid, however it is unusual among Maya structures in that its outlines are oval or elliptical in shape instead of the more common rectilinear plan. You can tell the difference between these buildings and others we've seen on our previous visits to Maya sites. As I've told you before, it was a common practice in Mesoamerica to build new temple pyramids atop older ones. Here you can see that a newer pyramid was built on top of an older one but centered slightly to the east, so that on the west side the old pyramid has been preserved, with the newer temple standing above it."

"Check it out, Gasp," Alex insisted, "Pretty cool, huh?"

"Notice," Roberto continued, "the western staircase of the pyramid is situated so that it faces the setting sun of the summer solstice.

"Come on you guys, let's climb it." Gaspar yelled, starting to climb on all fours, while his pals scurried behind him and Peugeot took the lead, dragging his leash behind him.

When they reached the top, Hanuman took in the view over Uxmal and exclaimed, "I can't believe this place, you guys. If I hadn't met you on the beach … I may never have experienced this, and to have an archaeologist like Roberto as our guide makes it even more interesting. Gasp, I can't thank you enough, dude. This is amazing!"

"You're very welcome, Han. We're just as happy

having you along with us, so the feeling's mutual.

"Yes," Roberto chimed in, "and thank you for your compliment about the archaeologist part. I was a professional archaeologist when I got out of school, but those days are long behind me. Now it is my pleasure to be an archaeological tour guide and with clients like you guys, I couldn't ask for anything more." Roberto informed them. "Would you like to hear a little bit more about the pile of rocks we're standing on?" he asked, before continuing.

"Carry on," Gaspar implored as he took a seat on the stone platform to take in the view while putting an arm around Peugeot's neck, pulling the seated dog closer to him.

"As I've already told you, this structure features in one of the best-known tales of Yucatec Maya folklore called, *El Enano del Uxmal* or *The Dwarf of Uxmal*, which is also the basis for the structure's common name, *The Pyramid of the Magician*. Multiple versions of this tale are recorded, and the story was further popularized by John Lloyd Stephens in his influential 1841 book, *Incidents of Travel in Central America, Chiapas, and Yucatán*. In the version told to Stephens in 1840, the pyramid was magically built overnight during a series of challenges issued to a dwarf by the King of Uxmal, as part of a competing trial of strength and magic. As the story goes, the king lost due to the magical orchestrations of the dwarf's mother who was a bruja … you know … a witch."

"Magic, that's what this place is, magic." Gaspar

evoked Roberto's words under his breath in a stage whisper into Peugeot's cocked ear.

"I love that tale, Roberto." Alex told the guide.

"Yeah, man, I like how the dwarf's mother orchestrated the competition to make her son the king by building a huge pyramid, using magic instead of union labor." Hanuman approved.

"What else should we be looking at from this vantage point, Roberto?" Gaspar asked, standing up to look around some more, while Peugeot stood up to mimic his master's every move.

"The Governor's Palace is over there," Roberto said pointing north, "it covers an area of more than 1200 square meters. I suggest we climb down and head over to those buildings." He pointed to another group nearby. "Those are called *The Nunnery Quadrangle*." Roberto told them as he started his descent.

Reaching the Nunnery Quadrangle, Roberto explained that the buildings really comprised a government palace with stunning horizontal architectural emphasis and mosaic-like decorations. Standing in the courtyard they admired the east building of the quadrangle, which was backed by the very vertical pyramid which they had just climbed down, right behind it. Nothing Roberto told them had prepared them for the magnificence of the grand pyramid at Uxmal. Set in a deep courtyard, a thousand steps rose heavenward in front of them. Although the pyramid was only partially excavated on one side, with the other three sides still completely covered with dirt and jungle, the structure took the boys' collective breaths away. Another amazing ruin that Gaspar decided was one of his favorites, even though it only consisted of one, very falling-down wall, was the one Roberto told them was called *The House of the Doves*.

"How long after the Spanish conquest did Uxmal survive, Roberto?" Gaspar questioned, while standing in front of The House of the Doves.

"It's interesting you should ask because the people here, the Xiu, allied themselves with the Spanish and helped them conquer their neighbors. Early colonial documents suggest that Uxmal was still an inhabited place of some importance as late as the 1550s, but no Spanish town was ever built here, and Uxmal was later largely abandoned." Roberto exclaimed.

"Wow, traitors to their own people," Alex exhaled. "Maybe because they sided with the Spanish. That's why the place is still in such good condition?"

"You have something there, Alejandro. Even before the twentieth century restoration work began, Uxmal was in better condition than many other Maya sites. It may be due to their alliance with the Spanish, but I think you can tell that this city was also unusually well-built. Notice all the well-cut stones set into a core of concrete and how they didn't rely on plaster to hold the buildings together, like we've seen elsewhere. The Maya architecture here is matched only by that of Palenque in elegance and beauty," Roberto gushed.

"I can see how the Puuc style of Maya architecture really predominates here," Alex extrapolated. "And thanks to its good state of preservation, it's one of the few Maya cities where people like us can get a good idea of how the entire ceremonial center really looked in ancient times," he enthused.

Before leaving Uxmal they explored The Governor's Palace, a long low building atop a huge platform, sporting one of the longest façades in pre-Columbian Mesoamerica. They also saw a large ballcourt where Hanuman told Alex and Gaspar that the Maya used human heads instead of soccer balls in their athletic competitions. Roberto deciphered an inscription in the ballcourt informing them that the stadium was dedicated by the ruler Chan Chak K'ak'nal Ajaw. Roberto also told them that before the decipherment of his corresponding name glyphs, Chan Chak K'ak'nal Ajaw had only been known by archaeologists and scholars as 'Lord Chac'.

"I'm glad they cleared that little bit of misinformation up," Hanuman joked, before they moved on to the next group of monuments which included The House of the Turtles and The South Temple as well as a number of other temple-pyramids, quadrangles, and monuments of significant size and varying states of preservation. Along with the buildings, the group studied a series of stone stelae which had been unusually grouped together on a single platform. The hieroglyphic inscriptions on the stelae depicted the ancient rulers of the city. Mysteriously all the stelae showed signs that they had been deliberately broken or toppled in antiquity. Roberto told them that they had been re-erected and repaired in the twentieth century. He also showed them evidence of a possible war or battle found in the remains of a wall which encircled most of the ceremonial center.

"Uxmal was interconnected with all the great cities of the Yucatan. See that large raised sacbé over there," Roberto pointed, " it links Uxmal with Kabah which is about eighteen kilometers south of here. Even though we're inland, Uxmal even had a port."

"Wha-da-ya mean, Roberto?" Alex was asked quizzically.

"The island of Uaymil is just to the west of here on the gulf coast. Uaymil was the official port for Uxmal providing the people access to the Maya's extensive circum-peninsular trade network."

"Roberto, you keep showing us over and over again, how the Maya were one of the most advanced civilizations on earth," Gaspar piped up. "And now you've proved it again. As a civilization, the Maya are mind-boggling."

"And not just in ancient times, Gaspar. Uxmal has had an interesting history in modern times as well. Because it is located near Mérida along the road to Campeche, Uxmal was not hard to get to and has attracted many visitors since the time of Mexico's independence. Jean Frederic Waldeck published the first account of the ruins in 1838. John Lloyd Stephens and Frederick Catherwood made two extended visits to Uxmal in the early 1840s. Catherwood was an architect/draftsman who reportedly made so many plans and drawings that they could have been used to construct a duplicate of this ancient city. Unfortunately, nobody knows how or why, since the turn of the century most of Catherwood's drawings of Uxmal have been lost."

"Sounds like you'll have to pick up the slack where Catherwood left off, Al," Gaspar kidded his pal, the budding young architect who throughout this trip was always sketch book in hand, drawing everything he saw.

Désiré Charnay took a series of photographs of Uxmal in 1860 which inspired Empress Carlota of Mexico to visited Uxmal in 1863. In preparation for Empress Carlota's visit, in an attempt to protect her sense of Victorian decency, the local authorities had all statues and architectural elements depicting phallic themes removed from the ancient façades.

"People were such prudes back in the 1860s?" Hanuman shook his head sadly.

"Back to square one," Alex complained. "More architectural elements depicting phallic themes."

"Come on, Al. We all thought the Phallic Temple back at Chichén was your favorite monument," Gaspar giggled.

"I hope you're not joking," Hanuman chimed in.

"I can see that Uxmal is also where Frank Lloyd Wright got a lot of inspiration for his concrete block architecture," Alex spoke up proudly.

"You're quite right, Alex," Roberto complimented him. "Although I'm not sure Wright ever visited Uxmal, he was certainly influenced by the Maya. Someone famous who did visit here a little more recently was Queen Elizabeth II of the United Kingdom. She was here in 1975 for the inauguration of the site's sound and light show. When the presentation reached the point where the sound system played the ancient prayer to Chaac, the Maya rain deity, a sudden torrential downpour fell upon the gathered dignitaries despite the fact that it was the middle of the dry season. One of the dignitaries present that evening was my friend, Gaspar Antonio Xiu, descendant of the noble Maya lineage, of the Xiu."

"Hey, Gasp, maybe we should call you Gaspar Xiu, and pawn you off as Maya nobility, since you're such an important land-owner down here?" Alex joked.

"Very funny, Al and not a bad idea, if ya don't mind my sayin' so," Gaspar laughed while Peugeot barked approvingly.

CHAPTER 18

THE DOCTOR'S HOUSE REDUX

THAT EVENING, AFTER SEEING THE AMAZING SOUND AND LIGHT SHOW AT UXMAL, THE TRAVELERS CAMPED OUT under the stars, leaving the next morning for Celestún with a stop along the way at Okintock, a small site full of interest where it took less than an hour to comprehensivly tour the ruins. Gaspar was pleased that they didn't linger at Okintock as he was anxious to get back to Hacienda Huayrocondo. When they finally reached The Doctor's House, Felix and Angela were waiting for them with expectation. Alex was the first to sprint from the SUV and throw his arms around his parents, who were more than happy to see him safe and sound and home again. Gaspar followed up the rear, running up to Felix and Angela to give them each a big abrazo, while

Peugeot ran happy circles around the group, barking his own greetings, happy to be back at The Doctor's House.

"This is Hanuman," Gaspar introduced the new member of their group. "Hanuman, these are Alex's parents, Felix and Angela."

"I'm very pleased to meet you," Hanuman shook the parents' hands. "Alex and Gaspar have told me so much about you."

"You remember our guide, Roberto," Gaspar re-introduced his other pal. Roberto stepped forward and joined in the homecoming, shaking Felix's hand and bowing slightly from the waist towards Angela.

"Okay, guys. Let's see the house!" Gaspar demanded; his voice full of excitement. "Come on, Peugeot, I can't wait to see the transformation!

Felix and Angela stepped aside deferentially to let Gaspar and Peugeot lead the way. Gaspar could already see just by the exterior of the house, that a lot of changes had taken place. The entire structure had been given a fresh coat of whitewash over its old adobe walls and the windowpanes had been meticulously scrubbed clean. The windows' wooden mullions and frames had been given a fresh coat of sap green paint, which the designers washed with an ochre glaze to make them look even older than they actually were.

Once through the front door, Gaspar stopped short in sheer amazement and so did Mr. Peugeot. The old terracotta tiled floors were not only spotlessly clean but shining with several coats of polished wax. The cracked and stained walls and ceilings had been given a clean, bright coat of white paint and the old ceiling beams had been stained and varnished a deep walnut. Gaspar was especially happy that his clever decorators had stenciled geometric black and white designs around the doors and windows in a Spanish colonial motif in keeping with the age and character of the house. Gaspar was thrilled to see that the antique seventeenth-century furniture was for the most part exactly where the doctor had placed it so many years ago. The antiques now glowed within an inch of their lives, having been rubbed with beeswax by caring hands. The broken-down upholstered pieces had been thrown out and replaced with new, comfortable and stylistically appropriate slipcovered sofas and club chairs that looked like they had always been there.

Peugeot especially liked the black and white cow-hides that the decorators had scattered here and there over the polished tile floors. The puppy soon spread out on one and rolled back and forth over the coarse cow hide with pleasure.

Gaspar realized that a team of electricians must have been called in to rewire the house, as good-looking table lamps with white linen shades, wrought iron wall sconces and iron chandeliers were now blazing soft light throughout the room.

"So far so good," Gaspar beamed. "Did the work go smoothly, Felix? Did the decorators run into any trouble or was there a minimum of drama?"

"Oh, señor, it was like an invasion by conquistadors around here," Felix bemoaned. "They arrived like a plague of locusts, four decorator assistants and ten workmen. They were very polite to us, but barely spoke. They just took over, like robots. It was amazing and educational," the simple man threw in, shaking his head disbelievingly at the memory.

"Every day was a revelation, Gaspar," Angela sang. "I loved watching them work. They even allowed me to help, and sometimes asked my opinion, which was genuinely nice. Wait until you see the bedrooms and the courtyards!" she trilled.

"Lead on, Angela," Gaspar commanded, as the group trooped off as one to see the rest of the renovations.

The library was a wonder, all shipshape and ready to be enjoyed. The bookshelves had been washed with a sap green glaze, and a deep green rag rug covered the polished tile floor. All of the dark, Spanish colonial furniture now glowed with beeswax and the tabletops held artistically placed photographs, pre-Columbian artifacts under glass and other decorative pieces, while the walls retained their old framed maps. The doctor's books, which Uncle Charlie had removed to La Rinconada decades ago, had been replaced with equally interesting if slightly fewer precious volumes interspersed with interesting native Mexican decorations. Surveying the titles, Gaspar saw a section on Mexico, Maya, Aztec,

Inca, as well as a section on Spanish colonial architecture, geography, biographies and other shelves stacked with novels and murder mysteries.

"A good well-rounded collection of books," Gaspar approved out loud, making a mental note to congratulate Margaret Stewart, his librarian back at La Rinconada, on her excellent choices especially where the leather bindings were concerned. While Gaspar glanced along the shelves, Peugeot stood up on his hind legs, mimicking his master perusing the volumes.

The dining room looked just like it was supposed to as far as Gaspar was concerned. The antique trestle table was set with old pewter candlesticks centered by a ceramic Mexican bowl full of red roses. The white walls were adorned with the same paintings that the doctor had placed there, but now they glowed, having been cleaned and revarnished. He especially approved of the deep red velvet draperies hanging from the original wrought iron rods and rings, and that the tile floor had been left bare, just like the doctor had liked it.

"Let's check out the kitchen, lady and gents," Gaspar suggested. "Come on, Peugeot."

"Oh, Gaspar, the kitchen. Even Elvira will approve, wait and see," Angela predicted.

Walking through the swinging door from the dining room, they first entered a newly configured butler's pantry with shiny white ceramic tiled floors and attractive new white painted cabinetry. Gaspar appreciated that the tiled counters and backsplashes were all done in traditional blue, white and yellow glazed Mexican tiles.

The next swinging door took them into the kitchen proper, which had been completely transformed into a gleaming white operating room from floor to ceiling with countertops and backsplashes in the same traditional tiles as in the butler's pantry. New stainless-steel appliances had replaced the non-existent ones that the doctor had never enjoyed way back when. More importantly, the previous staff, Juano and Carmen were present, dressed in pristine embroidered Mexican finery, ready to serve.

"Juano, Carmen, what a transformation!" Gaspar greeted his staff.

"Bienvenidos, Señor Gaspar," Juano greeted his teenage boss enthusiastically.

Then in her charmingly accented English, Carmen introduced Gaspar to the rest of the newly acquired staff. "This is Rosario, Isabel, Julia y Manuel. Julia is our cook. Isabel and Rosario are the housemaids and serving girls, and Manuel helps Juano with the gardens and maintenance.

"I am pleased to meet you all." Then to Angela, Gaspar commanded, "to the courtyards, Angela."

Stepping outside, he couldn't believe his eyes as they traveled from courtyard to courtyard, five in all including the connected stable yard. Each of these spaces had been transformed with splashing fountains, potted geraniums, trailing bougainvillea, wisteria, and honeysuckle vines.

Groups of iron furniture with cushions made of rough but colorful native cloth had been placed here and there, under large white canvas umbrellas. Electric lanterns had been installed on the walls, and others holding candles were scattered around the area as well. Each of these elegant courtyards was surrounded on four sides by bedrooms. One by one the group checked out the new sleeping arrangements. The decorators had created two master suites, one for Peter and Elvira with five guest bedrooms for their friends, and one for Gaspar with five guest bedrooms for his friends.

Elvira and Peter's bedroom was huge and included a sitting area with views out to the beach and the Gulf of Mexico. Their en suite dressing rooms and bathrooms were all that Gaspar could have asked for ... clean, simple and efficient. Peter's dressing room was all white plaster with dark wood cabinets. His bathroom had been painted sky blue against dark wood cabinets and ceiling beams with a scattering of blue and white Mexican tiles for pattern, white rag rugs and blue and white towels. Elvira's dressing room had whitewashed walls and cabinetry against red tiled floors and dark ceiling beams. Her bathroom was pale pink painted plaster with pretty painted garlands of Mexican dahlia pinnata flowers scrolling around the doors, windows and tub. Pretty pink towels and rag rugs completed the look. The accompanying five guest bedrooms attached to the master's serene courtyard were each decorated individually. The recurring theme in each of these were whitewashed walls, colorful Mexican tiles and dark beams. Each of these commodious suites was identifiable by their predominant colorings. One being predominantly white, one yellow, one green, one blue, and the last one done in shades of pink, all with impeccably appointed private baths. What Gaspar was inspecting today was a far cry from the ramshackle accommodations he'd left behind only a month ago.

Moving on to the accommodations that the decorators had set aside for Gaspar and his friends, the first room he saw was his own. Like Elvira and Peter's suite, Gaspar's was also on the beach, facing the Gulf of Mexico. A big old Spanish canopy bed filled the room, draped in red plush. The contrast between the dark wood, whitewashed walls and the ecclesiastical red plush pleased Gaspar's *inner Spanish grandee*. His dressing room and bath were enormous, again mostly whitewash, dark wood, and touches of deep red.

"Perfect," was his satisfied pronouncement, as Peugeot sprang up onto the bed and lazed happily against the pillows.

Next came the five guest suites. These were younger and slightly more masculine versions of the guest rooms they'd seen in Elvira and Peter's courtyard. Here the decorators had used bold stripes, checks and solid colors in bright shades along with nubby fabrics and rag rugs. Like in Gaspar's room, they used an almost minimal monastic arrangement of good solid but comfortable furniture. Gaspar approved of the decorators' choices as well as their arrangements. Of these five guest rooms, three had one large king size bed each, and the other two had two double beds each. The arrangements suited Gaspar's plans to a tee.

"Choose your poison, Alex. Which room shall be yours?" Gaspar asked his friend.

"I'll take the one with the big bed next to your sitting room, if that's okay," Alex was quick with his choice.

"My thoughts entirely, maybe we should put a door through to the sitting room so we can talk all night," Gaspar suggested.

"Good idea, Gasp," Alex concurred.

"What about you, Han? Which room appeals to you?"

"I'll take one of the monk's cells, the other one with the big bed if you don't mind. I can't tell you how long it's been since I've been able to spread out my entire six-foot-two body on one bed at the same time," he joked.

"Perfect, that suite is yours," Gaspar proclaimed. "We'll call it, The Hanuman suite. Remind me to call the decorators and tell them to send over some *monkey stuff* to brighten the place up, Al."

"Roberto, which one do you like?" Gaspar asked the driver inclusively.

"That one will be fine, señor," Roberto said, pointing to the green and blue striped room.

"Perfect," Gaspar agreed. That settles our

accommodations for the time being. Now let's see the next courtyard, Angela," Gaspar suggested, moving forward, Peugeot prancing along after him.

The next courtyard held the staff quarters. The decorators had arranged four compact apartments with two bedrooms, a sitting room, bathroom, and a kitchenette each. One was set up for men, and one was set up for women. Another was set up for Angela and Felix, and the other for Juano and Carmen. All of them were bright, white and comfortably furnished.

"Well, that was quite a tour and a real revelation. Thank you, Angela for being our guide. Now tell me, is everything working exactly right? The electrical, the plumbing, the roof. What about heat and air conditioning, did they do that too?" Gaspar needed to know.

"Gaspar, they did everything. Come with me to the stable yard. They even bought six Palomino horses and a new SUV for you. Look," Angela insisted, pointing to the stables, each with a pretty horse's head sticking out, nodding equestrian greetings, while a shiny new car sparkled in the stall across from them.

"Do we have grooms, too?" Gaspar asked, hoping that the decorators hadn't forgotten to supply them.

"Of course, señor," Angela smiled. "*Paco, Chico, Flaco, ven a conocer a su jefe*," she called in Spanish over the stable yard.

Heeding Angela's call, three Mexican lads not much older than Gaspar and Alex came running at a clip from their quarters at the end of the courtyard.

"These are your grooms, señor," Angela told Gaspar proudly before introducing the three grooms who wore jeans, crisp white shirts and blue and white bandannas tied at their throats. "This imp is Paco, this cowboy is Chico, and this roustabout is Flaco," she beamed, introducing each of the lads to their boss.

"Con mucho gusto, Señor Gaspar," the three boys hailed their young employer in unison.

"Con mucho gusto," Gaspar smiled back. Then in his best *Spanglish* he addressed them as a team. "Este tarde, cuando llo acavo almuerzo, nosotros quieren … ummm … caminar en caballo, para ver la hacienda … ummm … . hasta alla," he said pointing towards the towering mountain, "vamanos juntos." He finished not sure at all if they had understood his gringo-accented attempt at Spanish but they all nodded with huge idiotic smiles pasted on their happy faces, so he figured one way or another, if they were lucky, they'd all get a horse ride to the top of the mountain that afternoon.

"Gaspar, you just said, 'this afternoon, when lunch acava, we quieren, ummm walk horse, to see the finance … up there'," Alex laughed.

"Yeah, well, they seemed to have gotten the message," Gaspar laughed. "Okay," Gaspar exhaled, dismissing the three grooms with a smile and a wave. "How about lunch, Angela? Let's say in an hour. That will give us guys time to move in, take a swim in the gulf and put on our riding duds. Wha-da-ya say, fellas? Does that sound like a plan to you? I'll meet you on the beach in twenty minutes." Gaspar called across the courtyard before closing his door. Alone at last, he tore off his grimy five-day-old clothes and threw himself onto the bed which was soft and wonderfully comfortable. Happy in his new environment, Gaspar rolled around on top of the comforter, and dug his face into the luxurious down pillows. Finally getting up, he went into the bathroom and ran the water in the tub. Instantly, clean, clear hot water spilled out of the spout. *Not bad*, Gaspar thought, *all the comforts of home*. While he waited for the tub to fill, he grabbed his phone and called Los Angeles. He wanted to tell his decorators exactly what he thought of them. Reaching an answering machine, he left a long-detailed message telling them exactly how he felt, and how really pleased he was with everything he saw. Pressing *end* on his phone, he smiled wondering what Peter's reaction would be when the bill arrives. He next called Brewster in Peter's office … to talk business. Brewster picked up on the first ring.

"Brew, it's Gasp. I'm back at The Doctor's House in Celestún. Mom and Peter are on *Floridablanca* headed to Tierra del Fuego … I hope! Alex and I came back here and let me tell you, the house is amazing. Did you get the bill from The Duquette Studios in L.A. yet? They even bought me six palominos and an SUV, and I'm not even old enough to drive. Those guys are too much, the absolute best! So wha-da-ya say?" he asked, as he slipped into the steaming tub.

"Gasp, the bill is for a million five hundred thousand!" Brewster choked on his words. "And their fee is an additional four hundred and fifty thousand. That's almost two million dollars!"

"Brew, how much have you paid them already?"

"We gave them seven hundred and fifty thousand as a deposit."

"Brew, pay them the balance, and send them an additional fifty thousand *love money*, you know … like a tip. Then get on a plane and get down here. You gotta see this place. It's amazing and cheap, at twice the price."

"But, Gaspar, wait a minute. You can't pay them more than they want!" Brewster protested.

"Brew, hasn't Peter ever given you a bonus for *job well done*?" Gaspar asked him. "Well, this is one of those. If you could have seen this uninhabitable ruin when we got here and what it looks like now, you'd understand. Write a fifty-thousand-dollar check and bring it with you. I'll write a personal thank you note, and we can overnight it from here to L.A. Now *don't* argue with me, and bring your brother, Scott. We don't have a tennis court here yet, but there's plenty of room to build one if we want, and a pool too, so it will be good to get Scott's opinion as to where we should build them and besides, we'll have a lot of fun together down here too.

"Gaspar, cool it with the spending, buddy. Hold off

on everything until I get there," Brewster implored.

"I don't understand, Brew. What's the problem? Am I having financial difficulties?" Gaspar asked facetiously.

"No, but … "

Gaspar cut him off, not waiting for any further argument. "See you later, Brew," he pushed *end*.

CHAPTER 19

THE DOCTOR'S SECRET

Gaspar skipped the swim before lunch and luxuriated in his deep tub, while Peugeot snored softly on the bed. While he'd been on the phone with Brewster, Manuel had deposited his bags in his room. Stepping out of the tub, he dried himself and then rummaged through the duffel bags looking for some appropriate riding duds. He settled on a clean pair of jeans, a blue T-shirt and a long-sleeved red checked shirt. He rolled up the sleeves and tied a red bandanna around his throat. In the hall he found a great old sombrero, part of a collection that the decorators had found somewhere and used to decorate the doctor's hat stand. "Come on, Peugeot, let's go," he commanded his best friend to follow.

Searching around, they found their pals, similarly dressed in jeans, waiting on the terrace next to the beach

271

where Angela and her gang had set up a festive lunch table in the shade of the palm trees.

"I hope you and Felix are going to join us for lunch, Angela." Gaspar insisted.

"Thank you, Gaspar, we would love to join you." Angela smiled.

"Felix, I hope you'll join us after lunch for a gallop to the top of the mountain," Gaspar enticed his trusted caretaker.

"I would like that very much," Felix beamed having been invited to join in the fun.

"I also have some news to tell you … Brewster and his brother Scott are on their way here. They should get in sometime tomorrow. So, Angela, after lunch, do me a favor and tell the staff to expect two more guys to stay … we'll put them in the beige and brown room," he told her without a second thought.

"It will be like a family reunion to have the Wharton boys here." Angela sang happily.

Roberto, these guys are great friends, Brewster works for Peter, and his brother is my tennis pro. It would be great if you could pick them up at the airport tomorrow and bring them here. I'll let you know what time as soon as I find out."

"Para server te, Señor Gaspar." Roberto replied elegantly.

Lunch was a merry affair, with nothing but compliments for Julia's cooking. The Mexican lady's albondigas soup, arroz con pollo, grilled vegetables and sweet corn with drawn butter was about the best meal they'd had since leaving Florida. Also included in Julia's hearty repast were homemade corn tortillas, refried beans and a piquant salad too, not to mention a dessert of fresh mangoes over vanilla ice cream with powdered coffee sprinkled on top, a new taste sensation for Gaspar and his assembled friends.

"Julia is a wonder, Angela. We sure are lucky to have her in the kitchen. I might even learn to like coffee if it's gonna taste like this," Gaspar laughed, taking another heaping spoonful of his rich dessert.

"Don't eat too much, patron," Felix warned Gaspar. "You don't want it coming back up during the horse ride."

"So, Felix, which one of the grooms will we be taking with us on this adventure?" Gaspar asked.

"Chico, señor. He knows the area and will take good care of us," Felix pronounced without hesitation.

"Then, Chico it is," Gaspar announced. "Let's get going, guys."

Together the riders with Peugeot leading the pack, quick-stepped to the stable yard. When they got there, they found all six palominos saddled and ready for action, with the three grooms each holding two of the steeds by their bridles.

"What are the horses' names?" Gaspar asked Chico.

"You must tell us, señor. They are *your* horses." Chico answered logically.

"Oh, okay." Gaspar agreed. "Well … let's see … I

think the best way to do this is for each of us to choose our favorites. Then we'll work out the names from there. Which horse do you think would be the best for me, Chico?"

"This should be your horse, patron. He is the most beautiful, the strongest, the most intelligent. This should be your horse!" Chico declared again with more emphasis, handing Gaspar the reigns to the most handsome of the six steeds.

"Perfect, my thoughts entirely. I'll call him *Hippocrates*, in honor of Doctor Mendoza y Mendoza." Gaspar proclaimed, grabbing the reins and climbing onto the saddle. "Al, you choose next."

"Choose this one, Señor Alejandro. She is a good horse, gentle, but heroic. A very brave horse, señor," Chico insisted.

"Very well," Alex agreed. "If she is so brave and heroic, then I shall call her *Hero*, after the Greek," Alex proclaimed taking the reins in his hands.

"For you, señor Felix, may I suggest this steed. This horse, he has stature," Chico assured Felix.

"Then I shall call him, *Nobles*," Felix told them, pronouncing it *No-Bless* as he climbed on.

"This looks like a good steady horse for me," Hanuman decided without any prompting, taking the reins from Flaco's hand. My horse shall be called *Ajit* which means invincible in Hindi. He shall become a legend in these parts."

"Roberto took the reins from the horse that Paco was still holding and said, "this looks like a good ride. I shall call him *Chac*, after the benevolent Maya god."

"And my horse, she shall be called *Chiquita*," Chico said grinning, as he jumped up into the saddle.

"What a stable," Gaspar enthused. "Al, remind me to get signs for each of the stalls, and by the way, something tells me we're gonna need a brand too. Al, maybe you could design us a brand for this place. The hacienda has a name, *Huayrocondo*. That's what the harbor master told me it was called the day we arrived. Now that we've got horses, its gotta have a brand!" Gaspar insisted.

With Peugeot trotting by their sides, the group rode in a pack across the dirt road in front of the house, and through the big gates that pierced the wall surrounding the huge hacienda. Gaspar had been told, as far as the locals were concerned, that his land, '*had no boundaries*'.

"When we arrived here, the harbor master told us that the doctor owned not only the house, but the biggest hacienda in the area, which is situated all around the *Pico de Huayrocondo*. That's the name of the mountain top." Gaspar informed the assembled horsemen. "He also told us that the hacienda was a land grant from the King of Spain to a conquistador ancestor of Doctor Mendoza y Mendoza. The name of the original owner was El Capitan Ignacio de Mendoza y Mendoza, who was not only a conquistador but also the Perpetual Governor of Yucatán. The harbor master also said that the land grant is so vast that no white man has ever crossed it from one end to the other. Apparently it's bordered by two rivers which run on each side of the Pico de Huayrocondo, but the legend around here is that the hacienda has no boundaries and that it extends all the way to Chichén Itzá or possibly even the Caribbean Sea!" Gaspar relayed the story that they'd been told on arrival several weeks ago to Alex, Felix, Hanuman and Roberto.

"What do you think you'll find here, Gasp?" Alex asked.

"I really don't know. I guess I'm wondering if there is an old colonial house or the remains of an old colonial house somewhere else on the property. I don't think that the beach house, The Doctor's House, would have been the main house on a property as large as this. Somehow it doesn't seem right.

"It certainly is a grand house," Hanuman complimented his host.

"Yes, but don't you think, if you were a conquistador and the King of Spain gave you this property and made you the governor of the province, that you'd have something a little better fortified than a house on the beach, exposed on all sides not only to the elements but to the unruly natives as well." Gaspar put his thoughts into words.

"I see what you mean, Gaspar," Roberto joined the dialogue. "I think you have something there. Like you say, it doesn't make sense."

"But there aren't any other structures anywhere else," Alex lamented. "Just look around guys, nothing, not even a rock pile, just the mountain and this gently sloping earth."

"Do you think it was a cattle or sheep ranch?" Gaspar asked. "What would have been the traditional crop or use for such a property by a colonial? Why would he have wanted this land if it didn't have some economic significance?" Gaspar asked himself and the others.

"Well, let's think this through," Hanuman said, as he rode alongside Gaspar. "We know from what we've seen on our trip that he could have grown corn. He did have the water from the two rivers, which is really rare in Yucatán. He may even have been considered rich, just on that score."

"He couldn't have had cattle because the land is too arid, not enough grass to feed cattle," Roberto decided. "He could have had sheep. They like to eat scrub, but Yucatán hasn't a history of sheep farming."

"And yet he was rich," Gaspar pondered. "Of course, he could have been rich from collecting taxes for the king, or he could have been rich from leasing out farming plots to poor miserable mestizo farmers … "

"Or he could have been rich because he found oil, or silver or gold," Alex sang, as if in rapture.

"Yeah, but if he'd found gold, Doctor Mendoza y Mendoza would have known about it and told Uncle Charlie and Cousin Eugenia. If they had known anything like that, if this property had anything of value to offer, neither of them would have left it to rot, uncared for all these years."

"Why do you think they even kept the property, if they didn't like it or use it?" Hanuman asked.

"I've read my great-uncle Charlie's diaries," Gaspar lied, "and I can assure you they kept this place strictly for sentimental reasons. Uncle Charlie was rich, but it wasn't because he owned property in Yucatán. The rents in Florida are what kept him in clover. What I'm interested in is what kept the conquistador who founded this earldom in clover," Gaspar pondered the question with exasperation.

"Earldom, what's an earldom?" Alex asked.

"It's like a county. The man with the most land in the neighborhood was a count or an earl, if the King of Spain acknowledged them as such," Gaspar stated.

"I will ask my cousins if they know any legends about *Huayrocondo*," Felix opened his mouth for the first time since leaving the stables."

"That'll be great, Felix. I appreciate it," Gaspar assured him.

"How about we see how fast these babies can run," Hanuman suggested. "Let's race to the top of the mountain!"

"Taa-daa, da, dat, ta-da-dat, ta-da, dat, ta-da, daaa," Gaspar sang the traditional trumpet call for a horse race to begin … and they were off with Peugeot taking off after them, barking all the way.

Hanuman took the lead on Ajit, followed by Gaspar, then Chico, Roberto, and Felix. Soon Felix's Nobles had taken over Roberto's Chac while both Hanuman and Gaspar now trailed behind Alex with Hero in the lead. Faster and faster, higher and higher, and closer and closer to the base of the mountain, they raced. Scrambling upwards the horses vied for position as the pastures, house and seacoast diminished behind them. As they neared the top of the peak, Felix pushed Nobles ahead until he and Alex were neck and neck, while Gaspar on Hippocrates, regained second and Hanuman fell behind Chico and Chiquita, followed by Roberto who was too terrified to press Chac any further forward.

"The winner," Alex called, as his father reigned in Nobles at the top of the hill.

"Great race, Felix," Gaspar congratulated his care-taker. "What a close finish, Al."

"Yeah, I had no idea my dad was such a jock," Alex laughed, clasping his father on the shoulder as their horses panted under them.

Everyone had a good laugh, and jeered Roberto and Hanuman for coming in last. Finally settling down, they surveyed the land from on high.

"This is quite a vantage point," Gaspar marveled, looking out over his domain. It's kind-a hard to believe that I own … as far as the eye can see," he exclaimed dubiously.

"Let's follow around the peak and look out in every direction to see what the rest of the place has to offer," Alex suggested.

"Good idea, Al. Let's see how far we can ride today without running out of time," Gaspar decided. "Come on, Peugeot, you don't want to be left behind," he called to his panting hound.

The group of happy riders cantered their palominos over the rocky earth, following each other around the top of the Pico de Huayrocondo. They surveyed the land in all directions from the sea behind them, to the rivers far off in the distance on each side of them, to a spot way off on the horizon where Gaspar thought he saw the two rivers turn into one. Try as hard as they might, none of them could see any structures. There was nothing at all man made anywhere in the distance.

"Next time we come up here, I've gotta remember to bring some binoculars." Gaspar chided himself impatiently.

Having ridden around the entire peak and having discovered nothing of value or even a clue as to how the land may have been used four hundred years ago, they dismounted to stretch their legs and give their horses a breather. While the others stretched and walked around, Gaspar sat on a low rock with Peugeot at his side, sharing his canteen of water with the pooch while looking around. Just then Hippocrates decided to take a leak right in front of him and Peugeot, which wasn't exactly what they'd come up on top of the mountain to see. Lacking any other activity, he and Peugeot watched the horse pass water, as if mesmerized. It wasn't until Peugeot started barking that Gaspar came too and focused again on the scenery.

Later that night, after a hearty dinner in the dining room, Gaspar excused himself and turned in early. Lying in bed with Peugeot stretched out at his feet, he zoned out thinking back over the day's adventures ... the tour of the house, the lunch on the beach, the ride on the horses, and then it struck him. What was it about that horse peeing in front of him that he couldn't get out of his mind? The question kept coming back to him, repeatedly, until he finally fell asleep.

CHAPTER 20

BREWSTER TO THE RESCUE

T HE NEXT MORNING AFTER BREAKFAST, GASPAR JOINED
ALEX FOR A SWIM IN THE GULF AND THEN TOLD HIS
pal that he would be taking the morning off to do some
reading. Being such a close friend, Alex knew that *taking
the morning off to do some reading* was Gaspar's subtle way
of telling him and the world, that he wanted to be left
alone. Alex took the hint graciously and informed his
pal that he was going into town and would be back in
time for lunch.

After Alex left the house, Gaspar and Peugeot went
to the stables, where he ordered his horse Hippocrates
saddled up. "I'm taking him out for a ride," Gaspar
informed his groom Chico.

"Shall I saddle up Chiquita too, señor?" Chico asked
optimistically, hoping to accompany his master.

"Not today, Chico. I'm going to ride alone this morning."

"Si, señor," Chico replied, crestfallen. "Hippocrates will be ready en un minuto."

Before too much time had passed, Gaspar was in the saddle and on the other side of the road, passing through the main gates of the hacienda with Peugeot leading the way. Urging Hippocrates forward, he galloped up his sloping land to the top of the Pico de Huayrocondo. Dismounting behind the clump of scrub at the exact place where he'd seen his horse pee the day before, Gaspar undid his button fly jeans and took a whiz while Peugeot looked on, quizzically. Gaspar watched fascinated as his piss disappeared into the parched ground, as if it were going straight down a drain. "*Curiouser and curiouser,*" Gaspar whispered to Peugeot, channeling *Alice in Wonderland*, as he formulated a plan before getting back on his horse for the return ride back to the house.

"Come on, Peugeot, we don't want to be late for lunch," he urged the poodle to run along.

•••

In the best tradition of the Yucatán, Gaspar had taken to having a siesta after lunch. He'd sent Roberto to the airport in Mérida to pick up Brewster and Scott. It would be at least another hour before the Wharton brothers were scheduled to arrive, so Gaspar retired to his ecclesiastical cell with Peugeot for a lie down. When he closed the door and turned around, he found Uncle Charlie waiting for him.

"Gasp, I like the way you've taken to having a siesta." Uncle Charlie approved his nephew's newfound Mexican ways, as Peugeot acknowledged the old ghost's presence with a deep growl and several slightly friendlier barks.

"Peugeot, mind your manners … I'm glad you could drop by, uncle."

"Drop by, what are you talking about. I've been here the entire time. That was a great swim we had this morning, you, me and Alex, and that pony ride yesterday nearly did me in," the old ghost complained, rubbing his bum.

"Oh great, I wish you'd give me some kind of a sign. It's nice to know who you're traveling with, if you know what I mean," Gaspar cajoled the phantom. "By the way, if you don't mind my asking, who or what are you made up for today, uncle?"

"I'm channeling Pancho Villa, that old sidewinder," was Uncle Charlie's simple answer.

"Of course, you are." For some reason, Gaspar wasn't surprised. "Are those *bandoleros* really necessary?" Gaspar asked pointing to the rows and rows of bullets crisscrossing Uncle Charlie's chest. "Aren't they a little heavy considering the weather?"

"The weather? Gasp, when you're a ghost like me, you never consider the weather. It makes no difference, hot or cold, it's all the same to me. What I'm interested in is style and you gotta admit Pancho had style, don't ya think?" Uncle Charlie did a mock pirouette to show off his newfound finery.

Gaspar had long ago given up trying to figure out his sartorial kinfolk. "You win, uncle, you always win. I always give you first prize for style!" Gaspar exclaimed and Peugeot let out a sharp bark in agreement. "So, tell me ... what's on your mind, Charlie," Gaspar asked, getting comfortable, stretching out on his bed.

"I wanted to talk about what's on *your* mind." Charlie was emphatic. "I liked what you were saying on the ride yesterday, and I like the way you think. You were right you know, saying that I only kept this place for sentimental reasons. It's true. I kept it for my adopted daughter, Eugenia Floride. This was her family house, not mine, not ours. Those were her ancestors you were talking about, Gasp. Our family, that means you and me, only got this place by default ... a fluke."

"I know, uncle, but what a glorious fluke. Did you ever stop to think what made Doctor Mendoza y Mendoza so rich? Did he ever tell you the source of his wealth himself?"

"Rich? Doctor Mendoza y Mendoza? *rich*? Who told you that? The doctor wasn't rich. He was well-to-do, but land poor. He barely had two pesos to rub together. The family did have money at one time, that's for sure. You're right about this hacienda, absolutely no possibility in the way of farming or livestock. It's nothing but a rock pile. But old Ignacio, the one who came here almost 400 years ago, in 1635, he had money, lots of it. Maybe it was because he was the largest slave trader in the new world, who knows? Whatever the source of his income was, and it was vast, dried up or was lost at least 200 years ago. That's about the same time that the doctor's branch of the family inherited the place."

"Wait a minute. Are you telling me that the doctor was not the *direct* heir? That he was *like I am to you*, a distant second cousin twice removed or something like that?"

"Well, if you want to put it that way … yes," Uncle Charlie replied sheepishly.

"But, uncle, that explains everything. The old boy, Ignacio, probably had a palace in Mérida and this was just his beach house. The miles and miles of land meant nothing to him. When the king gave it to him, neither he nor the king knew it was worthless. It must have been the slaves and the tax collecting that gave him his power, prestige and wealth. By the time the doctor came around in the nineteenth century there was probably almost nothing left, just the house and the books and his private practice."

"Well, yes, I can attest to that. *I* am the one that ultimately made the doctor *rich*," Uncle Charlie reminded Gaspar proudly. "*I* am the one who found Gasparilla's treasure and restored Dr. Mendoza y Mendoza's family's prestige!" Uncle Charlie puffed himself up like a prized pigeon.

"That's all well and good, uncle. But there had to be something more … " Gaspar pondered. "Old Ignacio, the conquistador, would never have settled for such a useless piece of property. Yesterday Alex mentioned gold. I wonder if the locals ever pan for gold in those two rivers. I think I'll ask around and find out," Gaspar decided.

"You probably have something there, Gasp. But I'll be *dimmed* if I know what." Charlie scratched his head

"Did you see that horse try and pee on me and Peugeot yesterday?" Gaspar blurted out-of-the-blue, taking Uncle Charlie aback, and himself and Peugeot a little bit too.

"Yes, I did kid," Charlie answered. "What of it."

"I don't know, uncle. For some reason I can't get the sight of that horse, taking a leak right in front of me, out of my mind."

"Well it's not every day that you get to witness that kind of action up close and personal," Uncle Charlie laughed. "It was like a fire hose going off."

"Oh, uncle, that's not the point. I just can't put my finger on it," Gaspar complained in exasperation.

"And let's hope you never do, Gaspar."

"What?"

"Put your finger on it!" Uncle Charlie teased, howling with laughter as he disappeared through the whitewashed adobe wall.

•••

Later the sound of Roberto's car pulling up woke Gaspar from his fitful dreams. He quickly got up and ran from his room with Peugeot hot on his heels, to meet his arriving guests. Gaspar and Peugeot reached the entrance hall just in time to watch Manuel open the front door as the Wharton brothers bounded inside.

"*Bienvenidos a Huayrocondo*," Gaspar greeted the two brothers from where he stood under the living room arch.

"Hey, Gasp, you've gone native on us, in Spanish no less," Scott Wharton joked as Gaspar's tennis pro ran forward to shake the hand of his student and hopeful future tennis champ.

"*Si, si, señor*," Gaspar answered grinning from ear to ear. "And that, Scott, is the extent of my repertoire in Spanish," Gaspar informed his champion tennis teacher.

"That's good, cause all I speak is English and none too well, I've been told," Brewster Wharton, Gaspar's lawyer and Peter's law partner confessed, shaking Gaspar's outstretched hand. "Good to see you looking so happy, buddy, and you too, Mr. Peugeot," he grabbed the poodle and scratched his ears lovingly.

Looking around, Scott Wharton gave out a low whistle. "Whooooooeee, what a set up. Show us everything, Gasp," Scott begged from his seat on the ground where he was nuzzling Peugeot.

"Yeah, I'd like to see what two million buys these

days," Brewster added facetiously.

"Would either of you like a cool drink or something to eat before we get started?" Gaspar asked graciously, "or do you need to make a pit stop first, to wash up," he added discreetly.

"Something to drink, that would be nice," Scott accepted Gaspar's suggestion.

"Lemonade, or beer, or anything in between that you can think of. The kitchen is fully stocked and so is the bar." Gaspar told them.

"Lemonade, for both of us," Brewster ordered, receiving a nod in the affirmative from his brother.

"Great, Manuel, *tres limonadas, por favor*," and then to his guests, "let's get started. Lead the way, Peugeot. Manuel will catch up with the drinks when they're ready."

An hour later, they had seen every nook and cranny of the old house and all its five courtyards. Gaspar had showed off all the restoration work and all of the new decorations that the designers from the Tony Duquette Studios in Los Angeles had provided for the project. During the tour, Gaspar pointed out the guest bedroom that Scott and Brewster would be sharing, which was located off the same courtyard as himself, Alex, Hanuman and Roberto.

"If you guys want separate rooms, there are five others available off the other courtyard. But if you don't mind sharing, then us guys will all be together over here." Gaspar expounded, "I like to think of this courtyard as a *garconier*, you know … bachelor quarters.

Without a word, the Wharton brothers made it clear that they were happy to share by throwing themselves down onto their respective beds in the beige and brown bedroom, which had been decorated with native Mexican furnishings. Gaspar also threw himself down onto the sofa, which had been placed against the wall opposite the beds, and Peugeot jumped up to join him and from there they held court.

"So, now that you've seen the house, wha-da-ya think, guys?"

"Fantastic," Scott was the first to speak.

"Amazing," Brewster piped up. "I'd love to see some of the before shots of this place. If it really was the wreck that you described, the transformation is remarkable. I can see why you're so happy, Gaspar. This is quite an establishment."

"Thanks, guys. I think so too. I told the decorators to take the before shots so I'm sure they did. I can't wait for my mom and Peter to see it. Boy will they be surprised."

"So, Gaspar, what's on your mind. Why did you insist we come down here?" Brewster asked.

"Well, Brew, first, I wanted you to see this place and understand that two million wasn't a lot of money considering how much the decorators had to do to pull it all together. Second, a lot of stuff has happened to us on this trip, and I just feel better having you and Scott nearby, at least for the next week or so. I can't put my finger on it, or put my feelings into words, but something tells me that our Yucatán adventure may just be beginning," Gaspar told his pals, cryptically.

"So, what do you want us to do, Gasp?" Scott asked.

"Just enjoy yourselves … swim, ride, look around. If you have any suggestions as far as improvements go … just let me know

"So, when do we eat?" Brewster asked.

"Why don't you guys chill out and do whatever you like for a couple of hours. We can meet up on the terrace around six o'clock for drinks before dinner."

"You've got a deal, Gasp. Thanks for inviting us down. This is going to be a lot of fun," Brewster chuckled, slapping Gaspar on the back as he and Peugeot left the room.

CHAPTER 21

LEARNING THE DRILL

AT DINNER THAT NIGHT, GASPAR FILLED IN HIS NEWLY ARRIVED GUESTS ON THE JOYS OF CELESTÚN. "Tomorrow," Gaspar suggested, "We can all go check out the *Celestún Biosphere Reserve*."

"Gasp, where do you get this stuff?" Alex marveled. "What's the Celestún Biosphere Reserve?"

"It's all around us, Al. All the raw land surrounding Huayrocondo, and the town. It's a 147,500 acre preserve ... the *Parque Natural del Flamenco Mexicano*, or The Celestún Biosphere Reserve."

"Wow," Brewster chimed in. "That would be about six-hundred-square kilometers," he marveled.

"That sounds about right, Brew," Gaspar agreed. "It's a wetland reserve that is the winter home to vast flocks of flamingos, as well as herons and other wild bird species.

It's set within the *Petenes Mangroves Ecoregion.* Supposedly more than two-hundred species of birds pass through on migration, or live there, year-round," Gaspar enlightened his guests.

"Celestún's ecosystem is unique," Hanuman joined the conversation, "because of a combination of fresh water from the estuary and salt water from the Gulf of Mexico. This place was one of my first stops when I got to Yucatán. It's world famous," Gaspar's free-spirited friend, Hanuman informed them.

"From what I've read, the reserve also has two types of pelican, large white Canadian ones and smaller gray Mexican ones," Gaspar threw in.

"Sounds like a great visit," Alex enthused. "Are there any ruins inside the park?"

"No, Alex," Roberto set him straight. "There are no ruins here. Celestún is a little short on ruins, I'm afraid."

"I wonder why that is," Scott pondered. "With all the fresh water, sea life and bird life here, you'd think Celestún would have been a Garden of Eden to the Maya," Scott offered.

"You're right, Scott," Roberto agreed. "Perhaps the Maya understood the need to respect a natural paradise like Celestún. Perhaps they made a conscious effort to preserve it, like a sacred place. Even today, Celestún is protected as a hatching ground for endangered sea turtles. It has been an ongoing project of wildlife conservationists to protect the sea turtles from our encroaching civilization," Roberto informed them.

"That's very interesting, Roberto. You really think that the Maya were the first conservationists. I like that point of view," Gaspar approved. "It's interesting that you think they had a deep-rooted respect for mother earth. Do you have any evidence or is it just a supposition?" After his own experience at the Seminole Spring back on Perdido Isle, Gaspar took what his friend had to say very seriously.

"It is just my supposition, señor ... but over and over again, we can see here in the Yucatán ... areas rich in natural resources which the Maya left untouched except for a temple to the gods, constructed almost like a shrine or offering, giving thanks for their abundance," Roberto explained.

"That's a very interesting observation. Roberto you should write a paper on it, as I think it would meet with popular acceptance." Gaspar suggested.

"What else can you tell us about your new domain, Gasp?" Brewster asked.

"Juano and Carmen, my caretakers, explained that one of the busiest times of the year is Semana Santa, when the local Maya villagers from around the region come to Celestún to celebrate. The Catholic traditions of the local folk are abundant during holy week, when the town's patron saint is floated out to sea surrounded by candles and visited by the patron saint of nearby Kinchil."

"What's the name of the town's patron saint?" Alex asked.

"I've been trying to find that out. Everyone I ask has a different answer," Gaspar laughed, "One guy even told me it was Chac Mool!"

"When is Semana Santa?" Scott asked, just a little embarrassed, for not knowing.

"It's the week after Christmas, stupid," Brewster scolded his brother, giving him a shove.

"No, it's not, Brew," Gaspar laughed. "It's the week before Easter.

"We missed it by two months," Alex added. "But maybe next year we can come down for the celebrations. Wha-da-ya say, Gasp? Let's take the guys to the town square tomorrow to check out the action, anyways," Al suggested. "There's always something interesting happening down there."

"That's because the municipality of Celestún embraces and attracts various carnivals, dances and musicians to its town square on a regular basis. I've been into town three times, and each time there's been something new and different happening in the plaza," Gaspar told them. "I can't wait to show you guys."

"Sounds like fun," Brewster trilled, "even if it isn't Christmas!"

"I'd love to see everything I possibly can while I'm here," Scott agreed.

"After we see the plaza, and if we get bored swimming,

fishing, diving, riding, and camping out around here, then Roberto can take us to Campeche and Edzna, to see the archaeological sites there." Gaspar suggested grinning from ear to ear.

CHAPTER 22

EL PICO DE HUAYROCONDO

AFTER DINNER, BREWSTER AND SCOTT GOT TO KNOW HANUMAN AND ROBERTO A LITTLE BETTER WHILE conversing and nursing their night caps near the fire. They also brought Alex and Gaspar up to date with the latest gossip and goings-on back home on Perdido Isle, after which Gaspar and Peugeot excused themselves early, Gaspar feigning exhaustion.

When he got to his room, he called the stables and gave Chico some specific instructions. Dressed to go out, Gaspar told Peugeot to stay put and be a good boy before he stealthily made his way to the stables. He wanted to make sure that nobody knew what he was up to and tonight, he feared Peugeot might be in the way. When he got to the yard, Chico was waiting for him with Hippocrates saddled and loaded up for a little moonlight expedition. Gaspar had instructed Chico to tie a kerosene lantern, a long, coiled rope, a canteen full of water and a flat shovel to the horse's saddle. Proud of his thorough planning, Gaspar fingered the book of matches he'd placed in the pocket of his jean's jacket to make sure they were still there.

"Remember, Chico, this is *our* secret. You *have not* seen me tonight. You *did not* saddle Hippocrates, and you *did not* tie a shovel, a rope, a canteen and a lantern onto his saddle." I'll be back in a couple of hours," he told his bewildered groom. "When I arrive back, I'll knock on your door, so I hope you're a light sleeper."

"Si, si, señor," Chico answered in the affirmative.

Gaspar was convinced that the boy *hadn't* a clue what he'd just told him or what he was talking about, and that he had just promised to do a lot of things, though he had no idea what those things were. Riding quietly out of the stable yard, Gaspar headed out onto the road. He passed through the big gates, which he romanced had rusted in an open position a hundred years ago and raced up by moonlight to the base of the Pico de Huayrocondo. Continuing on to the top of the peak, he dismounted and tethered Hippocrates to one of the scrub bushes which he knew would conceal his lantern light and his presence from the road and The Doctor's House below. Touching a match to the lantern's wick, it made a huge circle of light on the ground. Perfect, Gaspar thought to himself, as he looked for the place where he'd peed earlier that day. Unscrewing the top of his canteen, he spilled a pool of water onto the earth and watched it immediately drain away. This was the place, all right.

Taking the shovel, he began to work the earth around the selected area. The dirt was soft and fine, and he was able to move it away without any trouble. Under the first thin layer he found rocks, lots of them, as if they had been part of a landslide. Moving his lantern in for a closer look he discovered that the loose rocks were actually cut stone. Gaspar pondered this for a minute and then came to and started frantically digging and prying the rocks away. Before he knew it, he'd cleared an area about three feet in diameter and had removed many heavy stones. Suddenly, the remaining stones fell downwards, as if the keystone in an arch had given way. At the first movement of the rocks, Gaspar jumped backwards. Now what remained of his three-foot diameter excavation was a deep dark hole about five feet by five feet. Unwinding his rope, he tied one end around Hippocrates middle and carried the other end over to the hole in the ground.

Grabbing the lantern in one hand, Gaspar tied the rope to its handle. Laying on his stomach, he lowered the lantern down into the pit. What Gaspar saw made his heart stop. The lantern revealed a staircase, leading straight down under the Pico de Huayrocondo. The top of the nearest step was a good twenty feet below him. Sprawled on his stomach along the edge of the opening

301

he looked down into the deep hole and followed the circle of light from the lantern. What he saw was a sheer wall of debris which blocked him from seeing any further up the staircase. Scooting around counterclockwise a little further along the edge, he could now follow the descent of the stairs, but the ring of light only extended so far. There was only one thing for Gaspar to do. He had to get down there and check it out firsthand.

Pulling the lantern back up, he untied it and set it on the ground. Then tying the rope around his waist, he picked up the lantern, and using Hippocrates for weight, lowered himself down into the pit until his Nikes touched the first exposed stone step. Untying the end of the rope from around his waist he secured it to a large rock that had earlier tumbled there. He hoped that it would act like an anchor for Hippocrates, who he certainly didn't want to wander off at this point.

Now by the warm glow of the lantern light, Gaspar started down the steep Mayan staircase, which he was forced to descend, as usual, on his butt, one step at a time. The steps led to an opening into a vast room whose walls were stepped upwards. Gaspar couldn't believe his eyes, but in the dim light he realized that he was inside a man-made pyramid, not some natural cavern, but an ancient Mayan monument. It didn't take Gaspar a minute to realize that it was not only a sacred tomb or temple, but also a repository for extraordinary treasure. Quickly he took out his phone and started snapping pictures like crazy. Piled all around him were golden idols, unlike any he had seen previously. There were large golden statues, standing as high as three feet tall, with the tiniest talismans being only two or three inches in length. He couldn't see as much as he wanted with just the single lantern, so he decided to do a quick reconnaissance around the perimeter of the room and then head out.

Behind the main altar, which stood immediately opposite the stairs, Gaspar spied a crude opening which led to a rough tunnel cut from the raw earth. Stepping through only a couple of feet, he decided to save further exploration for another time. Right this minute, all he wanted to do was get out of there. Coming back around the big altar, which he had only minutes earlier stepped behind, he was startled to encounter a figure in a flowing golden robe standing with his back to Gaspar. *Yikes, why didn't I bring a knife or something to protect myself with*, Gaspar thought. That's when the man turned around and lo and behold, it was Uncle Charlie.

"Uncle Charlie, you scared the *bachi bozouks* out of me. I know you'd never knock, or ring the bell, even if there was one or even if you could … but a simple *yoo-hoo* would have gone a long way tonight … thank you very much," Gaspar complained.

"Yoo-hoo, what … I'm speechless, Gasp," Uncle Charlie proclaimed. "And for me to admit that I, Carlos Munoz-Flores y Gaspar, am *speechless*, is saying a lot.

"How did you know about this place?" Gaspar asked him.

"Know about it? I didn't know about it! I followed you. I figured you were up to no good, and if you *were*, I wanted to join in the fun. Heck, Gasp, every time I turn around, you're finding more treasure. This is quite a haul, my boy, quite a haul. You need to be incredibly careful about how you handle this one, baby," Uncle Charlie warned him.

"You're telling me! I'm flabbergasted, but I can't believe that you and Doctor Mendoza y Mendoza didn't know about this."

"You think if he or I had known about this, that I would have gone sailing off with that murderous servant, Moises in search of Gasparilla's treasure when this pot of gold was sitting right in our own backyard. You think I would have left this rock pile and gone gallivanting all over the world with Mayan treasure starring me in the face, right across from the front door of The Doctor's House," Uncle Charlie said, sitting down on a rock ledge near a pile of golden objects.

"I think this is all we can do for tonight, uncle. Let's climb out of here and come back tomorrow with some proper equipment." Gaspar suggested with a trembling voice.

"Good idea, Gasp. Come on boy … lead the way."

With his lantern in one hand, Gaspar bent down and picked up a little souvenir of his night out, a small golden statue of Chac Mool, which he shoved into his jeans' pocket. Climbing on all fours up the steep stairs, he had to place the lantern down on the step in front of him each time, before moving up to the next step, which made for very slow going. Finally, unable to go any further because of the debris blocking the rest of the staircase he reached the top step where the dangling rope was. Untying it from the rock anchor he tied it back around his waist tightly.

"Uncle Charlie, give me a hand. Go outside and scare Hippocrates into pulling me out of here, but not too quickly, please."

Without answering, the old ghost went topside. Whispering in the palomino's ear, he successfully urged Hippocrates backwards ever so slowly.

Reaching the outside world, safe and sound, Gaspar placed the lantern on the ground in front of him, then hauled himself out of the pit.

"What an adventure," Gaspar squealed with glee. "Let me find some brush to cover up the hole I made, uncle, and we'll start down the hill together."

CHAPTER 23

GASPAR TAKES ACTION

WHILE RIDING BACK DOWN THE HILL, GASPAR HAD
TIME TO DISCUSS HIS PLANS FOR HIS NEWFOUND
treasure with Uncle Charlie. To his amazement, Uncle
Charlie agreed with him one hundred percent. "My
thoughts exactly," the old ghost concurred.

The next morning, Gaspar and Peugeot were up and
about early, with Gaspar full of anticipation regarding to
his big news. His first bit of business was to call Señor
de Montijo at the Instituto Nacional de Antropología e
Historia at the Dzibilchaltún site. His next two calls were
to Lieutenant Jacobson's pal, Admiral Jose Luis Sorzano
y Artieda, and Captain Morgan's friend, Major Ugarte.
Then he made the most important call of all and that one
was to Major Portillo. He told the same story to each of
these Mexican officials but customized the end of each

conversation to suit his individual goals.

Having taken care of business, he put on some swim trunks and a T-shirt and went out to the terrace with Peugeot where one by one his similarly clad guests were assembling for breakfast. Carmen and her helpers were there ready to serve them a delicious selection of huevos rancheros, fried bacon, Mexican hot chocolate, coffee and thick slices of homemade bread slathered with butter and guava jelly.

"What's on the agenda today?" Brewster asked after they were seated and digging into the delicious repast.

"We're going into town to check out the plaza," Alex reminded him.

"Actually, I have something I want to show you guys first," Gaspar informed them cryptically.

"What's that?" Alex asked.

"It's a surprise, but I promise you'll like it," Gaspar insisted. Let's have a swim after this and then I want to take you out for another pony ride."

"Oh, Gasp, my butt's still sore from our gallop the day before yesterday," Alex complained.

"Ya gotta get back in the saddle, Al, or you'll never get used to it," Gaspar cajoled him.

"Count me in," Brewster sang.

"Me too," Scott seconded.

"Can't wait," Roberto chimed in.

"I'm cool with another ride," Hanuman chanted.

"All right, we'll head out at ten. That will give us time

for swimming," Gaspar told them, getting up from the table and heading for the water. "Last one in's a rotten egg, he called over his shoulder, pulling his T-shirt off over his head, while Peugeot barking ferociously ran behind him and into the water.

By eleven o'clock, the group had assembled near the stables where Chico, Paco and Flaco had prepared the saddled steeds. Each of the saddles had a kerosene lantern attached and Gaspar's had a long- coiled rope, hanging from his saddle as well.

"These are my grooms … Chico, Paco, and Flaco." Gaspar introduced the Wharton brothers to his stable boys. *"Estos son mi amigos Señor Brewster Wharton y su hermano, Señor Scott Wharton,"* Gaspar introduced the grooms to his guests. "This is my gorgeous horse, Hippocrates, and this is Al's horse, Hero. Felix named this horse Nobles the other day. You can ride him, Brew. This is Hanuman's steed, Ajit. It means invincible in Hindi. And this one is Chac. Roberto named him after the benevolent Maya god. Scott, you can ride Chiquita, that's Chico's pony right over here."

Introductions completed, the group jumped onto their saddles and with Peugeot trotting alongside, followed Gaspar out of the stable yard at a clip. The minute they passed the big iron gates they were off, and the race was on. Gaspar led the way, followed by the others, who were finding it hard to keep up with Hippocrates. Reaching his goal, he was followed by

Brewster, Hanuman, Alex, Scott, and finally Roberto who came in last yet again.

"Okay, guys. I've got something to show you," Gaspar announced. "What you are about to see will be mind-boggling to many of you. I've found something, and I not only want you to be the first to see it, but I also want you to be the first to know what I plan to do about it.

The others looked at each other with wide eyes, as they watched Gaspar take the rope from his saddle and unwind it before tying one end of it around Hippocrates middle.

"Okay, men, light your lanterns, please." Gaspar instructed them, lighting his own and passing the book of matches to Alex, who passed it on to Brewster and down the line.

With little effort Gaspar removed the brush, exposing the gaping five-foot-wide hole in the ground which he'd excavated the night before. While the others lighted their lanterns, Gaspar put Peugeot into the big canvas bag he'd brought along.

"Al, I'm going down first, then you lower Peugeot down, and then send the lanterns down, before you each come down, one by one." Gaspar explained his plan.

He then tied the rope around his waist and with Hippocrates help, lowered himself down into the pit and said, "This way, gents, follow me."

When he reached the bottom, he untied the rope from his waist and called up to Al to pull it up and send down Peugeot. After Peugeot reached the bottom, the lanterns were lowered then one by one the rest of the party entered the pit. Oohs and aahs could soon be heard emanating from deep underground. The last man down the rope was Roberto. When they were all assembled, Gaspar led them on their butts, lanterns in hand, step by step, down the steep stairs and into the massive Mayan treasure room.

For the most part, his five companions were speechless, but finally Roberto spoke up, with a quaver in his voice. "This is the Temple of Chaaac Mooool." the archaeologist stuttered. "Señor Gaspar, you've found ... *The Legendary ... Lost ... Temple ... of Chac Mool*. Gaaaspaaar, this is probably ... the most important ... . archaeological find of the ... twenty-first century," Roberto exhaled in an audible whisper, visibly shaken, eyes bulging for all to see.

"What are you going to do about this, Gaspar," Brewster asked seriously.

"I'm going to give it to the Instituto Nacional de Antropología e Historia of course, Brew, but that's why I'm glad you're along. I want to give the treasure and the temple, but not the land around it. You see ... I've been giving this a lot of thought. I'll even pay to have the temple uncovered and restored. It will be my private dig, but I don't want to give the land away, and especially not what's underneath it.

"Well, I'm not sure about Mexican law, but something

tells me you're going to be in the driver's seat on this one, Gasp. Have you any idea what it'll cost to underwrite the archaeology on a place like this?"

"I think if we do it privately, we can't lose. But let's cross that bridge when we get to it," Gaspar insisted. "For now, I just wanted you to see what I found. There are probably many more rooms full of treasure around here, but that can all be uncovered later. Don't you think, Roberto?"

"Yes, yes," replied the wide-eyed, distracted archaeological tour guide and historian, as he continued picking up gold artifacts and reverently putting them back down again exactly where he'd found them.

"Try not to move things around too much, guys," Gaspar implored the others. "We need to get all this stuff photographed in situ, like they did at King Tut's tomb. You know … for posterity … like they show on the History Channel," he insisted while Peugeot kept busy sniffing every inch of the chamber.

"So, what's the next step?" Still in awe … Scott, could barely get the words out.

"I've already called Señor de Montijo at the Instituto. He'll be here tomorrow morning, and we'll see what he has to say," Gaspar laid out his plan. "Right now, let's keep this as our little secret, and get back home in time for lunch."

"Don't you think you should place some guards on the site?" Brewster suggested.

"No, Brew. If we do that, it will only call attention to the place and before you know it the whole neighborhood will be up here with pickaxes and shovels," Gaspar warned. "Let's just let sleeping dogs lie for today, because something tells me that by tomorrow, this place will be jumping with archaeologists, and reporters."

F. Catl

CHAPTER 24

THE DOUBLE CROSS

AFTER DINNER, GASPAR AND PEUGEOT SAID GOODNIGHT AND HEADED TO THEIR ROOM AND HIS PALS DID THE same. One by one, by a pre-arranged plan, Gaspar, Peugeot, Alex, Brewster and Scott met near the stables, where Chico had their horses saddled and ready for them. Quietly in the dead of night the four friends rode back up the mountain.

Tying off their horses, out of site, they made their way back to Gaspar's hole in the ground, and entered the newly discovered Temple of Chac Mool for the second time that day exactly as they had done earlier except instead of tying the rope around Hippocrates middle, they found a heavy boulder to attach it to instead.

For this trip, they'd brought flashlights, and as planned, they silently hid behind the main altar, waiting to see what might happen. If Gaspar's guess was correct the temple would soon be visited by *The Jaguar* and his gang. Around midnight they heard rough footsteps, and watched a dim light grow brighter from the direction of the staircase. They heard the clatter of objects being thrown down from above and heard the movement of what seemed like several people lowering themselves into the pit.

Who they saw approaching came as a total surprise to everyone ... everyone except Gaspar, that is? It was Major Portillo, the skunk, and he was leading a group of eight men into the vast chamber. Each man carried two large duffle bags in his hands. Quickly Portillo and his men started stuffing treasure into their duffels. Gaspar, Alex, Brewster and Scott watched silently from behind the altar. They had no intentions of stopping the thieves who outnumbered them two to one. Before too long, they were surprised to hear the clatter of more feet on the staircase, when a booming voice shouted, "*Stop in the name of the law!*"

It was Hanuman who stood there, weapon drawn, surrounded by six men in uniform, also with pistols drawn at the ready. Portillo ordered his men to attack, throwing a large gold idol at Hanuman who caught it like a quarterback and charged forward, followed by his men.

That was all Gaspar, Peugeot, Alex, Brewster and Scott needed to see, in order to jump out from behind the altar and join the melee. Gaspar and Alex, working as a team, managing to knock out one of the men and tie him up right where he lay using the sleeves they'd ripped off his arms to bind him. Brewster made quick work out of another of Portillo's cohorts, and Scott was giving all he had to one of the other Mexican thugs. Gaspar watched Portillo making a run for the tunnel behind the altar and saw Hanuman running after him in hot pursuit, flashlight in hand. As the crook, followed by Hanuman, ran through the tunnel Gaspar, flashlight in hand, and Peugeot fearlessly followed hot on their heels.

"Hanuman," Gaspar shouted to his pal.

"Gaspar, what were you guys doing here?"

"Waiting to see who the traitor was," Gaspar panted, catching up with him.

"You better stay here while I try and catch up with Portillo," Hanuman shouted.

"You know him?" Gaspar was impressed.

"He's been a prime suspect of mine in a series of antiquities thefts. Tonight, I was tipped off that he was coming to Celestún to check out a new find, and I knew it had to be this one.

"I'm the guy who tipped him off," Gaspar panted, running to keep up with his hero, while Peugeot barked fiercely from behind.

"*You* tipped him off? Good work man," Hanuman praised his young compadre on the run.

Just then they heard a terrific scream from up ahead, followed by a heavy thud and a deep groan. Gaspar knew it was Portillo and wondered what horrible fate had just befallen the rat. Peugeot raced forward barking furiously. Stopping short, Gaspar and Hanuman heard Peugeot's frantic barking along with a whimpering moan from far below.

"Down there," Hanuman shouted, shining his light over the edge of the narrow path. They were standing on a ledge looking over a deep cavern. The ledge dropped off, fifty feet to the stone floor below. Gaspar and Hanuman raced ahead, following the path until they came to the bottom where Peugeot was growling over the prone body of Major Portillo. Portillo was still alive, but bloodied and unconscious. While Gaspar calmed Peugeot down, telling him what a good dog he was, Hanuman extracted two pair of shiny handcuffs from his pocket and clamped them onto the unconscious Portillo's wrists and ankles.

"Gaspar, you and Peugeot stay here with Portillo and I'll send Brewster and Scott down with some lanterns and a couple of my men to haul him out of here. Hold down the fort, Gasp, I'll be right back."

"Alone with the unconscious criminal, there was nothing Gaspar could do but sit on the ground against the rock wall and stroke Peugeot's fur while using his single flashlight to look around. Shining his light here and there against the rough cavern walls he soon realized that he wasn't in a natural cavern at all. He was in a mine. Better yet, it was an ancient Mayan mine. If his eyes didn't deceive him, it was a *gold mine*. Gaspar hugged Peugeot closer and whispered in the pup's ear, "We sho is rich now, mister."

It wasn't long before Brewster and Scott arrived with lighted lanterns and their own flashlights.

They were soon followed by two of Hanuman's uniformed men, who were prepared to carry Portillo out.

"You all right, Gasp?" Brewster asked solicitously.

"Better than ever," Gaspar sang, boxing Peugeot's ears.

"How 'bout you, guys? No injuries, I hope." Gaspar wanted to make sure while keeping his new secret to himself for the time being as he watched the policemen carry Portillo's unconscious body out of the cavern.

"Couldn't be better," Scott beamed, rubbing his knuckles.

"Haven't had this much fun since I played football at Tulane," Brewster bragged.

"Hey, guys. What is this place?" Gaspar asked, shining his flashlight around.

With the addition of the two kerosene lanterns that the Whartons had brought with them, and all three of their flashlights, their eyes were becoming accustomed to the soft light. It wasn't a minute before Alex came out onto the ledge shining his light around too.

"Hey down there, are you guys all right?" Alex called down from above.

"All's well down here, Al," Gaspar spoke up.

"What is this place?" Alex asked.

"You tell us, Al," Gaspar coaxed him.

"Looks like a mine to me," Alex answered.

"Precisely, Al … It is a mine … a *Maya gold mine*!" Gaspar let fly.

"What!" Brewster cried.

"Of course, it is," Alex echoed.

"Are you kidding," Scott threw in.

"Nope, check it out. That's gold," Gaspar said nonchalantly, shining his torch up onto the cavern walls and tracing long veins of gold with his light."

"I can't believe it, Gasp, but why am I surprised?" Brewster yelped.

CHAPTER 25

THE HONEYMOON'S OVER

Upon exiting the cave, Gaspar, Alex, Brewster and Scott found pandemonium outside. From the base of the Pico de Huayrocondo they could see a Mexican frigate and a huge motor yacht anchored off the beach in front of The Doctor's House. The house itself was lit up like a Christmas tree, and from Gaspar's vantage point it looked like a lot of activity was going on both inside and outside the old hacienda.

Closer at hand, an entire battalion of federales had taken Portillo and his men into custody and were getting ready to drag them down the hill in handcuffs. Hanuman had taken control of the situation and was giving orders left and right, setting the record straight. The entire hilltop had been illuminated with floodlights from a chopper, which hovered noisily overhead, adding to the general din and confusion.

Hanuman stepped forward and extended his hand to Gaspar. "Captain Joel Westerbrook, Gaspar," he re-introduced himself, officially. "I'm a special agent with Interpol and I had a hunch that one way or the other, you'd lead us to *The Jaguar* ... and I was right! We had our suspicions about Portillo, but you put the lid on it for us, Gasp," Hanuman beamed, clamping the embarrassed teenager on the shoulder. "We finally caught the wild-cat, red-handed."

"Wow, Han, I mean Captain Westerbrook," Gaspar blushed. "We had no idea," Gaspar spat out his words awkwardly, while looking over at Alex for help. "You not only fooled me and Alex, but you fooled everyone ... even Peugeot here!" He chuckled, bending down to pet the befuddled pup.

"Well, I'm sorry to have been deceitful, but my cover is part of my job. As far as my friends go, and I'll always consider you guys to be my friends, I'm just Hanuman, the new age adventurer. But where crooks are concerned, I'm all Interpol, all the time."

"What's happening down at The Doctor's House?" Gaspar asked, changing the subject.

"Well it seems that someone around here not only called the Mexican navy but also the federales. Have you met Major Ugarte?" Hanuman asked, waving the federale over. Major, may I present my friend, Señor Gaspar Brown."

"*Con mucho gusto, mayor*," Gaspar greeted the policeman in his best Spanish. We have a mutual friend in Captain Morgan on Perdido Isle, Florida."

"*Si, si, Señor Gaspar, mi amigo, Enrique Morgan me llamo y llo stuvo esperando tu llamada.*" Major Ugarte assured him of his mutual friendship for Captain Morgan.

"Gracias, mayor, para tu ayudo con este problema." Gaspar thanked the major for helping out using his best gringo Spanish.

"Gaspar, I'm impressed. You know more important brass around here than I do, even if some of them did turn out to be crooks," Hanuman smiled. "By the way, I think you have some more business to attend to down below," Hanuman nudged him, nodding down towards the house.

"Major Ugarte and my men will seal off the area and keep a twenty-four-hour guard on the site until the proper authorities can take over."

"I called Señor de Montijo at the Instituto Nacional de Antropología e Historia this morning. I asked him to meet me here in the morning ... but I haven't told him why yet. I thought it would be a big surprise for him," Gaspar giggled.

"I'll say," Hanuman exploded. "Like Roberto enthused this morning, this is probably the biggest archaeological find of the twenty-first century and you're the guy who found it, Gasp!"

"Yeah, and right in my own back yard," Gaspar threw

in, so that there would be no doubt that he knew the boundaries of his private property.

"Better have some smelling salts ready when Montijo gets here," Hanuman chuckled. He wagged his head in disbelief at all the strings Gaspar had pulled and tied up neatly in a bow in order to solve the mystery of the recent antiquity's thefts in the Yucatán.

Saddling up, the four friends trotted their horses down the hill and over to The Doctor's House. Not wasting any time taking the horses around to the stables, they just left them by the front door in the midst of dozens of uniformed Mexican sailors. Chico, Paco, and Flaco appeared in an instant and took the palominos off their hands the minute the boys dismounted.

Inside the house Angela and Felix along with Carmen and Juano were running around in a dither, not knowing exactly why an admiral of the Mexican Navy and his entire crew had descended on The Doctor's House in the middle of the night.

When Gaspar and his friends entered the room, Angela and Felix stepped forward to greet them and get some assurance from the *patron* that all was well. Realizing that the boss had arrived at last, Admiral Jose Luis Sorzano y Artieda, stepped forward and introduced himself.

"Thank you for coming, admiral," Gaspar greeted the illustrious Mexican naval officer. "Our mutual friend, Lieutenant Jacobson told me I could rely on you."

"Señor Gaspar, from what I am hearing from the federales up on the hill, you have pulled off a magnificent coup. It seems that we have not only captured *The Jaguar*, but also his fence. I believe you know Señor and Señora Balaian," he said, motioning towards the sofa.

Sitting sullenly on one of the sofas were Mr. and Mrs. Balaian. From what Gaspar could tell, they were not at all happy to be paying a visit to Gaspar Brown at this time of night. The billionaire and his wife were both wearing evening clothes and around her neck, Madam Balaian had on a most magnificent ruby necklace.

"Yes, we know each other, admiral," Gaspar spoke in a low voice. "But how is it that Señora Balaian is wearing my mother's ruby necklace?" Gaspar whispered to the admiral in confusion.

"We just picked them up, off of their yacht. This is the way they were dressed when we arrested them. They were anchored just offshore, no doubt to receive *The Jaguar* and the loot. We have found a great deal of Maya gold artifacts hidden in a secret hold onboard their ship, but what is this about your mother's necklace," the admiral hissed softly, concern in his voice.

"She's wearing it, admiral. That *is* my mother's ruby necklace," Gaspar confided to the admiral quietly. "What I can't figure out is how Madam Balaian got it. Let me make a call, admiral, so we can clear up this mystery."

Taking the admiral by the elbow, he ushered the distinguished old sailor into the library where Gaspar called his mother onboard *Floridablanca*, waking her up from a deep sleep. He put the phone on speaker and while she was still groggy, asked her his simple question.

"Hi, mom, sorry to wake you up. I'm just wondering, are you missing your ruby necklace by any chance? You know, the one you wore to your wedding."

"Funny you should ask, dear, it has gone missing. We invited some people on board for a little party, and the next day when I went to look for it ... it was gone. I didn't make a fuss about it because you said it was costume. It's odd you should be calling about it now in the middle of the night."

"Were Mr. and Mrs. Balaian among the people you invited that night?" Gaspar asked point blank.

"The Balaians and about fifteen other people," Elvira seemed a little wider awake now.

"That's all I need to know for now, mom. The necklace has been returned here, to The Doctor's House. It must have been taken by mistake, and whoever took it sent it back. It'll be here for you when you return.

"Oh, that's nice, dear," Elvira said sleepily. "Have a good night and give us a call tomorrow when you have a free minute, darling," she sang, before hanging up.

"Admiral Sorzano, my mother thinks that they're fake rubies, but actually they are not. She has one real necklace which she usually keeps in the bank, and an exact copy in crystal that she wears now and then ... but that necklace is the real one ... I can assure you ... she has just confused the two." Gaspar explained, telling a version of the truth that he hoped the sailor would better understand.

Without a word or a gesture, Admiral Sorzano walked back into the drawing room with Gaspar in tow. Walking over to the sofa, he stood in front of Señora Balaian and outstretched his hand. Without his saying a word, Madame Balaian slowly unclasped the necklace and reluctantly placed it in the stern admiral's upturned palm. A look of immense hatred covered her face as the distinguished officer walked back over to Gaspar and handed him the sparkling trinket.

"Thank you, admiral. My mother will be delighted to get this gawdy piece of costume jewelry back. She just loves this kind of old junk," he chuckled, placing the priceless treasure in his pocket.

At that moment, Portillo was escorted roughly into the room. Seeing the Balaians sitting there he started screaming insults at them in Spanish, accusing them of tipping off the authorities and leading them to Celestún. Little did he know that it was Gaspar who had entrapped them.

Gaspar still wasn't sure which one of these characters, Portillo or Balaian was really *the Jaguar*. He figured that someone he had called was either *the Jaguar* or was tipping *the Jaguar* off, so he figured it stood to reason that *The Jaguar* would sooner or later show himself.

"Señor Brown, let me introduce you to *the Jaguar*," the admiral said, gesturing towards Major Portillo. "You have helped capture the most notorious antiquities thief in the world. And I believe you already know his accomplices, Señor and Señora Balaian. They were the … how do you say it … the fence for Major Portillo's nefarious acquisitions."

"Yes, admiral, I do know Mr. and Mrs. Balaian. I called them last night and told them that I'd found a small gold figure of Chac Mool that I thought they'd like to see. And I told them that I found a lot of old gold items while digging in the garden here at The Doctor's house, but the little statue was all I was willing to sell right now."

"And what did they tell you, my boy?"

"That they weren't interested in anything second rate and couldn't take the time to come to see me."

"Very interesting," the admiral smiled.

"I am also well acquainted with Major Portillo. I also called him and in the strictest confidence told him that I thought I'd found The Lost Temple of Chac Mool. He asked me where, and I told him. We made a date to meet here the day after tomorrow. I told him that I had to leave early this morning for Uxmal with my friends who had just arrived for a short visit, and that I wouldn't be around until then."

"Very clever, very clever indeed."

"So, me and my pals hid out in the temple and low and behold, Major Portillo arrived with his thugs to rob the joint," Gaspar finished up.

"Yes, but to have contacted my friend Ugarte, and

Interpol as well as the top suspects … well, that was a stroke of genius, Gaspar!" The admiral thumped the teenager on the back, nearly knocking Gaspar over while Peugeot barked his appreciation as well.

"Thanks, admiral, but Interpol was all Hanuman's idea. He met us on the beach back at Tulúm and wormed his way into our confidence. Hanuman's the one who made the arrest. I'm sure he was probably watching me as closcly as he was watching the crooks. Han's such a great detective that he must have known or probably guessed exactly what I was up to before even I was aware of it."

"That's only partially true, Gasp." Hanuman stepped forward. "Yes … it's true … I wormed my way into your friendship and am awfully glad I did. I hope all of us will stay good friends forever, dude," Hanuman insisted, giving Gaspar a big abrazo. "As for knowing what you were up to … yeah, your right, but I promised Craig, I'd have your back. I had to tell him the truth, man or he never would have let you go off with me and Alex and Roberto alone. Dude, that guy's like a rabid guard dog, where you and your family are concerned … to say … man's best friend, doesn't really describe Craig's loyalty and concern for you and Alex and your parents!"

Gaspar blushed at all the attention. "Well, Admiral Sorzano, Major Ugarte and Captain Westerbrook, I'm glad I could be of assistance. Just to let you know I will be meeting with Señor de Montijo tomorrow morning to turn the temple and its contents over to the instituto.

It is also my intention to fund the archaeological research team, as well as the excavation of the lost temple. But I also want you to know, right this minute, that I couldn't have done it without the help of my friends ... Alex, Brewster, Scott, Hanuman, Felix, Angela, Juano, and Carmen, and Chico and Flaco and Paco ... and Mr. Peugeot here and Roberto too. Hey, where is Roberto anyhow?" Gaspar asked, looking around the room.

"I checked on him, Gaspar, when all the excitement was happening. The man was snoring like a buzz saw, fast asleep in his bed, so I didn't have the heart to wake him," Angela confessed.

"Wow, we're going to have some fun ragging him in the morning!" Gaspar laughed, while the others joined in the joke, chuckling loudly including Peugeot, who barked uncontrollably while running laps around the room.

"Speaking of morning," the admiral stood up, "I think it's time to put these crooks to bed and get my men back into their bunks too. Good night, Señor Gaspar Brown. Goodnight, good people," Admiral Sorzano y Artieda smiled jovially as he headed for the door, while teams of sailors escorted the unhappy criminals out of the house in his wake.

Once outside, the admiral turned Major Portillo or as he would forever be remembered, *The Jaguar* and his rich accomplices Señor and Señora Balaian over to Major Ugarte and the federales, along with all of their scurvy henchmen, one of them who just happened to be called, Diego. Gaspar was pleased that the gang of antiquities thieves would soon be reunited with Joe and Mike who Han told them had been rotting in a Mérida Jail since Gaspar and Alex apprehended them at the Caves of Balamka'anche'.

Walking the admiral to the shore where his tender awaited, Gaspar witnessed the powerful man's command to his sailors, to impound the Balaian's yacht, "ATL", which Hanuman later explained to Gaspar and his pals was the name of the powerful Aztec water god.

Little by little the house cleared out. Juano and Carmen, Manuel, the grooms, the housemaids and the cook all departed for their quarters. Closing up the house and turning out the lights, Gaspar, Alex, Hanuman and the Wharton brothers finally went to bed, exhausted by the excitement.

•••

The next morning when Gaspar and his guests dragged themselves to the breakfast table, they were energized to recap the events of the previous evening. Despite their late night, the kitchen staff managed to rustle up a hearty breakfast which the boys enjoyed tremendously. When Roberto arrived at table they enthusiastically and dramatically rehashed the events of the previous night for the amazed benefit of "sleeping beauty", Roberto's new nickname.

"I can't believe you slept through the entire fracas while the federales ransacked your room and your car too." Alex told Roberto facetiously

Everyone got a good laugh out of Alex's joke, even Roberto admitted sheepishly, "As you see, I'm a very sound sleeper, amigos. I only wish you had asked me to join your stake-out inside the temple," Roberto complained.

"Well, Roberto, I didn't ask you because I didn't know if you were part of The Jaguar's gang or not. The only way for me to find out was to not invite you to join us … that way … if you did show up … then I would have known that you were one of them, get it?"

"I understand now, Gaspar." Roberto laughed, "and I don't blame you either," he said good naturedly. "I am one of you … and not one of them, and very proud of it, señor." Roberto insisted.

"Gaspar, I'm impressed by your presence of mind calling in the federales and the navy, I guess you didn't invite me to join the stake-out for the same reason that you didn't invite Roberto." Hanuman wondered.

"Well, Han, we like you so much, but let's face facts, you were also a bit of an unknown quantity to us … so … I thought it best not to invite you to the stake-out either … but when you arrived with your cops in tow … nobody was more surprised than I was and nobody is more impressed than I am either … a special agent for

Interpol, *wow*! Now that's a job I'd like to know more about."

"All in good time, my friend, all in good time," Hanuman chuckled. "But first I have a confession to make and it's not very nice, but it's the truth and part of my job, so please don't take offence, okay. You see, Gasp … I tapped your phone … I listened in on your calls to Ugarte and Sorzano, and Montijo, and Portillo … and your stable boy too and I figured you were trying to lure one or all of them over here … and you did and it worked. If I hadn't done that however … me and my men would have missed the entire shooting match, so I guess I did the right thing? Sorry dude." Hanuman blushed.

"Not to worry, Han. I would have been disappointed had you not tapped my phone." Gaspar smiled, happy to have been a person of interest to Interpol. "By the way, Han … I'm not so sure that Portillo is *The Jaguar* … I think that Balaian is *The Jaguar* … what do you say?"

"I'm with you on that, Gasp, but let's see what comes out in the wash … we've got the whole gang and someone's gonna spill the beans before this thing's over." Hanuman assured his teenaged pal.

"Gaspar," Brewster butted in. "I know you well enough to ask this. Tell us right now … what's your next step? What's your real plan? I know you have a master plan all laid out in that brilliant brain of yours. I should have suspected as much when you told me that you wanted to give the temple to the instituto but not the land and not what's under the land. Did you know all the time that there was a gold mine under that temple?" Brewster admonished him.

"Well, Brew, I do have a plan. And no, I didn't know there was a gold mine under the temple, but I've always thought it would be a good idea if someday I could find a gold mine in my own backyard and all the good things I could do … you know, if I had some real money to spend." Gaspar chuckled at his inside joke. "Besides, if you're gonna give something away, you may as well keep the mineral rights to what's underneath it … don't you think, Brew?"

"Smart man," Brewster acknowledged. "Now tell us what we can expect next."

"Well, Brew, some of this has been on my mind for several weeks, and some of this just occurred to me last night. We have a lot to think about, not just for me, but for the people of Celestún, and for the people of the Yucatán too. Take this house, for instance. We don't need a beach house in Yucatán, but we don't want to give it up either. I think it will make a great hotel, a boutique hotel, a great boutique hotel, nonetheless. We could put in a pool and a tennis court or two … and we can stay here when we want to, but it can be used and enjoyed by others and give employment to a lot of locals … all year long."

"I like the way you think, Gasp," Scott spoke up.

"Then there's the temple and the Maya treasure,"

Gaspar continued. "It belongs to Mexico and to the Mexican people, but I don't want it hanging around in the state that it's in for years and years while the bureaucrats figure out how to raise the money and how to spend three times more than they need to, to make it happen. I want to fund the archaeologists and restore the temple and open it to the public. For that I figure we'll need to fund an expedition from Stanford or Carnegie, or some other institution that wants to bid on it. By making it a competition we ought to be able to bring this in on a realistic budget."

"Gaspar, you're a veritable *free enterprise capitalist*," Brewster insisted.

"It's called private enterprise in the public sector," Gaspar told him.

"You make me want to go back into archaeology again." Roberto blurted.

"If that's what you want, Roberto … you can be the resident archaeologist, the expert on the site, the explorer who helped discover it." Gaspar promised, to Roberto's obvious delight.

"Go on, Gaspar. I like the direction this is going," Alex urged him on while Peugeot barked in full-throated agreement.

"I think the original gates to the hacienda should remain. Some kind of attractive parking lot has to be built there, but it has to be beautiful to look at from The Doctor's House. Then I think some type of easy access up to the temple, maybe mini-buses or trams, something like that. But it's what I want to do on the other side of the mountain that really turns me on."

"What's that, Gasp? Tell us your vision," Alex implored.

"I see a resort, a low-rise hotel building, a golf course, several swimming pools, tennis courts, the works. It will have to be beautiful to look at from the top of the Pico de Huayrocondo. I'm not sure what I'm talking about ... maybe a Spanish hacienda, but somehow, I see it more Mayan ... a Maya village, but twenty-first century, authentic, not a pastiche. Are you getting this down, Al?"

"I can see it, Gasp. What a vision, what a project."

"Will you want a yacht harbor, and a landing field, too." Scott asked.

"Hmmmm ... I'm not so sure, Scott. It's not a bad idea, but for now I think I'm dreaming big enough. The real job is going to be for Brewster and Peter and a team of Mexican lawyers. They'll need to figure out a way to get the government to approve our plans, in exchange for giving the temple to the instituto, and also in exchange for allowing us to underwrite the site and make it happen the way we want it to happen," Gaspar insisted.

"That won't be easy, Gasp," Brewster assured him. "But it shouldn't be the hardest thing in the world either and definitely not impossible. What you want to do for the people of Mexico is not only reasonable but should be commended."

"Well then, when Señor de Montijo gets here, we can go over some of this with him, wha-da-ya say, Brew."

"Strike while the iron's hot, Gaspar, but you haven't even discussed the gold mine yet."

"Oh yeah, the gold mine. I guess I haven't told you about '*Huayrocondo Mines*' yet! 'H.M.' for 'Huayrocondo Mines' should be an easy symbol to look up on the big board of the New York Stock Exchange, don't you think, Brew." Gaspar hoped he'd finally amazed his lawyer-in-training. "We'll need to find a CEO and a CFO or maybe we could lease the mine to Dome, although I think it's a good opportunity for us to branch out into something international. By the way, speaking of which, I'm hoping that Mike Fitzpatrick back home will be up to building the infrastructure around here. The resort should keep him busy, that's for sure, and maybe he can help the archaeologists in shoring up and uncovering the temple.

"Gaspar, you won't mind if I call in some reinforcements, would you?" Brewster asked.

"Brew, it's all in your hands now. Just let me know where you want me to sign," Gaspar told him over his shoulder, as he headed for the beach with Mr. Peugeot prancing by his side.

"I'm right behind you, Gasp," Alex called as he ran across the sand to catch up.

As one, the two teenagers and Peugeot ran into the surf without a care in the world, little knowing that *The*

Mystery of the Ashkenazie Acquisition, would be awaiting them back home on their return to Perdido Isle.

CATÁN LEGACY